About the Author

Nick Rogers is an avid cricket and punk rock fan. He was fourteen during the summer of 1976. He is a mathematician who works in the City of London. He watches cricket and football regularly through following Essex County cricket and Ipswich Town football club. Musically, he still likes pogoing to the likes of The Damned, Stiff Little Fingers and Sleaford Mods.

1976 - Punk, Cricket and London's Burning

Nick Rogers

1976 Punk, Cricket and London's Burning

Olympia Publishers
London

www.olympiapublishers.com
OLYMPIA PAPERBACK EDITION

A CIP catalogue record for this title is
available from the British Library.

ISBN: 978-1-78830-778-9

This is a work of fiction.
Names, characters, places and incidents originate from the writer's
imagination. Any resemblance to actual persons, living or dead, is
purely coincidental.

First Published in 2020

Olympia Publishers
Tallis House
2 Tallis Street
London
EC4Y 0AB

Printed in Great Britain

Dedication

To Vicki, Claire, Amanda and Jack

Acknowledgements

To Billy Idol, Suggs, Peter Ackroyd, Iain Sinclair, John Rogers, Don Letts, Gene Vincent, WG Grace, Bessie Bellwood, Siouxsie Sioux, Poly Styrene, Viv Albertine, Joe Strummer, Paul Simonon, Mick Jones, Viv Richards, Michael Holding, Clive Lloyd, Tony Greg, Graham Gooch, Fred Titmus, David Steele, Bob Willis, Ian Dury, Chaz Jankel, Roland Matthes, Kornelia Ender, Bob Marley. Thank you.

Prologue

"Gin and drugs are my inspiration."- TS Eliot

A cricket match was to be played at Bromley Common in Kent on Monday 9 July 1739. The game was billed as between "eleven gentlemen of Kent and eleven gentlemen from any part of England, exclusive of Kent." The team of Kent was described as "the Unconquerable County." The description was optimistic as this would be their first game.

A second match was scheduled to take place between the same teams at the Artillery Ground in Bunhill Fields, Finsbury on Monday 23 July 1739.

July 9th arrived. Kent won the toss and batted first. William Broad opened the batting. He was the star of the team. He had a decent eye and plenty of time to play the ball. Also, he played straight and late, mainly in the 'v'. His late cut was a wonder to behold, and only surpassed by a lofted straight drive that was pure artistry. Three players had never played before but were business friends of William Broad. A huge wager was being made on the game. The wager was 20 gallons of gin to the winning captain. William Broad was captain of Kent. William Cordell was Captain of the Rest of England.

Gin was the drink of London. At one time in London, there was one gin distillery for every four houses, and gin was plentiful enough to be sold for a penny a piece. Following a series of reforms, gin moved out of the bathtub… and into the gin shops. From a bottom-shelf tipple that was sometimes laced with turpentine or lethal when distilled incorrectly, gin began to transform into something quite a bit more highbrow or maybe not.

Pushed forward by social reformers such as Joseph Jekyll, The Gin Act of 1736 attempted to curb gin consumption by instituting a 20 shilling per gallon excise tax as well as a £50 annual license for all gin sellers. Passed in 1735, it was set to take effect in September 1736. The law proved immensely unpopular and provoked public rioting. King George II issued a proclamation requiring compliance with the law and an end to public disorder against it.

Kent won the game easily scoring 52 runs with the Rest of England falling short, scoring a paltry 32. At the end of each over, the players would have a tot of gin. The scene was Georgian England in all its splendour. The ladies of the players had their parasols to protect themselves against the fierce summer sun. The food was sumptuous and plentiful. There was much drinking and merriment in the crowd of several hundred. William Broad had talked of this game of 'cricket' for years. He was adamant it had existed since Tudor times and was the 'king' of all sports. Henry VIII had played a form of the game in Greenwich. He had dreamt of this day for years. After years of explaining it to friends, a game of cricket had been arranged. The rules seemed simple. There were bats and a ball and you had to hit something called a wicket. People bowled and batted and it was eleven a side. What could go wrong?

The dispute was over the dismissal of William Broad. He had nicked off to the wicketkeeper but refused to walk. There had been clear contact with the bat and the wicketkeeper had taken a clean catch. The hastily written rules explained this was a dismissal and a wicket for the bowler. William Broad had bribed the Umpire with gin and his finger stayed down. He declared confidently, "Not out." The bowler was furious. Nearby fielders were sledging William Broad. He was unaffected, marking out his crease whilst insults were being hurled his way.

His retort was concise. "Desist you idiots. They've come to see me bat. I'm the entertainment here. Not you lot."

William Broad's proclamation made the atmosphere worse. Threats were made and a brief melee occurred on the pitch where weapons were drawn. The Umpires managed to calm the players and an uneasy truce existed for the rest of the game. At the end William Broad was not out for 35 out of a total of 52. He was the best batsmen in the team by some distance. Once again, his late cut was exquisite and his forward defensive was watertight to befit the importance of the occasion. However, he was savage on anything short, preferring to score off the back foot.

The Rest of England fell 20 runs short of a winning total. William Broad took 6 wickets for 9 runs. He was fast and accurate with a little bit of nibble outside off stump. He had smashed William Cordell's middle stump out of the ground with a fast thunderbolt of a delivery for a first ball duck. He eyeballed Cordell and sent him on his way with "Call yourself a cricketer. You're not good enough to play this game." Broad make quite a show of the dismissal. Cordell was furious.

William Broad took the last wicket to end the game with a fast, brutish, rising delivery that took the edge of Edward Davis's bat through to the wicketkeeper. The Rest of England players were furious and marched off the pitch refusing to shake hands with the Kent players. William Cordell had to be restrained from physically attacking William Broad. "Your bowling was too fast Broad. You intimidated our batsmen. You said this was a game for gentlemen. My men were in danger."

Several other facets of Broad's behaviour had infuriated him during the game. Broad had verbally abused some of Cordell's team. The wager of 20 gallons of gin wasn't honoured. The game for late July at Bunhill Fields was cancelled. But this wasn't the end of the matter.

After the match, Cordell issued the challenge of a duel to William Broad. Cordell's second was Charles Ford and he delivered the letter to William Broad's residence in Bromley less than 3 hours after the finish of the game. The duel was to take place between at Hampstead Heath Park between William Broad and William Cordell 7 days hence on July 16th 1739 at 6am. William Cordell was laying down the challenge.

Events over the next few days became complicated. William Broad's second was Daniel Hyde. Both seconds over the next few days negotiated a truce. They agreed that if William Broad delivered 20 gallons of gin to William Cordell the challenge would be dropped. William Broad agreed reluctantly. So far, the challenge was not common knowledge and William Broad feared for his business interests and life. William Cordell was known to have a steady hand, good eye and was a good shot. On July 14th 1739, 20 gallons of gin was delivered to William Cordell who lived in Bristol.

William Cordell fell ill soon after taking delivery of the gin. He was a serious gin drinker. An investigation took place into Cordell's illness. The outcome in the Courts, later in 1739, was that William Broad had poisoned the gin with turpentine with an intention to cheat and maim William Cordell. William Broad was sentenced to death.

William Broad was to be hung on June 12th 1740 on The Tyburn Tree. He was sent to Newgate Prison immediately. From Newgate Prison he was sent to Tyburn and hng until his death. On the evening of June 11th, the sexton at St Sepulchre's church, opposite the prison, would proclaim to William Broad;

"All you that in the condemned hole do lie,
Prepare you, for tomorrow you shall die.
Watch all, and pray, the hour is drawing near,
That you before Almighty God will appear.
Examine well yourselves, in time repent,
That you not to eternal flames be sent,
And when St Sepulcher's bell tomorrow tolls,
The Lord above have mercy on your souls."

Twelve chimes from the handbell at the stroke of midnight June 11th was the 'death knell' for William Broad.

Despite the popularity – or perhaps because of the growing crowds – the gallows were eventually moved from Tyburn and from 1798 public executions took place at Newgate Prison. Never an actual tree, Tyburn Tree was the site of public hangings from 1196. From 1571, a wooden scaffold was erected in a triangular shape, able to host three hangings simultaneously, perfect for a waiting crowd eager for some entertainment.

Hanging days were public holidays. The large crowds were there for the spectacle, not only for the death itself but the dramatic speeches that preceded the hangings. It was drama and theatre with cruelty. The formula was outstanding. A last minute confession or defiant denial was the cherry on the cake. It's these speeches that led to the tradition of public speaking and eventually Speaker's Corner being established near this site.

The crowd was over 100,000 from a London population of less than a million. The execution was to take place at 8am. People had started lining the route at 8pm the previous evening to get the best view. The crowd was inebriated on gin already. Food stalls lined the route. People were mixing wormwood beer and gin. The mix was dangerously drinkable and very intoxicating. Salacious behaviour was everywhere. Men and women were in various stages of undress. This was the FA cup final of 1740. People would spit at William Broad as he walked the route to Tyburn, a walk of nearly 3 miles. They would throw dog excrement as well. He was fair game for any form of abuse so long as he got to Tyburn in broadly one piece. William Broad was incoherent under the influence of gin and wormwood. He had bribed the governor of Newgate prison sufficiently. Cricket had its first victim and fatality.

Halfway on the journey to Tyburn, William Broad was offered a further concoction of wormwood beer with something extra at Resurrection gate in St Giles in the Fields. This was tradition. The 'something extra' was a closely guarded secret passed on by the Minister of the church. However, the church had a classic herb garden, inspired by the works of Nicholas Culpeper, Spitalfield's favourite son. All sorts of wonderful and hallucinogenic plants were grown there.

William Broad's speech before his hanging was defiant, having achieved some resemblance of sobriety, when viewing the Tyburn Tree. He spoke for himself, "I am the finest cricketer in the country."

The crowd hissed and booed. The crowd wanted repentance and humility. They wanted to see a broken man.

"I am no cheat. William Cordell is a cheat. I did not poison him with gin. I'm the finest bat and fastest bowler in all England. Yes, I bribed the Umpire a little. But that's nothing." The crowd was in a rage. They hissed and booed. The Marshalls were struggling to hold them back.

William Broad spoke, "Future generations of the Broads will clear my name. I die in the name of cricket. I'm the best bat and fastest bowler in England."

Five minutes later, William Broad was hanged. John Thrift was the hangman. He took over half an hour to die and refused to leave this world quietly. The crowd was euphoric, delirious and dangerous. Fireworks littered the sky. Wormwood beer was flowing faster than the River Thames. The atmosphere was akin to Smithfield's Fair.

On May 1787, Thomas Lord had acquired seven acres off Dorset Square to create the first Lord's cricket ground. The Marylebone Cricket Club was formed soon after.

On August 21st 1787, a Kent XI was to play a match against a MCC XI at Lord's. William Broad and Thomas Lord were captaining the respective teams. William Broad was a Kent landowner in the Bromley area of the county. He had connections with the London Dry Gin company. Gordon's had opened a distillery in the Southwark area in 1769, later moving in 1786 to Clerkenwell. Thomas Lord was born in Thirsk, Yorkshire 1755. His father was a Roman Catholic yeoman, who had his lands sequestered for supporting the Jacobite rising in 1745 and afterwards he had to work as a labourer. The Lord family later moved to Diss, Norfolk, where Thomas Lord was brought up. Thomas Lord moved to London in the late 1770s and was employed as a bowler and general attendant at the White Conduit Club in Islington.

The match was tense with a growing personal friction between the respective captains. They both had considerable egos. History was repeating itself. Kent batted first and scored 191. William Broad had top scored with 84. He scored mainly on the leg side, pulling and hooking anything short with aplomb. His onside drives were magnificent. A century looked a certainty before he became over confident and was bowled playing across the line. He cursed himself for his stupidity.

"They were throwing pies out there. How could I get out to that rubbish?" William Broad's team mates knew better than to speak with him for an hour. Such was his anger than he sent a plate of chicken pies flying with his bat. The irony was lost on him.

Thomas Lord took 7 Kent wickets for 65 and was the MCC's star bowler. The MCC started well. Thomas Lord came into bat with the MCC requiring 12 with 3 wickets left. William Broad came onto bowl and dismissed two MCC batsmen in consecutive deliveries. 8 runs were now required for the MCC with Thomas Lord still at the crease. This was captain versus captain. There had been a fair amount of gamesmanship between the two already. In between innings the MCC had accused William Broad of spiking their drinks. Gin was at the centre of the controversy again. William Broad was on the board of a London Gin company who were supplying the refreshments for the match. In return Kent accused the MCC of time wasting and applying a solution to the ball to make it swing through the air more. Players had squared up to each other on more than one occasion. In the end William Broad dismissed Thomas Lord with MCC's score at 189. William Broad had bowled an aggressive short delivery that hit Lord full in the face. Lord had then toppled over onto his stumps, dismissed hit wicket bowled Broad. Kent had won by 2 runs. As the MCC walked off Thomas Lord, still bloodied and shocked, came up to William Broad and hit him with his glove. In Regency England there was no greater insult. He didn't need to say anything.

That night, a letter was sent by the second of William Broad to Thomas Lord issuing a time and date for a duel. There was no letter of apologies. The duel was to take place at Hampstead Heath at 6am the next morning.

The weather on August 22nd was warm and bright. Hampstead Heath looked wonderful in its summer splendour. William Broad was shot through the heart. William Lord was as accurate with a pistol as he was with his bowling. William Broad was quick but had splayed his bullet too far down leg side. His peers would not charge him. This had been a matter of honour over a game of cricket. There was no greater crime than spiking a gentlemen's drink to win a game of cricket. The 'Gentlemen' was well within his rights to extract retribution.

The Broad family of Bromley had suffered 2 violent deaths this century at Tyburn and Hampstead Heath over the sport of cricket. The family felt cursed. William Broad's wife was visited one week after his death. The visitor Mary Abbott was a complete stranger to the family but knew a great deal about the two deaths. The Broad family was desperate to lift the curse and would listen to any suggestions. The visitor explained there was no solution until the son of the seventh generation of the recently deceased William Broad saved 1,000 souls or was forgiven by the President of the MCC. This person would have the gift of sight. However, this gift of 'sight' was not explained. This story was passed down the generations of the Broad family, with considerable embellishments. On November 30th 1955, William Michael Albert Broad was born in Stanmore, Middlesex. He was the seventh generation descendent of William Broad, shot on Hampstead Heath August 22nd 1787, or great-great-great-great-great grandson. Also, he was the ninth generation descendent of William Broad hung at Tyburn. His father was excited. Maybe the Regency curse would be lifted. He would call himself Billy Idol.

The rock n'roll singer Eddie Cochran died at age 21 after a road accident, while travelling in a taxi in Chippenham, Wiltshire, during his British tour in April 1960, having just performed at Bristol's Hippodrome theatre

The taxi driver was driving far too quickly and lost control of the vehicle, crashing into a lamppost on Rowden Hill. At the moment of impact, Cochran, who was seated in the centre of the back seat, threw himself over his fiancée (songwriter Sharon Sheeley) to shield her and he was thrown out of the car when a rear passenger door opened in the collision's force. He was taken to St Martin's Hospital, in Bath. He had suffered severe head injuries, and died at 4:10 p.m. the following day, Easter Sunday, 1960.

Eddie Cochran's body was flown home and, after a funeral service, was buried on April 25, 1960, at Forest Lawn Memorial Park in Cypress, California.

Sharon Sheeley, tour manager Pat Thompkins and the singer Gene Vincent who were also in the taxi survived the crash. Gene Vincent sustained lasting injuries to an already permanently damaged leg that would shorten his career and affect him for the rest of his life.

Gene Vincent never recovered mentally, in addition to his physical woes. The mental wounds were even worse. There was no greater guilt than surviving a crash and seeing your best friend die. He was a shadow of himself and struggled with the demons of this night in the Wiltshire countryside. He died in 1971 at the young age of 36. He lived in England for a large part of the 1960s and felt more appreciated here than in the States. His life was unfulfilled and vowed, on his deathbed in California, to return to England to reclaim his previous glory. He had to get back to London. He heard that to make it you had to play Camden and Hammersmith. England owed him for the loss of his greatest friend and the pain of his all too short life.

Gene Vincent came back in spirit late March 1976. He bumped into Billy Idol outside Sainsbury's on Bromley high street. He had been waiting 5 years for this opportunity. Billy Idol recognised him immediately. They got talking about rock n'roll and the career of Gene Vincent. Billy Idol explained the burgeoning Bromley and London punk scene. Gene Vincent was hooked. Billy was relaxed in his relationship with the spirit of Gene Vincent. He saw no problems being friends with a spirit and a legend of rock n'roll. It was all in a day's work for the bashful confident descendent of England's greatest cricketers hung at Tyburn and shot on Hampstead Heath; he had been told it was his mission.

Gene Vincent saw Joe Strummer perform for the 101ers at the Nashville on April 3rd with Billy Idol. He was bowled over with the charisma, passion and energy of Joe Strummer. Strummer was going to be the new frontman of rock n'roll. He was like a reincarnation of Eddie Cochran. Gene felt an immediate connection and knew the career of Joe Strummer was the reason for his return. He could make amends for the tragic death of Eddie Cochran and could think of nothing else for days. He had to mentor Joe Strummer for the legacy of Eddie Cochran.

Siouxsie Sioux was walking along Bromley high street late March 1976. Her appearance made her stand out and attracted critical attention. However, Siouxsie wasn't interested. She was special. Her detractors weren't. Goiswintha was waiting for her as she turned into the road where she lived.

"Hi, Siouxsie, can we have a chat?" Goiswintha looked ethereal and gothic. Siouxsie felt a natural connection. This was someone who would 'get here'.

"Of course. My house is over there. My parents are out." Siousxie felt she was born for these moments. Finally, there was someone she could truly connect with.

"I'm Goiswintha, Queen of the Visigoths."

"Hi Goiswintha. I've been waiting for you. Thankfully, you've made it. I've dreamt of this moment for years."

"It's time for you to learn your purpose. You have talents. It's time to use them."

"It's the future isn't it? I've always had it."

"Yes. But you've never really used it before. You've just played with it."

"True. It's never required in Bromley. Nothing ever happens in Bromley. It has no future, present or past."

"That's not strictly true Siousxie. This punk rock thing is about to explode. Bromley is the centre of it all with your friends. Bromley is rich in history. You've got to know where to look."

"Thank you! So what can I do for Bromley? It's the King's Road in Chelsea where the action is."

"You need to help Billy Idol. You need to use your gift wisely."

"I'm always helping Billy. He's lovely, but useless without me."

"I realise that. Foresight allows you to shape events and change the future."

"So what's Billy got to do with this?"

"He's got to work with 2 returning spirits."

"Who are the spirits?"

"Gene Vincent and WG Grace. They're two legends in their field. Billy is going to help them."

"With what?"

"Punk rock and cricket."

"That's a strange combination."

"There's one more thing, Siouxsie."

"Something else?"

"Come back with me to the Thames. Chelsea Physic Garden is the place. It's where you'll meet Masters Gerard and Culpeper for your inauguration. There are some other special people I want you to meet."

At Vauxhall bridge Marc Bolan, Ray Davies and David Bowie were there to meet Siouxsie.

"What about the Garden. I thought we were going there?"

"We are Siouxsie. Vauxhall Bridge is important as well."

"These are the guardians of London, Siouxsie."

"So this is the new Queen of the Thames then?" asked Ray Davies. "Welcome Siouxsie. Let's take you to Chelsea."

"It's so nice to have a good Bromley girl for once." David Bowie was impressed.

Marc Bolan had his say as well. "I just love the way she is. She's perfect."

Chapter 1

'Reality leaves a lot to the imagination' – John Lennon
'There's nowhere you can be that isn't where you're meant to be' – John Lennon

Siouxsie Sioux and her band, the Banshees, were rehearsing at the cemetery in the early hours. This was the perfect place to fit their mood. Also, they couldn't find anywhere else to practise that inspired them and didn't offend the locals. The dead of night bought out the best in the Banshees as creatures of the dark. They had broken into the mortuary, connected their equipment to the electrics, whilst trying to avoid disturbing the clientele, and set up their instruments. The gravestones added to the aesthetics they required to perform at their best. They were hoping to get a first gig sometime in late summer at the 100 Club in London's Oxford Street. Flashes of lightning could be seen in the distance somewhere over Bexleyheath. The sound of thunder shook the gravestones violently. The Banshees were invigorated from the drama. Siouxsie was, like the Queen of the Visigoths, all dressed in black with a presence to match the night and her punk royalty status. Bats were circulating around the Banshees as they practised.

The Banshees were raw. Luckily, the cemetery was remote enough not to attract too much attention other than some local wildlife, and Siouxsie loved the cemetery, especially at 2am in the dead of night. Billy Idol was with the Banshees that night along with Steven Severin and Sid Vicious. They were part of the 'Bromley Contingent'; punks from suburban London, saving and giving hope to people from the tedium of bank clerk's houses, privet hedges and dull concrete shopping centres promising a new utopia and spewing out resentment, boredom and mediocrity instead.

There was a new energy surging through London and the country. Punk rock was about to explode in the capital. People had enough of listening to prog rock, glam rock and the Bay City Rollers. Their music made you want to avoid the school disco, Radio 1 or any other outlet for bland and soulless music. You wanted to go out and smash up a Yes LP or vomit and spit on a poster of Rod Stewart. Rick Wakeman was talented, perhaps too talented, but wasn't a voice piece for a generation frustrated with boredom, unemployment and a declining racist Britain. You were surrounded by music so vacuous and unappealing that you wanted to go out and pogo to something decent with rage and anger flowing through your veins. Rebellion was in the air and it needed a conduit. Punk rock was that conduit – vibrant, aggressive and refreshing. Suddenly, you felt that you had some serious volts going through your body and you'd been reborn. At last, someone was speaking your language and it was beautiful. Salvation had come and 1976 was the year it happened. Punks would call it Year Zero. Any music before didn't really matter with maybe the exception of the Beatles, The Who, Iggy Pop, Velvet Underground, The Kinks, Marc Bolan, David Bowie and rock n'roll. Not quite true with sober and intelligent reflection, but its how you felt back in 1976 as a callow youth with rebellious and awkward hormones flowing through you.

Where did the word 'Punk' come from? The dictionary defines it as a worthless entity. It's a general term of abuse. The Pistols and The Clash didn't consciously become punk bands. They wanted something new, rebellious, accessible and fresh. The British press initiated the name thinking these bands were about to destroy society and had become enemies of the state. The press loved a label and the label stuck like a limpet to rock.

Kilburn and the High Roads, The Adverts, Subway Sect, London SS, Cock Sparra, Eddie and the Hot Rods, The Stranglers, UK Subs, Doctor Feelgood, Sham 69, Ian Dury and the Blockheads could all lay claim to have created the form that is punk. All were performing around the mid 1970s. Britain at that time was watching shows on TV like the *The Two Ronnies*, *The Good Life* and *Man about the House*. This was gentle TV, unable to offend, other than through its mediocrity and tedium for young and rebellious teenagers. Swearing on TV was a no-go area. Punk blew all these sensibilities into oblivion. It was no surprise that 'alternative comedy' followed soon after.

There were many contradictions in punk. With the benefit of future sight, you'd see that bands would sell out for the middle ground and mainstream of mediocrity appearing on Radio 2. 40 years on and you'd see old punk acts just doing it for the money with a message that didn't make sense anymore. Malcolm McLaren would be embroiled in a bitter grubby dispute with Sex Pistols band members that damaged so much of what punk stood for. John Lydon would be paid a fortune to advertise butter on the TV. Sid Vicious poisoned himself and sadly did kill a cat after drugs had destroyed his once gentle humanity. You could go on. Age and nostalgia filter out the bad for many of us.

Paul Weller said, "I liked the attitude of punk." Adding, "But I also thought a lot of it was fake. We all saved up about pounds 20 to go to McLaren's shop and we went in to buy some mohair jumpers. We found we couldn't afford anything. We thought, this is bullshit. It was quite elitist, cliquey and art school. They were mostly middle-class kids with rich parents, and they'd run away to join the circus."

For Jon Savage, author of England's Dreaming, it was a time of "sun, sex, sulphate and swastikas. The circus had come to the King's Road."

Punk was imperfect. You didn't need a degree at the Royal College of Music to form your own punk band. Many artists of punk struggled with learning to play their instruments.

Joey Ramone nailed it perfectly. "Play before you get good, because by the time you get good, you're too old to play."

But for one great summer in 1976 it offered hope and salvation whilst listening to Viv Richards score runs for the West Indies on Test Match special. Test Match special and punk-the most unlikely of combinations. A little like a pilchard and jam sandwich with a topping of spicy mayonnaise.

Much later, Kurt Cobain hit its sweet spot. "Punk rock should mean freedom, liking and excepting anything that you like. Playing whatever you want. As sloppy as you want. As long as it's good and it has passion."

Shane MacGowan of the Pogues led a trail for punk soon after 1976 and reached the soul of punk just like Kurt Cobain.

"I'm not singing for the future.

I'm not dreaming of the past.

I'm not talking of the first time.

I never think about the last."

For some women, it was liberating and empowering. They could break away from the mute appendages of male dominated cock rock. Viv Albertine said with much emotion, "Punk was the only time I fitted in. Just one tiny sliver of time where it was acceptable to say what you thought."

The magnificent Poly Styrene said it better than anyone else. "Some people think little girls should be seen and not heard. But I think, "oh bondage, up yours!"

The popular British pioneers of punk rock were The Damned, The Clash, Sex Pistols and Siousxie and the Banshees. The Pistols were nihilists, aggressive and anti-establishment. They were full on 'fuck you'. With John Lydon there was no other way. They would burn out quickly such was their intensity. The Damned were plain daft but beautiful. Dave Vanian, Captain Sensible, Brian James and Rat Scabies were artisans and would prosper for over 40 years. They would get better and better. They were the 'fine wine' of Punk. Maybe it was all down to Dave Vanian not wanting to go back to his job as a grave digger. Rat Scabies and Captain Sensible had been inspired watching the famous pianist Mrs Mills perform at a theatre in Croydon. Mrs Mills would encourage the Captain and Rat. Nobody was better than Mrs Mills at working an audience.: The Banshees were dark, gothic and wonderfully weird with Queen Siouxsie Sioux leading from the front. Bromley and surburbia had shaped her in that she would rebel against it, albeit non aggressively. Her style spoke volumes. However, The Clash were just formidable and explosive, punching with a consciousness that would last in people's minds. They spoke from their own souls and it resonated with the people. It was heartfelt, raw and passionate. Maybe it was a little naïve. Mick Jones, Joe Strummer, Paul Simonon, Terry Chimes and Keith Levene were the original band members. Joe Strummer was the charismatic lead man, dripping in personality and energy; he had impressed as the frontman of the 101ers. Mick Jones, formerly of London SS and fan of the New York Dolls, was the solid lead guitarist with a talent in musical composition. Paul Simonon had style to make a man envious and feel sartorially inadequate. He was cooler than an ice box. The Clash spoke of the Westway and West London like cultural experts of the streets. Mick Jones was ambassador to the Westway. He had lived on the 18th floor in a high-rise flat, yards away from its splendour.

The Clash, aka the Strummer version, had got together the month before. Paul Simonon and Mick Jones had seen the 101ers at the Nashville with the Pistols on April 3rd. Both knew Steve Jones and Glen Matlock of the Pistols. The Pistols were a sensation that night. Paul and Mick knew a wind of change was blowing and the Pistols were orchestrating it. This was punk's epiphany. They weren't the only converts. The 101ers were history.

Joe Strummers' words captured the Pistol's crowning and the demise of the 101ers. "Anyway, they played. There was hardly any audience; it was a Tuesday or something. And I knew we were finished, five seconds into their first song I knew we were like yesterday's papers. I mean, we were over."

Joe Strummer's attitude to the 101ers changed from that moment. The marriage was over. The breakdown occurred after a gig not much later at the Golden Lion in Fulham. The Clash's manager, Bernie Rhodes, came to the dressing room after their performance with Keith Levene and went, "Hey, come with me; I want you to meet some people."

They went to Shepherd's Bush, to a squat in Davis Road. Joe met Paul Simonon and Mick Jones who he had seen at Lisson Grove dole office while collecting his £10.64 a week. Paul and Mick were already fans of Joe Strummer.

Immediately, they hit it off and started to practise. Within 24 hours, Joe Strummer was part of The Clash.

Joe would later explain, "It was the look of them more than anything else; you could see the new world."

Joe would describe The Clash succinctly and what they were about. "The day I joined The Clash was very much back to square one, year zero. Part of punk was that you had to shed all of what you knew before. We were almost stalinist in the way that we insisted that you had to cast off all your friends, everything you'd ever known, and the way you'd played before in a frenzied attempt to create something new, which was not easy at any time. It was very rigorous; we were insane, basically. It was completely and utterly insane."

In the summer of 1976, the West Indies Cricket team were touring England, trying to redeem themselves after a disastrous tour of Australia. They were talented but unproven. Maybe the wonderful exuberant talents of that team playing the best sport in the world would make the summer of 1976 a joy. They had a batsman in Viv Richards, who looked very special. He played attacking cricket that bought joy and excitement. He had skill, panache and talent in abundance as well. English players often looked timid and dull in comparison. West Indian fans certainly hoped so. 20 years on from the Windrush Generation and the West Indian community was treated worse than dirt, like unwelcome aliens, with all the crimes of humanity being thrown at them. The Windrush Generation had helped save the NHS and kept the transport system running, at the same time as living under deep suspicion in poor neighbourhoods with low wages, poorer prospects and enduring often the obvious contempt and open hatred of fellow British citizens. They need a saviour, something to prove they could be as good as anyone. The West Indies cricket team could be that saviour. On their day, they could play cricket to warm the hearts of even the most cynical. They just needed to do it more often, fulfilling their obvious talent, and their captain, Clive Lloyd was of a similar opinion.

"What do they know of cricket that only cricket know?" The question came from West Indian political intellectual, CLR James, in his book *Beyond a Boundary*.

James's question was essentially rhetorical. It underlined both the impossibility of understanding cricket without reference to its social and cultural context and the equal difficulty of understanding West Indian history and culture without reference to one of its defining popular activities

Viv Richards made his first-class debut for the Leeward and Windward Islands versus Jamaica in Kingston in January 1972 when he was 19. In 1974, he moved to England play for Somerset in county cricket on the recommendation of a Somerset committee member Len Creed. He shared a flat in Taunton with Dennis Breakwell and Ian Botham. Anyone who could survive a flat share with IT Botham deserved a knighthood. On 27 April 1974, Richards made his debut for Somerset against Glamorgan in Swansea. The toughest man ever to play cricket, Brian Close, was his captain and mentor.

Viv Richards made his Test match debut for the West Indies 1974 against India in Bangalore. He made an unbeaten 192 in the second test of that series in New Delhi. However, he struggled against the mystery Indian spinners in the other test matches. Chandrashekhar had him mystified with the skill of his brilliant leg spin bowling. In 1975, Richards helped the West Indies to win the first World Cup cricket final. Viv starred in the field, running out Alan Turner, Greg Chappell and Ian Chappell but scored just 5 with the bat. Clive Lloyd scored 102 that day promoting joy and celebration across the Caribbean.

At 2.10 am, the night sky started to resemble a light show. Lightning and thunder droned out the singular and hypnotic sound of the Banshees with rain now starting to fall heavily. Nature's fireworks illuminated the tombs and gravestones. The Banshees carried on regardless adding to the surreal atmosphere. Alternating blankets of light and darkness distorted any sensibilities. Billy Idol was howling and singing. Sid Vicious was snarling. Cats screeched and Dogs barked. Somehow, they all survived electrocution.

At 2.30 am, lightning stuck the tomb of WG Grace, arguably the most famous cricketer ever. WG's tomb lit up in a spectacular blue and silver light that shimmered around the tomb for an age. The Banshees were no more than 10 yards away and stopped playing to watch. Then a couple of the trees close to the tomb went up in flames from another lightning strike.

At this strike, Siouxsie started arguing with Billy Idol, who wanted to make a run for it.

"Look, Siouxsie, this is crazy. We're going to get fried if we carry on." Other Banshees started to grumble.

"We're going nowhere, Billy. Stop being a prat." There was menace in Souxsie's voice. Leaving wasn't an option.

Siouxsie's resolve lasted about ten minutes as the fire started to spread and sirens could be heard fast approaching the cemetery.

WG Grace's tomb was still shimmering when Siouxsie said, "I've had enough. This is too weird even for me. Let's get out of here."

This was a cue for the Banshees, Sid Vicious and Billy Idol to collect their equipment and to make a run for the streets of Bromley. Somehow, they avoided disturbing any of the clientele in the mortuary.

At 3am, the freshly released spirit of WG Grace was still trying to overcome the sight of the fast disappearing Banshees and his new scenery when a man with a quiff approached him.

"Hello, my name is Gene Vincent. You're WG Grace aren't you?"

"I am. How do you know my name?"

Gene replied, refusing to answer directly, "I've been waiting for you. I was getting impatient thinking you'd never cross over."

"Cross over? Have I come back as some form of spirit? Am I a ghost? What year is it?"

Gene didn't answer the questions. "Your tombstone was more lit up than the Empire State Building."

"What are you on about?"

"Who are you? What year is it?"

"I'm Gene Vincent, the king of rock n'roll. It's May 1976."

"I've never heard of you. I've been dead since 1915."

"Well you're back in the living now. What should I call you?"

"Call me WG."

"I'm the best performer there ever was apart from Ray Davies of the Kinks. And Eddie Cochrane."

"Really? You don't lack confidence."

Billy Idol returned to the cemetery with Siousxie. The blond dye in his hair was starting to run over his leather jacket. His eyes looked a foot wide. His hair stood up high and straight. The rest of the 'Bromley Contingent' was still running back to Bromley. He ran up to Gene Vincent and WG. Siouxsie looked disinterested.

"Sorry, chaps, I thought it best if I came back. There's a little explaining to do." Billy was out of breath, struggling to get his words out.

"I just lost my mind for a moment. It's this lightning. Freaks you out." The rain was coming down in buckets. Lightning was still illuminating the night sky.

Gene Vincent explained, "I've just mentioned to WG that we've been waiting for him."

"Very true. We've been waiting since March. I thought we'd missed the boat with you." Billy Idol sounded uncharacteristically serious.

Billy Idol explained briefly the history of Gene Vincent and rock n'roll to WG in a few soundbites. It was the way he spoke and expressed himself that made WG think it was more than a flash of lightning that was behind all this.

Gene Vincent, born Vincent Craddock, was born in Norfolk, Virginia on Feb 11th 1935. His early musical influences were country, rhythm and blues and gospel music. He had planned a career in the navy and, in 1955, used his $612 re-enlistment bonus to buy a new Triumph motorcycle. However, in July 1955, while he was in Norfolk, his left leg was shattered in a motorcycle crash. He became involved in the local music scene in Norfolk and formed a rockabilly band, Gene Vincent and His Blue Caps. In Norfolk, they won a talent contest organized by a local radio DJ, "Sheriff Tex" Davis, who became Vincent's manager.

In 1956, he wrote Be-Bop-a-Lula which drew comparisons to the great Elvis Presley. The song reached no 5 in the billboard chart and launched his career as a rock n'roll star. Vincent also made an appearance in the film The Girl Can't Help It, with Jayne Mansfield, performing *Be-Bop-A-Lula*.

On December 15, 1959, Vincent appeared in the UK for the first time on the *Jack Good's TV show, Boy Meets Girl*. He would perform in the UK many times treating it as a second home. He had a special connection to England. He loved England but hated cricket, that very English of sports. He'd never got his head around the idea of a game that lasted 5 days with breaks for cucumber sandwiches, Victoria sponge and milky tea. Cricket wasn't rock n'roll. It was its antithesis.

In April 16, 1960, while on tour in the UK, Vincent and Eddie Cochran were involved in a high-speed traffic accident in Chippenham, Wiltshire. Vincent broke his ribs and collarbone and further damaged his weakened leg. Cochran died from his injuries. The heir to Elvis Presley was dead. Gene Vincent never recovered from the guilt of losing his friend and the great loss to rock n'roll. He vowed to continue the spirit of Eddie Cochran.

In 1961, Gene Vincent returned to the UK and toured with Chris Wayne and the Echoes. He moved to Britain in 1963, touring with the Outlaws, featuring future Deep Purple guitar player Ritchie Blackmore as a backing band. Gene went on to play with the Beatles at their Shea Stadium concert.

Gene was a volatile character. He had problems with tax authorities in both Britain and America. He fell out with band members and married four times. Much of his money was spent on ex-wives. In 1968, in a hotel in Germany, Vincent tried to shoot Gary Glitter. He fired several shots but missed and a frightened Glitter left the country the next day.

Gene Vincent died at the age of 36 on October 12, 1971, from a ruptured stomach ulcer while visiting his father in California. He was buried in Eternal Valley Memorial Park, in Newhall, California.

Billy Idol was warming up the task of explaining who Gene Vincent was to WG. "He was better than Presley. Gene was the king of rock n'roll and rockabilly."

"His greatest song was *Be-Bop-A-Lula*. He sang other classics like *Crazy Legs*, *Blue Jean Bop* and *Wild Cat*."

WG looked confused. He would have understood more if Gene has been explaining nuclear physics in Russian. "You're into music and were famous. I know people like that."

Gene explained, "I've been dead since 1971. Died in California. I came back in spirit about 2 months ago. Billy and I bumped into each other in Bromley High Street. He's the seventh descendent of someone famous."

"I recognised him straightaway. I've been listening to his records for years," replied Billy, as if he was talking about shopping for your favourite cheese. "I've got the gift of sight."

"You died in California. Rock n'roll stars that die there don't turn up 5 years later in Bromley High Street," exclaimed WG. "This is ridiculous!"

WG went on. "Look. I think is all some weird dream. Maybe we're all dreaming. None of this can be true."

"Reality is perception." Billy Idol looked reflective. "What's real? Maybe it's the drugs we're taking."

"You look too young for this Billy. Are you on something? Opium?"

"Opium?! That sounds cool. Never tried it. Is it any good?"

"I was a doctor. In the late 1800s, it was very fashionable. I wouldn't recommend it long-term."

"Don't worry, WG. Nobody else can see or hear us." Gene didn't sound too confident.

"I still don't get why you'd end up in London," repeated WG.

"I loved London and the UK. Its where I was appreciated the most. It was a case of 'London's calling' I think."

At this point Billy started rolling about in laughter. He was soaked through with the rain. "That would make a great title for a song. I'll mention it to Siouxsie."

"Let's be serious now. So how come you're here? You're a long way from home," asked WG, trying to get more of a handle on Gene Vincent and who he really was.

"I've a mission to save rock n'roll. This country is going to save rock n'roll. Joe Strummer is going to be the saviour.

He's the lead singer of The Clash. I'm going to help him as his spirit guide."

"That's very noble of you." WG was at his sarcastic best. The years hadn't diminished him. "'Why isn't Billy Idol going to save rock n'roll?" said WG turning to Billy.

Ten seconds later, "Why isn't Gene Vincent going to save rock n'roll?" WG said, now turning to Gene Vincent.

Billy Idol answered first, "I'm going to be king of rock n'roll in a few years. This has come a few years too early for me. Nobody has the the charisma of Joe Strummer. He's going to be the greatest frontman ever. He's something really special. If you'd ever seen him with the 101ers you'd know."

Gene Vincent followed, "I was there at the Nashville in early to see Joe with the 101ers. He's something really special. He's got what Eddie Cochran had. He's that special."

"There's more to it than this, Gene. This is personal." You've got mee. My friend, Eddie Cochran, was killed 15 years ago just outside Bath. He would have been the king of rock n'roll. I lived and he died."

"So its guilt then? That's a good motive. Guilt is one of the most powerful emotions. You're onto something Gene."

"You've sussed me, WG. I was fucked up and drank too much. Four marriages and violent rages."

WG continued questioning Gene Vincent, "So why are you hanging about around here?"

"I was waiting for you and watching the Banshees. The Banshees are going to be big. It's a shame Siouxsie can't see me."

"But why me?" WG seemed even more perplexed. "I don't know the first thing about this rock n'roll or whatever you call it. Surely, Billy can help you find Joe Strummer."

Gene Vincent answered unconvincingly and a little too quickly, "Billy and Joe don't like each other. Joe wants to thump him. It's down to us."

Billy Idol interjected quickly, "It's complicated. Cricket is in my blood. I can't explain it now. It's connected, though. I will tell you when my head is straight."

"Now you're talking about cricket. I don't get it. All this lightning has played with your mind." WG was scratching his head, "Is this Siouxsie running the show here?"

The explanation sounded unconvincing, born out of fantasy. WG imagined that he knew little of the truth. There was more likelihood this was a dream, or something similar, for all of them. He decided to carry on with this charade. There was nothing else to do. With any luck he'd get to watch some cricket now he was back, albeit as a spirit. Surely, it was still a game and flourishing. That would be a consolation.

"I was a cricketer. I was into music hall as well. Bessie Bellwood, Marie Lloyd. I even saw the great Zaza at the Camden Theatre in 1901."

"Camden. I'd love to play there. I'm seeing Patti Smith there next week on the 16th." Billy Idol seemed genuinely excited.

The three of them sat in the cemetery whilst the police and firemen surveyed the site. Siouxsie was also there, but apparently she couldn't see Gene Vincent or WG. All she saw was Billy Idol having a deep conversation and dancing with himself. That was nothing new.

The torrential rain had stopped the fires from spreading. The police inspected the mortuary and assessed the break-in. They spotted that the tomb of famous cricketer WG Grace had been hit with lightning suggesting that either English cricket was about to be re-born or had died a horrible death.

Gene Vincent tried to explain, "I need someone to help me who's an outsider. All the punks seem to know each other. It's all a little incestuous. Now I've found you!"

"So where have the Banshees gone? Where do we go from here?" asked WG.

Nobody answered.

Eventually, Gene broke the silence, "WG and I will try and find The Clash tomorrow. We'll make a start and meet up with you tomorrow night at the usual place."

"Do I have a choice?"

"Of course you do. But do you have anything else to do?" Gene Vincent was smiling smugly.

"That's true. Also, I've missed London. London's been calling me for 61 years now."

The usual place was the George and Dragon pub in Bromley High Street.

Billy Idol and Siouxsie Sioux left and returned to Bromley. It seemed anti-climactic. The rain had stopped. Thunder and lightning was no more. Calm had returned. The sun was rising and early commuters, in grey suits, made their way to work. The wildness of the night had passed. London, in all its grey splendour was waking. The rising sun made no difference as if the grey was hard coded into London's DNA. People talked of a coming heatwave-more in hope than expectation. However, either the new cricket season or the possibility of a heatwave gave many commuters an extra spring in their step, dimming down the 'grey' momentarily. The spirit of punk rock was rising, getting stronger every passing day. Billy Idol and Gene Vincent were feeding off that energy.

John Robb from The Membranes talked of the heatwave of 1976 as sucking the greyness, coldness and post war bleakness out of Britain and bringing out a new hope. Upper lip stiffness and formality were consigned to history. Confusion, colour and a 'fuck off attitude' was taking hold. Long live rock n'roll.

Chapter 2

Beckenham Cemetery Part 2
May 10th 1976, 11AM

"Go where we may, rest where we will, Eternal London haunts us still." – Thomas Moore

Later that morning, Gene Vincent and WG were in conversation. They were still at the cemetery. Spirits needed their rest and the cemetery was as good as any other place.

Gene Vincent was expressing his relief at finding WG, though was worried he didn't have a handle on how to save Joe Strummer, other than a vague concept about mentoring him as to the spirit of rock n'roll. He was also singing endless renditions of *Be Pop a Lula*.

WG had thought about last night's encounters, with the same thought going through his mind. "I don't understand any of this. I get that you might be a spirit guide to Joe Strummer. Why am I here? It doesn't make any sense."

He kept repeating to WG, ignoring his argument. "Time is running out to save rock n'roll. I must get to Joe Strummer."

WG tried to summarize. "Let me get this straight. You met Billy Idol and he told you about a new band called The Clash whose lead man is Joe Strummer. He's going to be the next big thing. And he needs your input otherwise the world of rock n'roll will be lost forever?"

"That's right."

"You really have lost it. There must be more."

"I keep getting visions of The Clash."

"Really?"

WG was certain this wasn't his purpose and it lay elsewhere. He had no choice but to go along with this charade until something personal to him raised its head. He would have to endure Gene Vincent. A game of cricket would help though.

"We've got to make our way over to West London. That's where The Clash is playing. I keep getting lost. You know London so you can help me."

WG looked a little concerned. "London has changed since my time. I might struggle."

"I hear they're over at a place called the Westway. Some 'Clash' grafitti was sprayed onto one of the concrete pillars. Billy told me."

"I've never heard of the Westway," replied WG. "What's graffiti?"

"It's some writing on the side of a wall," responded Gene Vincent nervously. He realised it sounded absurd.

"I've come back to a mad, bad world. London is a lunatic asylum then?"

"We've nothing else to go on."

"Maybe that's true. Someone else must have given you some sort of clue." WG had gone beyond despair.

"The Banshees mentioned a place called Shepherd's Bush. It's where a soccer team called QPR play."

"Oh, I know where it is now. It's called football. I played for the Wanderers back in the day. I'm sure I played there."

The Westway was a raised dual carriageway 2.5 miles in length connecting Paddington with the outer reaches of West London. It was built in the early 1960s cutting through and over residential properties. You lived north or south of the Westway and it became an artificial border line for West End city living. The concrete snake that was the Westway and its noise dominated the surroundings. The Westway was a cultural icon in a weird brutalist fashion. Paddington Basin, close to the Westway, was a cesspit and rubbish dump, a forgotten relic and a derivative from the Regent's canal. Old dilapidated and graffiti strewn warehouses dominated its pathway. The salubrious surroundings of Warwick Avenue and Little Venice did little to alleviate the bleakness. 40 years on from 1976, the place would be unrecognisable. Shiny glass offices and apartments dominated the Basin. Beautiful landscaping with top restaurants and outdoor cafes frequented by high salaried professionals have become the order of the day. Residential flats and properties seemed to have undergone millionaire makeovers. The feel of The Westway in 1976 was very different.

A metaphor for The Westway and its eventual change in fortunes was Trellick Tower. The tower was designed in the brutalist style by Erno Goldfinger and opened in 1972. The location was between the Grand Union on its path to Kensal Rise and The Westway. The building became a magnet for crime, vandalism, drug abuse and prostitution in the '70s. Rapes, suicides were not uncommon. In 1991, Sand Helsel, Professor of Architecture at Royal Melbourne Institute of Technology made a BBC documentary praising Trellick Tower, which helped to change public opinion in its favour. The tower became a significant local landmark and was awarded a Grade II listing in 1998. The monthly rental values today reflect that of a desirable and fashionable neighbourhood.

The backdrop of the '70s Westway was a driving force for The Clash. It fed their anger, resentment and energy. The Westway was a contradiction of West London and London karma. Comparisons were everywhere: 'East London v West London'; 'Poor London v Rich London'; 'Downtrodden London v Sophisticated and Wealthy London'. The people living close to the Westway in squats and council high rise flats didn't feel 'West End rich and successful'. Cheek by jowl with Kensington just felt like a kick in the balls. The overall feel in 1976 was of quiet desperation and futility. The need for an escape was desperate. Humans weren't meant to live 20 yards away from noisy concrete juggernauts in rundown flats where the lifts didn't work and people were always trying to break in and steal the rubbish that counted for your worthless possessions. This was the energy behind The Clash. They had a right to talk about anger and frustration because that was tangible and littered the Westway like a London fog of yesteryear. This is what connected them to so many and made people love them. This wasn't the unconnected adoration to Rod Stewart, forgetting his roots, living the Hollywood dream in LA, and being someone, you'd never know. With The Clash, you could share the experience on a personal level. You knew Strummer, Simonon and Jones. They were your mates who'd give you a room for the night and didn't make you feel like lower class scum. You had to be mates because the Westway and London was awash with different music tribes who all hated each other and though nothing of playing out serious street violence on each other. Clothes were a way of identifying each gang. Punks stood out from the rest and were slaughtered habitually by rockers, teddy boys and skinheads. This was fight club for the streets.

QPR were the football team of the Westway. They had finished second to Liverpool in the first Division, comfortably the best season in their history, at the end of April. They had some stars in their team. Players like Gerry Francis, Frank McLintock, Don Masson and the great Stan Bowles were the stars. Their arch enemies were the aristocrats of post-2000 London in the form of Chelsea, their soon to be wealthier and more illustrious neighbours.

WG and Gene Vincent continued their dialogue.

"Take me over there later today when the punks have woken up," asked Gene.

"Won't people think I'm a little strange dressed like this?" When people came back in spirit, they were always dressed in the clothes they left in. For WG, this was a tweed suit and flat cap. Gene Vincent was wearing leather jacket, denim jeans and a leather glove.

Gene started to explain the reality of his situation. He sounded nervous and unconvincing. "Nobody can see you unless you want to be seen. Billy Idol's friend, Siouxsie, could see you back at the cemetery, but she's royalty. You're invisible to everyone else. I rather like what you're wearing."

"Thank you. I've no idea what you're dressed up as. If we're invisible, then how can we help anyone?" ventured WG, struggling to come to terms with the idiot in front of him.

Gene Vincent smiled, "It's all very simple really," contradicting himself, but trying to put WG at ease. "You just leave them your calling card. I'd leave it in the pocket of their jacket or their trousers." Gene showed him a collection of cards.

"Where do you get those from? You've got to be kidding me. You're making this up."

"Just trust me. It works. I'm not allowed to tell you until you've proved yourself."

"How come we could see Billy? Is he the only one we can see?"

"Billy is different."

"Is this a joke? I don't believe a word you're saying. Am I in a kind of limbo hell for eternity?"

"Honestly WG. It's true."

"No it's not. You're making this up. You're living in fantasy land."

May 10th was a warm day in London with Gene and WG making their journey over to the Westway via a train journey into the city from Bromley and then the Circle Line to Paddington.

WG and Gene made their way from Paddington tube to Paddington Basin.

"We've got to have a plan," suggested WG. "Your A-Z map says this is the start of the Westway, but that's all we've got to go on."

"We can't go into a pub and ask people if they know of a Joe Strummer," added WG.

"We might have to. I'm not sure what else we can do. Also, that's going to be easier said than that."

"You're the king of rock n'roll. You must be able to come up with something inspired. Otherwise, we're going to walk around this cesspit forever. We'll have to use one of your cards."

WG and Gene sat on a bench outside Paddington Station trying to come up with a plan, whilst watching busy London about its business. They came up with nothing.

After a couple of hours, WG suggested they go over to Little Venice for inspiration.

"It's a beautiful place and much nicer than around here. Also, it's on the way to Lord's cricket ground. That's where I played for England against Australia in test matches. You can see my name everywhere there."

"That stupid sport of cricket again. 5 days of doing nothing other than sipping tea and eating cake. How can that be a sport?"

"There's nothing wrong with eating cake. Very civilised if you ask me."

"It ain't rock n'roll that's for sure. England. The home of cricket, tea drinking and victoria sponges."

WG ignored the insult. "I'm not sure about this rock n'roll business as you call it. It's a lot of throwing yourself about. I'm much more music hall. Give me Bessie Bellwood anyday."

On the thread of teacakes and cricket, 1976 was a Mike Gatting's first full season as a county cricketer for Middlesex who played at Lord's. He played 79 test matches for England with skill and distinction. However, his equal claim to fame was his ability to eat huge quantities of food and especially cake. At one break for play due to rain, Elsie, Lord's famous and wonderful tea lady, saw him divulge a whole lemon drizzle cake after consuming 6 rounds of cheese and cucumber sandwiches and 22 mini pork pies. Gatting was a food legend. In the 2000s, the redoubtable Adam Richman may have made his name in a TV show called *Man versus Food*, but he was second division compared to 'Gatts'. In Gatting's case, there was only ever one winner.

WG and Gene sat on another bench, but this time looking over the wonderful vista of Little Venice. Canal boats chugged through on their journeys to the Grand Union or Regent's Canal. A few boats masqueraded as cafes. The place was a welcome relief from Paddington Basin.

WG looked pained. "I'm desperate for some cake. It's been 61 years. Why don't we go into that café over there? How does this spirit thing work? If we can't be seen, then do we go and take what we want? I guess that's why things mysteriously disappear."

"Look, WG, stop talking about cake. You can't eat anyway. That's all you cricketers ever talk about. Let's concentrate on finding Joe Strummer. I don't know how long we've got." Gene took a few pages of a daily newspaper from his pocket.

"What's that you're reading?"

"It's for you, WG," Gene look perplexed. "I've been collecting them for you. Billy suggested I do it. It's articles about cricket. All your crap talk about cricket and cakes has just jogged my memory."

"Are you making this up again? Let me have a look. Why is Billy interested in cricket? It doesn't seem his thing."

"Who knows!"

WG took the paper. WG eyes were drawn to an article on a cricketer with the name IVA Richards. The writer mentioned that this incredibly talented young cricketer was in risk of wasting an exceptional talent and he required help and guidance. The paper was from yesterday... yesterday's papers.

The article mentioned that he was touring England with the West Indies cricket team in the summer of 1976 and that they had already played a few matches.

Then a transformation took place for WG. The ground shook and the skies darkened for him. Lightning bolts struck everywhere. For a moment, he was back at Beckenham Cemetery. WG had never felt so excited. His whole body tingled and he didn't know why. Now, pure instinct was guiding him and smashing away his apathy and confusion. Truly, he felt reborn. His spiritual path ahead was clear with bright lights guiding the way. He would have done cartwheels the whole length of the Regent's Canal to Limehouse, if possible. He tried hard to repress his excitement, but knew why he'd come back. He didn't care about anything else. IVA Richards, or Viv Richards was his calling. Viv Richards was to him what Joe Strummer was to Gene Vincent. He just knew it. WG started to explain it to Gene Vincent.

"What's happened? Did you see that lightning?"

"No, WG. There's no lightning. Your imagination's gone into overdrive."

"Plans might have changed. I'm a cricketer. It makes sense. I've got to save a fellow cricketer. My calling is Viv Richards."

"Viv who? What are you on about?"

"Viv Richards. He's a young cricketer. That's why I've come back. Its all clear now."

"That's a relief, WG, but I've got to save Joe Strummer and the future of rock n'roll. That's much more important than some cricketer."

"Gene, you've got to tell me the truth. What's going on here? Why did you meet up with Billy Idol or was it the other way around?"

"I wasn't going to tell you."

"It might help if you did."

"When we meet up with Billy, later in Bromley, then we'll explain."

"That's helpful."

They sat there in stony silence for over an hour not talking to each other. WG was thinking if he could find out more about this cricketer. Whatever madness they were embroiled in was out of his control, but it would be nice to catch up with some cricket and to meet Viv Richards. He wanted to know more about IVA Richards. He didn't want to waste his time listening to Gene go on about saving 'rock n'roll' or whatever that was.

WG broke the silence, "I'm going to get a newspaper. I want to know what this man Richards is about."

"You know that you just go up and take stuff. Nobody can see you. I'll have a walk along the canal over there and see if I can pick anything up." Gene looked over to where the Grand Union started its journey to the Midlands.

WG was back on and firing on all cylinders now. "The only thing you'll pick up from the canal towpath is dog shit."

WG took several newspapers. The Daily Telegraph ran a full length article on IVA Richards. They would do a series of articles on players from the touring team. WG reread the article 30 times. The article talked about his troubles in Australia during the previous winter, but how he redeemed himself in the last 2 test matches with scores of 30,101,50 and 98 after a poor run of scores and humiliation from the pace of Lillee and Thomson. He'd followed this with 3 hundreds

(142,130 and 177) against India in the spring of 1976. There was still this doubt that he was an unfulfilled talent with suggestions, albeit faintly, of a suspect temperament. The article further suggested he was too arrogant, playing like a millionaire, thinking he was the world's best batsmen when he still had much to prove. WG felt a warm glow for IVA Richards. He kept repeating to himself, "I want to help this man. He's my type of cricketer." WG noted that the West Indies were playing Surrey at the Oval the day after tomorrow. Everything was coming together as if fate was playing its trump card. This was more than a coincident. He was beside himself with excitement. Cricket was like that. When it was your game it was more than a religion, more than passion. Cricket touched your soul. The game was a spiritual experience.

"I'm going to the Oval. Nothing's going to stop me. I've got to see Viv bat. He's going to be the new Victor Trumper."

Gene had come back from his stroll with no further progress on the whereabouts of The Clash, but with a fascination of the Westway. He listened to WG's new plans. "You'd better go then. I'll have to look for The Clash on my own. I can't believe a game of cricket is more important than discovering the re-birth of rock n'roll."

WG chuckled to himself, "The game doesn't start until the day after tomorrow. We've got the rest of the day and tomorrow."

"For what"? asked Gene. "I can't even find The Clash graffiti."

"I've got a feeling about Camden. It's a little way from the Westway, straight down the Regent's Canal for a few miles. I know it from years ago. Do you remember me talking about Camden Theatre?"

"I'm in your hands," Gene Vincent looked doomed to failure. "We might as well."

"Your enthusiasm is killing me. This is your show, Gene," WG didn't look too impressed.

They walked along the Maida Vale straight known as Maida Avenue where the houses were expensive, exclusive and well-protected. Residential canal boats lined the canal housing bohemian types and artists. London planes lined the avenue with a luxuriant leaf cover. The place smelt of money and was just out of the sound of the Westway when the prevailing wind blew. Punk rock bands didn't live here. They crossed over the A5 and came back onto the canal to pass Blow-Up Bridge. A tourist guide, who also played rugby for Ealing, the notorious, prop eating Donald Clarke, was explaining its history. His sidekick 'Lord Jasper' was providing a theatrical accompaniment to the history lesson.

The name for the bridge came about from an incident in 1874.

An account of the incident read "In the early hours of 2 October 1874, The Tilbury – a barge containing a concoction of coffee and nuts – exploded right under the bridge. Both boat and structure were immediately destroyed. Alongside its less volatile cargo, The Spectator would later report, "The perilous combination of two or three barrels of petroleum and about five tons of gunpowder."

"The three men aboard the Tilbury, one of whom, it's presumed, lit a match that ignited the blast were killed. Windows shattered a mile from the explosion. Residents sat bolt upright in bed, fearing an earthquake. The animals in the nearby zoo caused a hullabaloo. 'Dead fish rained from the West End sky'."

At this point, Lord's Cricket Ground was no more than 200 yards away and they were on the western edges of Regent's Park near to London Zoo. Lord's cricket ground was founded by Thomas Lord. Lord's is a place so special for cricket and especially English cricket that to say it resembled the cathedral of cricket would be something of an understatement. The place was a metaphor for Englishness and English identity. 'Hallowed ground' wouldn't even start to do justice in describing its importance.

A kink in the canal, just past the Aviary and close to the Feng Shang Princess took you on a straight path to Camden. Camden to Little Venice was like comparing punk rock to classical music. Camden was dirty, disheveled and vibrant. Some would call it seedy and reeking of drugs and cheap sexual encounters. Others would call it enlightened. Street markets were everywhere with modern day 'Fagins' lurking about. It was a place to have your wits about you. Camden was the definitive marmite location offering opportunities to musicians of all backgrounds and tastes. Numerous venues were happy to give bands a chance. If you were poor, then you would be given mean abuse and run out of town. Camden could make or break you. People were known to run up the hill as fast as possible back to respectable Highgate and Hampstead Heath.

Gene Vincent and WG entered the Hawley Arms in Camden thinking it looked a likely venue for The Clash. It was night time in Camden. Music blared out from the Jukebox. People of all musical sorts frequented the pace; rockabillies, punks, metal freaks, goths, soul lovers and much more. A man called Sir Johnny Green was reading poetry. He was the self-styled 'bard of Camden'.

"You could fit in well here, Gene," suggested WG. "There are at least 10 people in this pub who look like you."

Then a wonderful moment happened. 'Wild Cat' by a certain Gene Vincent came on the jukebox. People got up on the tables and started throwing themselves around. The place was rocking. Beer was being thrown about like confetti at a wedding. This pub was not for the gentile and faint-hearted. Sir Johnny Green gave up reading his poetry and joined in with the madness.

"It's fate, Gene. Get your card out and hand it over to one of those blokes. They'll never notice."

Gene went over to a man who looked like he could break you into two with a stare and had just come out of prison for GBH.

"Take this, mate. It's my card. It's my song."

The man with the stare took the card and put it in his back pocket.

"Fuck me! Where did you come from? Love the outfit and the quiff mate," he gave Gene a playful headbutt. Then he punched him quite hard on the chin. "That's for being Gene Vincent and dying young. Now you're a mate. I'm Dave."

Gene reeled from the blow. He fell into a chair and was steadied by a rockabilly husband and wife combo down from St Albans for the day. WG, invisible to all but Gene, quickly moved to his side. "Well done, Gene. This is your chance." They had ignored that fact that the couple from St Albans had helped Gene Vincent.

Gene took a few moments to come to his senses. The man who had hit him bought him a pint of warm ale. "Get that down you, mate. You'll feel a lot better."

"You hit me."

"Nah. That's my introduction. You're Gene Vincent. We're mates now."

They looked at each other for about 10 minutes before Gene built up the courage to ask him the question that had to be asked.

"I'm looking for a band called The Clash. Have you heard of them?"

"Of course. My best mate is the manager. Bernie Rhodes is the bloke you want. They practice just along the canal at Camden Road Depot. It's a train station."

"Are they there now?"

"They're always there practising even if it's away from their manor. They haven't got a gig yet."

"Manor?"

"You really are a stranger. We're North London here and they're over from the West."

"Where do they play there?" asked Gene.

"I hear they broke into Loftus Road, QPR's ground, the other day and started playing. They move fast so you've got to be quick."

Dave took another sip from his pint. "You're a dead ringer for Gene Vincent. I love Gene Vincent."

"Would you help me find The Clash?"

"I'll have a word with Bernie. Let me call him now."

Dave went to the bar to use the pub's telephone putting 10p in to get a line.

WG looked excited. "Well done, Gene. You did really well there."

"The man is mad. He hit me. I've had worse. It's the mad world of rock n'roll."

"You get hit in cricket as well. That ball is very hard. Fast bowlers are really mean. They're ruthless bastards."

"Stop talking about cricket. This is fucking rock n'roll."

"I can't stop talking about cricket."

"Is that Ray Davies from the Kinks over there?"

"Ray who?"

"Get back to your cricket WG."

5 minutes later, Dave came back.

"They're on the Green at Shepherd's Bush tonight in a place called 'The Goldhawk'. It's 2 mins from the tube station."

"Are they at The Goldhawk for long?" asked Gene.

"I haven't a clue mate. Joe's kicking off and Mick Jones has just hit Paul Simonon. So, it's a normal calm night."

"Thanks, Dave."

"No worries Gene Vincent. Come back to Camden soon. Camden loves you."

Life was moving at the speed of light.

Sir Johnny Green came over. "Who are you talking to Dave?"

"I'm talking to Gene Vincent."

"Have you gone fucking mad? There's nobody there."

"Of course there is. I've just been speaking to Gene Vincent," Dave looked convinced.

Sir Johnny Green looked to the sky. "Camden... oh fucking Camden. Full of fucking madmen."

Both Gene Vincent and WG shuddered. Camden had been an experience.

Gene and WG left the Hawley Arms and were looking totake the Northern line followed by the Central line to Shepherd's Bush. Camden was starting to warm up for the night. People, stoned out of their minds, stumbled along the streets. A couple of goths were being annihilated at the hands of a pack of rockers. Police sirens were an unwelcome backdrop to pub rock music. Violence permeated the air. Skinheads walked along the high road, menacing and unwelcoming, beckoning all and sundry to a ritual beating. Civility was about as visible as the old River Fleet that flowed under the mean streets of Camden. It was like an urban version of the film *Apocalypse Now*. WG started to panic.

"Don't be an idiot. Nobody other than that David can see me. You're invisible."

"This is nothing like the Camden I knew," WG lamented the decline of Camden in a moment of nostalgia. "In my day, the place had style."

"Forget it WG. We've got to get over to Shepherd's Bush for some rock n'roll. I'm done with Camden for tonight." Gene Vincent was struggling.

In the 1970s, the Northern Line could dampen the spirits of even the most optimistic person. The Central Line was cramped and over capacity. The journey to Shepherd's Bush was not something to look forward to.

"Get in you two. I'll drive you to where you want to go."

"Cheers my friend. Who are you?" WG was relieved.

"My name is Iain Sinclair. I'm a young writer. Now where do you want to go?"

"Shepherd's Bush Green."

"No problems."

"How come you can see us?" WG was intrigued.

"I just can."

"Fair enough." WG and Gene Vincent were too weary to push the argument. Camden had played them out. Nothing else was said.

Forty minutes later Iain Sinclair dropped them off. "Be careful of the Green."

"Why?" asked Gene Vincent, but Iain Sinclair was gone into the night, screaming past Shepherd's Bush theatre, as if his life depended on it.

"Nice guy. Strange though." Gene Vincent shrugged his shoulders, adding "Now it's all about the Clash."

WG looked weary. "It'd be easier finding the Holy Grail than The Clash. Is this some wild goose chase?"

"It was never going to be easy to find a saviour," Gene sounded evangelical.

"Do you think we should just let fate play its hand? Maybe we're trying too hard," WG sounded exasperated.

WG spoke, "The last 24 hours have been too hard and crazy. We've got to see this through. We must have some purpose, otherwise we'll spend an eternity in this in-between world. I don't want to be the lost soul of the Regent's Canal. I think there's a few of those already."

Gene lamented, "It's surprising we've not bumped into any other spirits. We could have done with the help."

WG and Gene walked along the Green at Shepherd's Bush. The Bush was calmer than Camden. The tree-lined Green was an oasis of serenity with The Goldhawk at the far end close to the Empire.

WG entered The Goldhawk first. They could hear The Clash. They were loud and aggressive. Gene Vincent hang back as nerves started to affect him. He had his stage. Rock n'roll was going to start again. This was its re-birth. He felt the weight of the moment.

The Clash was practising furiously in the basement. Gene and WG opened the door to the basement gently.

They looked magnificent. Joe Strummer was like an overworked piston on rocket fuel. Paul Simonon was cooler than an iceberg. Mick Jones looked like the Lord of the Westway. Terry Chimes was industrious, and Keith Levene was absent.

Gene froze. The sound was so pulsating and exciting. He was wired. This was as good as anything from the '50s and '60s. The problem was how to connect with Joe Strummer. He had to give him his calling card. But how to do it was beyond him now he was face-to-face.

WG was prompting him, "Come on, Gene. This is your moment. You've got to go now."

"I can't, WG. I just can't."

"What's the matter with you?"

"I don't know."

"You've got to do it. It's a waste of time me doing it."

"I'm in awe. They're too good. I can't do it. They don't need me."

"Is that it then?"

"Let's get out of here. I've heard enough."

"That's the anti-climax of all time," WG looked furious.

WG and Gene Vincent left The Goldhawk. The Clash was none the wiser to their presence.

They sat on a seat in the middle of Shepherd's Bush Green. They could hear The Clash playing, albeit faintly.

"What happened Gene? You froze."

"Rock n'Roll is safe in their hands. My work is done." Gene didn't sound convincing.

"No. It isn't. You choked when it mattered. Where do we go from here?"

"We'll keep trying. I'll be different next time."

"You don't believe in yourself. That's what this is all about."

"I do."

"I don't know much, but you're no king of rock n'roll that's for sure. You need to do this for Eddie Cochran."

WG's last comment had wounded Gene Vincent.

For WG, he could look forward to seeing Viv Richards at the Oval. He would be watching cricket again, the game he loved. He was worried about Gene Vincent though. Both of them felt a slight unease. Neither of them knew that the Green had supported one of the largest plague pits in London.

WG spoke first after a period of silence and a big sulk from Gene Vincent. "We've got to meet Billy at the George and Dragon in Bromley. Let's not fall out. I'm really trying to help you. We're in it together. We're a team."

"Thanks, WG. I appreciate that. Let's get a move on then. It'll be closing time soon. This place gives me the creeps. Something weird is going on here."

"I played football and cricket on Shepherd's Bush Green. I thought it looked familiar. It's coming back to me now." At last, WG had a smile on his face.

WG and Gene Vincent made their way south of the river to the George and Dragon in Bromley. The evening had been chastening. There was only 10 mins to closing time. Billy Idol was at the bar on his own.

"Where have you two been?" Billy Idol was clearly frustrated.

"We've been to Camden and Shepherd's Bush," Gene Vincent sounded starry eyed. He was doing his best to hide his inner turmoil.

"If I was alive I'd feel knackered," WG wasn't so ebullient.

"Any success with Joe Strummer?"

"No," WG and Gene Vincent answered in unison.

"What happened?"

Gene Vincent and WG looked at each other.

"I froze. I don't understand what happened."

"Keep trying. You'll get there. Siouxsie can see a bright future."

"Is Siousxie the lady that was with you last night?"

"She's the lady in black. Siouxsie has the gift of foresight. She can see the future."

"What's the story about you then Billy? You promised to fill us in."

"I've famous relatives. One of my descendantswas hanged at Tyburn. Another was killed in a duel at Hampstead Heath."

"Why did they die?"

"Both died over the game of cricket. You could say that I'm cricket royalty."

WG asked, "Is that why I came back?"

"It must be. It's too much of a coincidence. We weren't sure of your name though. We got lucky with you. We got the most famous cricketer of all time."

"You have a point, I have to admit. Good to hear something that makes sense for once."

"The 'Tyburn redemption' is what it's known as. My family 'the Broads' were wronged."

"I need to save the family name. The seventh descendent would be given the opportunity. That's me. It was foretold that a saviour would come to help me."

"Who said?" WG looked unconvinced.

"Mary Abbott. The last person to speak with my descendent hung at Tyburn. The story has been handed down the Broad family for over 200 years.

"WG! You must have come back for that reason. To save me!"

"It was cricket that killed them. It'll be cricket that saves me."

WG was adamant. "I've come back to help Viv Richards."

"Yes, I know. But you've come back to help me." Billy sounded earnest.

"Have I come back to help everyone? There's you, Gene and Viv. I know I was a doctor but this is crazy."

Billy turned to WG. "It looks that way WG. You're the saviour."

"That's an eclectic bunch WG," Billy was trying to sound impressed.

"That's true, Billy. Two idiots and a genius."

"Is Billy or me the genius?" asked Gene seriously.

"Neither."

"Are we that bad?" asked Gene and Billy together.

WG looked at both them as if they had the black death.

"I've got a lot of work to do with you two. Neither of you have any common sense."

"How come?"

"Both of you hate cricket. How can you hate cricket."

"It isn't rock n'roll."

"What's this Siousxie all about then?" asked WG. "She looks rather strange."

Billy and Gene laughed. "You old fart."

"Does she speak?"

"Not very often. She's royalty you know."

"Royalty. You're kidding me? Is everyone fucking mad around here?" WG was ready to give up completely.

She reckons her descendant was Goiswintha, the Queen of the Visigoths.

"Maybe I'm Julius Caesar. Of course she is. I'm sure that I'm still dead and somehow dreaming all this."

"Queen of the Visigoths?"

"They were knocking about around 570 AD."

"Goiswintha visited Siousxie."

"Stop it, Billy. Is this the drugs?"

"I don't think so."

"Are we allowed to speak with Siouxsie?"

"I'm not sure."

"She's very talented. She has the gift of foresight."

"What has she foretold?" asked Gene.

"It's a little hazy."

"Of course it is, but go on."

"Ok then. She says The Clash are going to become legends but they need your help Gene."

"What about WG's story?"

"Not sure. She doesn't like cricket. She needs to like something to foretell."

"That's typical. Why does nobody love cricket?"

"But you're here. You're central to all of this."

"Did you feel that when you die… you die?"

"No I don't."

"Do you believe that people are re-incarnated or come back in spirit form?"

"I do."

"Well then, what are we worrying about then? Let's go with it then."

"I suppose we have to."

"Just relax boys. We can do this." Billy was trying to be encouraging.

His naivety was overwhelming as was his boyish charms.

Normally, WG would have exploded in rage. Instead, he laughed.

"I have to admire your innocence. I like you Billy Idol."

Chapter 3

The Oval Cricket Ground
May 12th, 1976

'Cricket to us was more than play. It was a worship in the summer sun' – Edmund Blunden
'For once, cricket has claimed you, it never lets you go' – Marcus Berkmann

The temperature hit 24C in London. The West Indies cricket team was playing Surrey at the Oval in South London, their first real test of the tour. The Clash practiced in the basement of a Railway Depot in Camden having relocated from yesterday's venue. It was 'punk mobility' as Strummer called it. You had to be always on the run.

WG wondered around the Oval cricket ground around 9am waiting for the West Indies to arrive and thinking of ways he was going to meet Viv Richards. He saw the West Indies team bus turn into the Oval car park. Clive Lloyd, the team captain, was the first off the bus. The team looked resplendent in their cardinal red blazers. Viv was near the back of the queue waiting to get off the bus, talking to Lawrence Rowe and Gordon Greenidge. They were carrying their kit bags up the steps to the away team dressing room.

The game was to start at 11am and very few supporters were at the ground yet. The teams would have a net before the match on the outfield. There were a couple of hours to kill for WG. He just couldn't think of a way of getting close to Viv to give him his calling card.

Gene Vincent had decided to stay away still despondent from the encounter with The Clash. The mix of emotions was very strange. He hated cricket, but he didn't want to leave WG to fend for himself. He'd arranged to meet up with WG outside The Hanover Arms, a stone's throw from the Oval. Billy Idol had drunk there and recommended it. Gene was more comfortable in South London.

The penny dropped. WG knew now that Gene had got it all wrong. The experience at The Goldhawk had convinced him. He would just go up to Viv after today's play and announce himself. If Viv Richards has the 'eye' there wouldn't be an issue. He was the Grandfather of cricket and inferior to nobody. Nobody who had gates named after himself at Lord's needed to worry. This calling card story was utter rubbish. WG threw his cards to the ground in disdain. He had to talk some sense into Gene Vincent. The man was an idiot.

Surrey batted first. The West Indies opening bowlers Wayne Daniels and Andy Roberts were lacklustre and wayward. England stalwart John Edrich picked them off at ease, scoring quickly and using the bowler's pace onto the bat skillfully. He was well supported by Alan Butcher in an opening stand of 176. King and Jumadeen fared even worse going for 137 off 25 overs between them. Only the part time bowlers in Gomes and Fredericks provided any bite taking 2 wickets each. Clive Lloyd was none too impressed and laid into the team and particularly the mainline bowlers during the break for innings. Bowlers were reminded that every game counted and that the many fellow West Indians who had come to support them had been let down.

The batsmen in the West Indies first innings fared little better than the bowlers. Rowe, Fredericks and Kallicharran went for 18 runs between them. Viv Richards came in at 3 and started to dominate the bowlers immediately scoring 7 4's and a 6 at a run a ball. A big hundred looked there for the taking when Viv was bowled looking for an expansive drive against occasional bowler Alan Butcher. He hit his boot with the bat in anger. This was a gift wicket to Butcher.

WG watched every ball that Viv faced intently. He studied his foot movements, the straightness of his bat. He liked what he saw, though had concerns about his head position. WG could see that he saw the ball early and had plenty of time. There was something special about him. He pinched himself to be watching the game he loved. The game was broadly the same. The players looked different and the Oval had changed significantly. But it was still cricket and it was still batsmen versus bowlers. The rhythms of the game hadn't altered. The captain was still the conductor moving players around in the field, changing bowlers and deciding tactics. Bowlers still looked disgruntled when batsmen nicked them through the slips for four. Fast bowlers still looked moody and aggressive. Spinners were still reflective and scheming. The game was still beautiful. WG knew what he was going to say to Viv Richards.

The West Indies supporters came from all over the Caribbean: Jamaica, Antigua, Barbados, Trinidad and many of the smaller islands. They carried their conch shells and island flags proudly. Jerk chicken and Rum had been the food and drink of the day. The tunes of Bob Marley were everywhere.

Many offered plenty of vocal advice to their heroes. West Indies fans were not averse to giving out loud reprimands to a poor shot or a wayward delivery. Fast bowling and bouncers were adored. Big hits from the batsmen were obligatory. Every supporter was a cricket expert. A successful West Indies team would make them feel a foot taller, providing some light to many who suffered from a daily diet of abuse and harrassment. And then there was the weather to endure. Viv Richards had attended the Alf Gover cricket school in Wandsworth in the winter of 1973 to learn his trade. Rumour had it that he wore an overcoat to bed every night.

Viv and many of the other West Indies players were talking with their supporters underneath the stand at the Pavilion End. WG, resplendent with white luxuriant beard, approached Viv and shouted out, "Well played, Viv. You hit some good shots. You should have scored a hundred though."

The praise seemed a little formal and tinged with criticism. There was none of the 'in your face' warmth he received from fellow West Indians who had come along to support their team.

Nevertheless, Viv responded with a smile and a simple "Thanks" then adding with more contemplation, "You're right. I gave it away. Got too confident."

Viv looked at WG. He liked his directness and confidence. He recognised instinctively in WG there was a man who knew his cricket and that the slight criticism was well meant. He sounded like his father. And he looked familiar, but he just couldn't place where he had seen him before.

"You should murder these bowlers. Butcher was throwing pies out there." You've some big test match innings this summer." Then WG was gone. He was off to meet Gene

Vincent at The Hanover Arms just outside the ground. Viv shook his head, wondering why the man had suddenly disappeared.

Viv thought nothing more for the moment, other than thinking back to a couple of admirers who wanted to appreciate more of him than his batting skills. Later that evening, he left the ground on the team bus and saw WG again. This time, WG was chatting to a man with a quiff, as they passed the Hannover Arms, on route to their hotel. He noticed their outfits were as different to each other as it was possible to get. They looked as if they were going to a fancy dress party.

Viv thought this as strange and casually mentioned to a team mate Wayne Daniel, who responded, "I can't see anyone with a long white beard. That sun and those runs must have got to you today. Just think of all your admirers back at the Oval. Did you get their phone numbers?"

"My phone book is full enough," replied Viv, cheekily.

Several moments later, Viv added, "I only scored 46. Gave it away. It's been a good year so far."

Viv smiled and thought of all the centuries he had scored in 1976. Those big scores had fans back in the West Indies salivating at his success. Fellow Antiguans lapped up his runs. Gravy, his number 1 fan after family, wore his pink suit every time Viv got "serious runs" as he called it. Rum barrels were emptied. West Indians loved their cricket and embraced it with a style unmatched by any other nation. There was no pomposity and stiff upper lip in the Caribbean Islands. Cricket, music and life were their passions. Vivian Richards was following in the path of greatness: Headley, Weekes, Worrall, Walcott, Hall, Griffiths and Sobers. These were the creme de la crème: cricket legends of the highest standing. People would talk about them for decades if not centuries.

The team bus arrived at the hotel in Kensington after suffering a break down going over Chelsea bridge. "He's there again, Wayne, the bloke with the white beard." Viv just stood hands on hips, shaking his head, blinking his eyes as if somehow this would cure him of the human mirage.

"How did he beat us back to the hotel?"

"Have something to eat, Viv and don't drink tonight. I can't see no bloke with a long white beard." Wayne preached, adding, "Why are you losing it, Viv? You're freaking me out man."

"I'm not losing it, Wayne. He's for real. Honestly."

Viv walked to the hotel restaurant worrying he was hallucinating and 'telling lies' as his strict, God fearing father would say. Viv tried to put the man with the white beard to the back of his mind, but he knew there was something about him that was special. It was just some type of gut instinct that Viv trusted in.

WG was thinking about Viv and what he needed to say. He knew Viv was special but unproven. A few words might make him see that he was something special. The first test match was less than 3 weeks away and in Nottingham. After this match the West Indies would move onto Hampshire, Kent and Somerset. He had to meet him now as his range was London for the foreseeable future as he had to help Gene Vincent. WG knocked on Viv's door just before midnight. He'd left Gene at the Hanover Arms, soaking up the rustic atmosphere of South London. Spirits couldn't drink though, which was such a shame, given their name.

Viv woke up startled by someone banging on his door. "Who the hell is waking me up?"

Viv moved to open the door, willing to have an argument. WG spoke first, "I need to speak with you, Viv. Don't get angry with me. I mean to help you. You saw me yesterday. Do you remember?"

"Of course I do. There are not too many people rocking your look mate in South London. You told me off for getting out to Butcher."

The kindness in his eyes and voice placated Viv. "Just give me half an hour of your time. That's all we'll need. It'll change your life."

Viv thought WG looked unthreatening, so why not let him have his say and put this behind him. "OK, old man. Take a seat. Who are you? Why were you at the Oval earlier?"

"Listen to me Viv. Don't be freaked out, but it's WG... WG Grace."

"You're having me on. You're dead. That's it."

"You're right. I've come back in spirit to help you."

Viv looked disbelieving, "I'm dreaming this. This can't be true. No way."

"I don't know why this has happened, Viv. But I'm here now and I can help you. I'm your spirit guide."

Viv decided to let him in. Something told him he had to listen to the man.

"Don't worry, Viv. Nobody else can see me."

Viv knew the legend of WG Grace, albeit in very sketchy details. This wasn't out of disrespect. Viv loved the game of cricket in an uncomplicated fashion, just wanting to smack the ball to all parts of a cricket ground, with a warm Caribbean sun on his back. Batting was pure pleasure. The battle 'eye to eye' of batsmen versus bowler was enthralling. Bowlers were to be annihilated and humiliated in a sporting sense. He wanted to see bowlers tremble as they started their run ups and look in despair as the ball sailed into the stands from a vicious hook. The crowd baying for the bowler's 'blood' was pure music to his ears. Cricket was gladiatorial and brutal. Bowlers were trying to damage your reputation and your joy in batting. They had to be resisted and put to the sword. If he hadn't been a batsmen Viv would have been a boxer, citing Smokin' Joe Frazier, ex-Heavyweight Champion of the World, as his hero. Though a decent and gentleman, Viv became like a gladiator from Ancient Rome when he crossed the whitewash. The cricket ground was his Coliseum.

Gentle singles and padding away medium pacers and spinners were a sign of weakness to Viv. As was ducking bouncers from the men of speed. All challenges had to be met with a steely glare and complete dominance. The English approach to the game was more conservative and attritional, all about wearing down your opponent in mind. This was cricket of a bank clerk mind set. Timidness and negativity was everywhere. It was bad choir music to the pulsating sounds of punk rock. This was achieved whilst talking about what you were drinking that night in the pub and if there were decent sandwiches and cake in the 'break for tea'. Batsmen were naturally cautious and respectful that bowlers had a bag of tricks up their sleeves and were throwing down bombs at them. Bowlers were to be mastered but peacefully, never humiliated and put to the sword. Cricket was a pastime to be enjoyed after long, dull, grey and cold winters. The onset of spring and watery sunshine with the smell of 'willow on leather' was pure joy to an Englishman. The 'end of suffering' had arrived. Maybe it was just all down to the weather.

Another cause for the 'English malaise' was the Players v Gentlemens division in the game before 1962. Gentlemen played the game as amateurs in name only claiming expenses often much more than the wages of professionals or players. As Gentlemen they were men of means, education and background, having other careers and professional occupations. They had no need to play the game for a wage, looking down at such people who did, as grubby working-class mercenaries. A laissez faire attitude to the game ensued. This was cricket's equivalent of the English civil war, as seen by respected historians or The Clash. Royalist versus Parliamentarians. Upper class versus working class. Karl Marx would have had a field day writing about the game. Even in the 1970s, certain cricket writers like E.W Swanton would have this romantic image of the Gentlemen. All the ills of the game were brought on by the players, those 'grubby' working class mercenaries. To these people, only a Gentlemen, a man of education and more importantly, breeding, could be captain of England. The 'cut of your jib' was everything. No wonder England played like they did. As an Englishman, you would support your team but a part of you wanted the oppressed playing their colonial masters to play with flair and win. IVA Richards was the antithesis of everything English and you loved him for it, albeit with a little guilt in your soul and your English DNA. Every Viv Richards boundary was a snub to English arrogance, snobbishness and class-ridden pomposity.

In summary, Viv just hadn't done the history part of the game yet. However, he was its soul, and true heir to WG Grace. WG Grace had gates named after him at Lord's, the home of cricket. They were located close to the west end of the Tavern Stand and the main entrance to Lord's for MCC members. WG Grace was the Godfather of Cricket. He was a Victorian era superman. His list of achievements would make any mortal feel extremely jealous and completely inadequate. He was that special. However, WG Grace bought a ruthless gamesmanship to cricket. Once he was clean bowled and refused to walk. "Play on," he was heard to say, adding, "they've come here to see me bat, not you umpire."

In some eyes he was the original 'bad boy' of cricket, the enfant terrible. WG broke every convention about how to behave on a cricket field. In his breakthrough innings at Hove in July 1864, when to his "great annoyance" he chopped a ball on to his stumps. The 15-year-old Grace stomped off in a huff, displaying his anger to all. He had failed only scoring 170 when a double century was there for the taking.

Controversy was never far away. On 29th August 1882, he ran out an Australian batsman who had absent-mindedly wandered out of his ground, thinking the ball was dead. According to cricket's code of honour, Grace should have warned the batsman not to repeat his mistake. Yet he electrified the game, triggering two hours of almost unbearable excitement as the Australians, out for revenge, won the game, prompting a London newspaper to write a mock obituary for English cricket. Without Grace's alleged "cheating", the Ashes might never have been born.

In 1882 WG was already on the slide. WG's physical self-destruction is usually blamed on his prodigious overeating, but he was a formidable drinker as well. By the mid-1880s he routinely needed a lunchtime whisky and soda to fuel him through the afternoon's play, switching to champagne, wine and whisky chasers at the end of the day. The Music Halls were his sanctuary to alleviate the stress of fame.

Tragedy also struck him. He and his wife, Agnes, lost their only daughter Bessie to typhoid at the age of 20 in 1899. Then the sudden death of their eldest son Bertie struck them in 1905. "We know what it is to lose those that are dearest to us," WG wrote shortly afterwards to a recently widowed friend.

WG played from 1865 to 1908, captaining England, Gloucestershire, MCC and just about any other team he played for. He ruled cricket like a Victorian Caesar, even bigger than Bradman many years later. He bought the game into a style that we know of today. His technical innovations and enormous influence left a legacy. He excelled at everything cricket... batting, bowling and fielding. His captaincy was inspiring and if he wanted to, he could probably have made the best cricket lunches and teas known to man. His statistics were immense and mind boggling. 54,896 first class runs. 2,864 wickets. He played in the Test Match in 1882 that spawned the Ashes.

One of his famous quotes was, "Do not be content to stop the ball by simply putting the bat in its way – anyone can do that – but try and score off it too." WG Grace and Viv Richards were spiritual soul mates. WG Grace was back playing again. Every Viv Richards hook for 6 over square leg had part of him in that shot.

He died at Mottingham in South East London on 23rd October 1915, aged 67. His death shook the nation, compared in importance to the death of Churchill 50 years later.

Grace took part in other sports. He was a champion 400 metres hurdler on the track and played football for the Wanderers. He qualified as a doctor in 1879.

Viv decided to ask some questions of WG. "So, nobody else can see you?"

"Only you and some idiots called Gene Vincent and Billy Idol."

"Who are they?"

"Gene Vincent was a star in the 1950s and '60s... a rock n'roll legend. Whatever that is. Billy Idol is a delinquent from Bromley who likes something called punk rock. For some reason, I like Billy. He's got something about him. He's a kind and decent soul."

WG went through his test career that started in 1880 and ended 19 years later. He talked for over 2 hours about his life and career. Viv was enthralled. He wasn't sure if he was dreaming or hallucinating.

WG started to get serious. "You could be great, Viv. But you're making mistakes."

"I'm making runs. In Australia, I got a century and got 3 more against India."

"Everyone gets lucky. You got beaten 5-1 in Australia. Lillee and Thomson murdered you."

Viv was taken aback, "I've learnt from that."

"Make yourself great, Viv. There's no other cricketer I want to talk to. Forget the Chappells, Fletcher and that Lawrence Rowe. You're the one. Though that Michael Holding ran you close. You're lucky I prefer batting." WG had done his research over the last 2 days whilst Gene Vincent fretted about finding The Clash.

Viv didn't know if he should hit him or shake his hand.

"So, what have I got to do?"

"Be humble. Respect yourself and your opponents. Simple stuff. Play straight and don't try and hit every ball for 6."

WG continued, "You play across the line."

"Is that all?" Viv looked perplexed.

"Keep your head down. You're lifting your head too much. Hit the ball under your nose and a little later."

Viv was speechless but now enthralled. This was an audience with greatness. He'd been won over.

The time was 3am.

"I need to rest now, so I'm going to have to leave you Viv." The lecture had finished.

Viv was struggling to say anything. After some hesitation, Viv muttered weakly, "Will I see you again?"

"I'll pop over to see you at Lord's for the MCC match at the end of May. Then it'll be the first test match in Nottingham. I can't leave London too much as I've got to help my friend save rock n'roll."

"Rock n'roll. Why?"

"It's complicated."

At this point WG got out of his chair to leave. WG felt they were kindred spirits and really liked him. There was no better person to save the game.

"I'll be seeing you, Viv. And I'll follow your progress every day in the papers. Go and score big, my friend. Though you'll be murdering England though if you do."

WG was becoming emotional. "The game needs you. You're its soul and spirit. It's a responsibility so respect that. And from what I've seen today the West Indies people need you."

Viv knew he'd been visited by the almighty. He sat on his bed and pinched himself. He went to the bathroom and washed his face as if the water would bring his senses back.

The next day, the cricket world exploded. Several incendiary words from England cricket captain Tony Greig, "I intend to make them grovel," when referring to the West Indies and upcoming Test Series. Viv Richards and the rest of the West Indies team were furious. Tony Greig was born and raised in South Africa, 6' 7" and white. The insensitivities and gross racism of these comments would influence the forthcoming test series and taint Tony Greig's reputation. Though, to be fair to Tony Greig, he would apologize almost daily for the rest of his life and nobody in time thought the comments were racially motivated. The West Indies were keen to beat the old enemy, their former colonial masters, before the series. Now that level of motivation had increased tenfold.

Viv spoke of the team's initial reaction. "Wow. And I'll tell you, that was the team meeting. I think someone said to the skipper at the time, "Clive, are we gonna have the meeting?"

He said, "No, the meeting's over."

Viv Richards summarized the atmosphere. "You could see the looks on everyone's face, and I knew we were going to have a good summer".

The next day, the West Indies cricket team did hold a meeting with all the players, manager and officials involved. Most of the players were spitting fury at Greig's comments. A few talked about an official apology and even boycotting the upcoming test series. That was never going to happen. However, all of them wanted to rub Greig's face into the dirt. Revenge was going to be sweet. Every time Greig would come into bat, the bowlers would try that little bit harder and bowl faster. When he bowled, the batsmen would look to hit him to all parts of the ground and tried never give their wicket away to him. Greig was going to feel the heat.

The second day's play saw Clive Lloyd hit 152 not out and share a 204 run fifth wicket partnership with Larry Gomes. Gomes scored 85. They were the ying and yan of cricket. Lloyd was tall and powerful who liked to score quickly and played with aggression. He was the blueprint of West Indian batting, and on his day, totally devastating. The crowd were in physical danger when watching Clive Lloyd bat. Gomes was diminutive who scored mostly through nudging and nurdling the ball for singles, twos and threes. He didn't hit sixes often. He was uncaribbean in his style, often unstated, but very valuable and a fine cricketer. The West Indies declared on 316-5 with a slender lead of 13.

In Surrey's second innings, the West Indies bowed with more accuracy and intent. Daniels, Roberts and King bowled well sharing 5 wickets between them. Surrey were all out for 252. Jumadeen made up for his poor bowling in the first innings taking 3-72. Larry Gomes, the understated Gomes, took 2-31. The Wes Indies had 3 hours to chase down 240 to win the game. They opted for batting practise instead reaching 97-3 when the captains shook hands on an honourable draw. Roy Fredericks scored 42 not out playing with uncharacteristic caution and if he was having a net. Viv scored 13, dismissed by the leg spinner Intikhab Alam.

WG watched every ball of the 3 days. He was unseen and decided against contacting Viv Richards. WG loved many sports but cricket was special. Cricket was like marmite, but when you 'got it'; you really 'got it'. The rhythms and intricacies of the game were very special.

The great West Indian intellectual CLR James understood like few others. "Cricket is an art. Like all arts it has a technical foundation. To enjoy it does not require technical knowledge, but analysis that is not technically based is mere impressionism."

The next day, the West Indies moved to Southampton to play Hampshire. Hampshire were demolished with true Caribbean style. Hampshire batted first scoring 152 all out. Vanburn Holder took 5-44 with nagging accuracy and subtle seam movement and swing. Julien, Padmore and Holding took wickets also. Holding bowled with serious pace. Several Hampshire batsmen were hit. PJ Sainsbury was unable to bat second innings. Holding ran like an Olympic 400 metres runner. He was smooth in his approach with a loose limbed, nimble and a fast action. His action was pure poetry. He was like a Ferrari and Porsche rolled into one supercar. Pure pace bowling was a joy to watch if not to face.

Viv Richards opened the batting with Roy Fredericks in the West Indies reply. Gomes contributed again, scoring 56. However, it was Viv who got the headlines. He scored 176. The Telegraph called the innings 'majestic'. Viv played at a slower pace, keeping the ball on the ground. His scoring rate was barely above 50 though still very decent. He was dominant, but never brutal with the Hampshire bowling attack. The innings was played with the words of WG in his thoughts. His head was still and low, playing the ball in the 'V'. The West Indies declared on 371/6 and bowled out Hampshire for 131 to win by an innings and 88 runs. Padmore took 5-49.

However, it was Michael Holding who stayed in your mind, especially if you were a batsman. Graham Gooch, who played West Indies pace bowling better than anyone, would state, 'Nobody likes pace bowling, it's just that some play it better than others.' Holding had pace to burn. He hurt batsman. He gave batsmen sleepless nights.

Punk and its origins were a product of what was happening in Britain in the summer of 1976 in terms of economics, social history, fashion, weather and music.

The UK was in drought. The summer and autumn of 1975 were very dry, and the winter of 1975–76 was exceptionally dry, as was the spring of 1976. A swarm of Ladybirds engulfed a man on the Dorset coast at Lyme Regis in response to a huge growth in the number of aphids. The weather was blamed.

The first reading of a Race Relations Act took place in the House of Commons after being debated at committee stage for some months. The Act would be passed in December 1976. The Act was much needed. Sadly, it happened 20 years on from the Windrush Generation arriving. Too much blood had been spilt already.

The UK economy was barely coming out of the recession from the Oil crisis of 1973-74. Britain was an importer of oil, so the quintupling of the oil price in this period, had helped to bring inflation, unemployment, negative growth and a worsening balance of payments. In May, the GBP/USD exchange rate declined 15% to US$1.70/£1. It would fall to 1.55 before the end of the summer of 1976. The government and Bank of England had stopped supporting the Pound hoping a lower currency would kickstart the UK economy. Export led recovery and a surge in productivity were the mantras to bring back the good times. Economists talked endlessly about Britain's productivity malaise. For the middle classes, with their expense accounts, company cars and comfy offices, it was all down to the blue collar working classes 'not working hard enough' and being 'always on strike'. Trade Union leaders were the devils in disguise. The Daily Mail had all the answers and knew where the blame lied.

The defining economic blow to Britain came with the 1976 IMF Financial Crisis. In 1976 the UK Government had to borrow $3.9 billion (GBP 2.3 billion) from the International Monetary Fund (IMF), at the time the largest loan ever to have been requested from the IMF. Jim Callaghan, the Prime Minister, was saying, "What crisis?" The Daily Mail was crying in ecstasy at Labour's woes. According to the Mail, Britain was finished.

Only half of the loan was ever drawn by the UK government and it was repaid fully by 4 May 1979. Denis Healey, the Chancellor of the Exchequer, stated that the main reason the loan had to be requested was that public sector borrowing requirement figures provided by the treasury were grossly overstated. The politicians were blaming everyone but themselves.

The IMF loan meant that the United Kingdom's economy could be stabilised whilst drastic budget cuts were implemented. Even with the loan's security, the Labour Party had already begun unravelling into camps of Social Democrats and left-wing supporters, which caused bitter rows inside the party and with the unions. The mood had changed from Keynesian economics to the principles of Milton Friedman. Thatcher, Howe and Joseph were waiting to pounce.

Monetarism was to be the new religion. MV=PT had replaced E=M*c(Squared) as the formula of choice.

In the second week of May, the organisers of the annual Notting Hill Carnival started to accelerate their planning. They met at Mangrove Restaurant in Notting Hill. The restaurant was owned by Frank Crichlow, who hailed from Trinidad.

The Notting Hill Carnival is an annual event that has taken place in London since 1966 on the streets of Notting Hill each August Bank Holiday weekend. The Carnival had become one of the world's largest street festivals in 1975 and a showpiece for Black British culture.

The roots of the Notting Hill Carnival took hold in the mid-1960. A "Caribbean Carnival" had been held on 30 January 1959 at St Pancras Town Hall as a response to the growing hatred to the Caribbean community throughout the UK. In 1958, the Notting Hill race riots happened between August 29th and September 5th with 108 arrests. The backdrop of the riots had been an increase in violent attacks on black people throughout the summer. On 24th August 1958, a group of ten English youths committed serious assaults on six West Indian men in four separate incidents. Tensions were rising. 5 days later, a domestic dispute with racial overtones ignited Notting Hill. Later that night a mob of 300 to 400 white people were seen on Bramley Road attacking the houses of West Indian residents. The disturbances, rioting and attacks continued every night until 5 September The riots caused tension between the Metropolitan Police and the British African-Caribbean community, which claimed that the police had not taken their reports of racial attacks seriously. A Government report many years later would claim there was no racial motive behind the riots.

The 1959 event, held indoors and televised by the BBC, was organised by the Trinidadian journalist and activist Claudia Jones in her capacity as editor of influential black newspaper 'The West Indian Gazette'. The event was to show elements of a Caribbean carnival in a cabaret style. One highlight was the singing of calypso "Carnival at St Pancras." The Southlanders, Trinidadian All Stars, Cleo Laine and Hi–Fi steel bands dance troupe all performed. The Carnival ended with a Caribbean Carnival Queen beauty contest and a Grand Finale Jump-Up by West Indians who attended the event.

Another catalyst for the Carnival was the London Free School Festival at Notting Hill in August 1966. The prime mover was Rhuane Laslett. This festival was a more diverse Notting Hill event to promote cultural unity. A street party for local children turned into a carnival procession when a steel band went on a walkabout. By 1970, the Notting Hill Carnival consisted of 2 music bands, the Russell Henderson Combo and Selwyn's Baptiste's Notting Hill Adventure Playground Steelband and 500 dancing spectators.

Leslie Palmer, who was director from 1973 to 1975, is credited with getting sponsorship, recruiting more steel bands, reggae groups and sound systems, introducing generators and extending the route. He encouraged traditional masquerade and created the bridge between the two cultures of carnival, reggae and calypso.

West London was one of the birthplaces of punk. Further south to the Westway was the King's Road in Chelsea. In the summer of 1976, past a shop called Sex at number 430, there was a scruffy, pencil-written announcement. Someone calling himself Sid Vicious was looking for people to form a band with him. "No flares," was in the message.

The Sex Pistols soon brought Sid Vicious in to replace their sacked bass player, Glen Matlock. Sex, was where Malcolm McLaren and his partner Vivienne Westwood, ran a fashion emporium. The place became a meeting place and cultural hub for punks. Glen Matlock had worked there.

Malcolm McLaren, manager of the Sex Pistols, commented later: "For a few years in the seventies, the King's Road became the centre of the universe... 430 King's Road was us placing the black spot in the palm of the culture we wanted to see trampled into the ground."

The King's Road traded on its 1960s reputation as swinging London's trendiest street. Chelsea footballers and fashion icons like Twiggy and Raquel Welch would frequent its shops and pubs. Marc Bolan and Rod Stewart were the hipsters there in the early '70s. Glam rock took a hold for a while. Suddenly, there was change, a punk revolution. Glen Matlock watched the dying days of the old regime: "The fashion trend was for Oxford bags. The mainstream look was Chelsea Girl and Lord John. The King's Road was peppered with shops who'd do watered down versions of the Rock Star look, loon pants and star tops, tulip lapels, stack heels, horrendous stuff. Then there was the sub-Roxy Music look, Alkasura and Antony Price and the 'real' rock star stuff from Granny Takes A Trip, which was kind of cool."

There was revolution in the air, and the weather acted as a catalyst for change. In the long hot summer of 1976, to escape from the sun, there was no shadier place in the whole King's Road than the Roebuck pub. Truant schoolgirls mingled with drug dealers in the place where McLaren had introduced his new discovery, Johnny Rotten, to the other three Sex Pistols, Paul Cook, Steve Jones and Glen Matlock.

The Roebuck was notorious. One of the residents of the King's Road would recall walking past the Roebuck just as the police arrived: "Out of the windows, there came this enormous cascade of drugs, hurriedly thrown into the street. 'The raids were hysterical, 40 or 50 policemen from Chelsea nick descending on the pub and lining people up. The place was run by this huge bloke, called Fat Jack, with one eye and a bald head. The funny thing is that, years later, the Roebuck became a Dome Cafe. Inside, you'd see all the same people who used to do drugs in the pub, but now they weren't on drugs anymore."

The King's Road began in West London splendour and glamour – Belgravia, Sloane Square – but ended with a council estate in a district called World's End, where the McLaren's shop was. The Road captured the economic and social apartheid of West London perfectly. In that sense, it was like the Westway.

One character of the King's Road was Don Letts. He was born in London, and educated at Tenison's school in Kennington, next door to the Oval cricket ground. In 1976, he ran the London clothing store Acme Attractions in the King's Road. Acme was a clothing store selling electric-blue zoot suits and jukeboxes. The shop would pump out dub reggae all day long. Acme had to move to the basement, from the Antiques Market Antiquarius, after complaints about Don Letts's pounding dub reggae. Don was deeply inspired by the music coming from his parents' homeland, Jamaica. He would go on to play an integral part of The Clash's success in the coming years, as a respected and talented film maker.

Acme attracted punks. The shop's accountant was Andy Czezowski, who later helped to start up The Roxy, a London nightclub, so that people could go from the store and have some place to party. As most bands of that era had yet to be recorded, there were limited punk rock records to be played. Instead, Letts included many dub and reggae records in his sets and is credited with introducing those sounds to the London punk scene. Joe Strummer and Paul Simonon were already inspired by reggae. Don Letts helped them to the next level in appreciating reggae taking them to Notting Hill blue's clubs. Reggae and punk was a beautiful musical fusion. The Clash would infuse a reggae beat and theme into many of their tracks. Don Letts would be a DJ at the Roxy club for punk's 100-day event that started at the end of 1976.

On the evening of May 15th WG, Gene Vincent and Billy Idol met at the George and Dragon in Bromley. WG had been attending the West Indies tour match against Surrey up until the previous day. Gene Vincent had been walking along the Regent's Canal and onto the Grand Union, whilst WG was at the cricket, looking for The Clash. He could sense other spirits along the Canal but none had made themselves known to him. It was as if they were laughing at the futility of his mission. At Kensal Rise, he had seen someone who looked a dead ringer for Joe Strummer, but his overtures were ignored.

"How's it gone today, boys?" Billy Idol wasn't expecting miracles. He was happy, and almost victorious.

"Nothing. We went back to Camden. Seedy awful place," WG was almost nonchalant.

"Don't worry. I'm taking you back to Camden tomorrow."

"Oh no. I'm fed up with Camden, thanks, Billy."

"Look, WG, it'll be different. We're going to see Patti Smith at the Camden Roundhouse. She's over from New York."

"Will The Clash be there?" asked Gene Vincent.

"Defintely. Siouxsie has assured me. Apparently, Joe Strummer and Mick Jones are excited at meeting Patti."

"So that's our chance then Billy?"

"Has to be. Though it'll be busy. We can try and hook up after the gig."

"Will it be that easy? There'll be lots of people around." WG wasn't convinced.

"No problems. Just go up to Joe at the end. It won't be that busy. It'll be a walk in the park."

"Really?" WG wasn't impressed.

"It isn't rock n'roll." Gene Vincent was looking for another way. He was hoping their first meeting would be memorable with both of them singing *Be Pop a Lula* and Jayne Mansfield looking admiringly at him.

Billy Idol looked a little wild and almost unhinged. His hair was coloured green, red and blond. He was wearing chains and sporting a particularly dark eyeliner and lipstick.

"Is that make up you're wearing? WG had never seen a man in makeup before.

"Suits me doesn't it?"

"No."

WG looked as if he was going to explode. Billy didn't seem to notice.

"We're going up West tonight. Are you coming?"

"West?"

"Oxford Street. The 'Bromleys' are outside. We're hitting Louise's. It's the only club where we don't get attacked."

WG looked at Billy Idol. "That doesn't sound very promising. I think we might leave it."

"Juvenile, Steve Severin and Soo Catwoman are coming. You'll recognize some from the cemetery."

WG and Gene Vincent looked outside to where the Bromleys were congregating. Gene Vincent spoke first, "Is this a fucking freak show or something? They look like aliens."

Billy Idol got serious. "They're lovely people. They just look a little different. It's the spirit inside you and your heart that matters."

Surprisingly, WG nodded. "That's a good point, Billy. It is your heart that matters."

They exchanged a glance. They both understood. They were kindred spirits. The clothes and appearances were just mere props covering the important stuff.

Gene Vincent added, "Maybe it's the new rock n'roll. I might get to like it."

WG went up to Billy Idol. He placed his hand on his shoulder. "We'll see you tomorrow at The Roundhouse. Have a great night."

Chapter 4

Camden Roundhouse
May 16th, 1976

"To me, punk rock is the freedom to create, freedom to be successful, freedom to not be successful, freedom to be who you are. It's freedom." – Patti Smith

Patti Smith is playing the Roundhouse for the next two evenings. Punk firms from all over London gathered to pay their homage to the Queen of the New York punks like a gathering from a mafia wedding. Patti Smith was an American singer-songwriter, musician, author, and poet who had become an influential component of the New York City punk scene with her 1975 debut album 'Horses'.

The Camden Roundhouse was a performing arts and concert venue situated at the Grade II listed former railway engine shed in Chalk Farm, owned at the time by the Greater London Council. It was originally built at the height of railway building mania in 1847 by the London and North Western Railway as a roundhouse, a circular building containing a railway turntable. After being used as a warehouse since the late 1800s, the building fell into disuse just before the Second World War. It was first made a listed building in 1954. The Roundhouse reopened after 25 years, in 1964, as a performing arts venue. Jimi Hendrix performed there in February 1967and had his black Fender Stratocaster stolen from the side of the stage during the performance. The Doors with Jim Morrison had played there in 1968, being the only time he performed with them in the UK. The Rolling Stones also performed there in 1968, and Motorhead played their first ever gig at the Roundhouse in 1975.

WG and Gene Vincent had done no searching for Joe Strummer that day. Tonight would be when Gene and Joe Strummer would meet up and rock n'roll would be saved. They got to Camden around midday and took in its atmosphere. They visited the famous Electric Ballroom and toured the markets. They saw 'Sir Johnny Green' reciting poetry on Camden Lock to an audience of over 50. He was a local celebrity. Also, they had time to explore Hampstead Heath.

Just before 7.30 pm Gene Vincent and WG were outside the Roundhouse. Billy Idol was with them.

"Is this it then?" WG was less than impressed. "In my day, it was Wigmore Hall and Camden Theatre. The Bedford, Alhambra, Empire and Oxford were much better than this."

"What are you on about, WG?" Gene Vincent sounded nervous and distracted.

"London music halls. I'm talking proper Victorian London splendour and glamour. How I miss those days. This is all rather seedy."

Both Billy Idol and Gene Vincent looked at WG as if he'd just arrived from another universe. He was truly a man from a different era.

"I think you're in for a big shock, WG, then." Billy Idol was worried. Neither WG nor Gene Vincent inspired confidence. They were fishes out of water. Luckily, the fashions and hairstyles weren't too outrageous. Punk was in its infancy. The fashion was still developing. The Bromley contingent were leaders in the developing trend.

WG recoiled a little. "Oh no! Everyone here needs a good wash and a proper haircut." WG's enlightenment with Billy from the previous evening had disappeared.

"I like it. This is the new world WG." Gene Vincent wanted to be won over. He wanted to be distracted from the expectation over Joe Strummer. Joe Strummer was starting to become a monster for him. The irony wasn't lost on him.

At the Roundhouse, The Clash was there with Joe Strummer, Paul Simonon and Mick Jones representing the firm. Siousxsie and her Banshees take their positions just behind The Clash. John Lydon made some barbed comments to Joe Strummer about his outfit that was lost in the background noise. Siouxsie is dressed in black leather head to toe. Her entourage, The 'Bromley contingent' has the edge in numbers. The Pistols are in attendance looking menacing and ready for an argument with anyone. They're a safe and a respectable 10 yards away from The Clash, but that might not be enough. Deepest South London might be a better separation to stop this clash. Billy Idol is pouting furiously and talking to Tony James. The Damned are aloof and slightly distant from the other punks this night as Captain Sensible was in a furiously bad mood. Viv Albertine, Chrissie Hynde and other future punk luminaries are circulating, looking for their positions, drunk with excitement and anticipation. It's like a congress for punks. They look at each other, checking out outfits, attitude and fashion. Attitude and fashion to the DIY cause is everything. Nobody else outside the punk family counts. It's as if they're invisible. Comradeship to a common cause sits uneasily with contradictions to youthful jealousies and egos.

WG and Gene Vincent stand anonymously next to Viv Albertine. They sensed Viv was smiling at them. They have no idea what to expect. Gene Vincent is the more nervous of the two. Billy Idol waves to them.

Billy Idol seemed to be talking to himself.

"I can't believe people dress like this. Have they no standards?" demands WG.

Gene chuckles. "It's rock n'roll. It's meant to shock. People said the same about me and Eddie Cochran in the '50s. We're hip."

"Hip? You still look a mess. What's that grease in your hair? You and Joe Strummer have the same ridiculous haircut."

"It's the quiff. It's cool isn't it?"

"It's preposterous."

Gene Vincent changed tact. "Is that Ray Davies from the Kinks over there?"

"You keep going about him. Who is he?"

Gene Vincent changed tact. "Is that Ray Davies from the Kinks over there?"

"You keep going about him. Who is he?"

Billy Idol came over to WG and Gene Vincent. "How do you feel fellas?"

Gene spoke first. "Nervous. Do you think it's the time and place to meet Joe? They're a lot of people around."

"Might be perfect later as Joe and The Clash leave," reasoned Billy. "A meeting on the mean streets of Camden would be prophetic."

"Camden makes me nervous." Gene Vincent looked less than confident.

"Camden is where it's at Gene. It's the place to be. Camden and the King's Road, Chelsea."

The scene was set for the inevitable confrontation. Young men overloaded with testosterone and ego were going to determine the punk hierarchy. Siouxsie had other ideas though.

Joe Strummer walked up to John Lydon of the Pistols and fired the opening salvo. "You might learn something tonight John. The Clash is number 1 now. You've had your moment. Yesterday's papers. Good for fish and chips and nothing else." Two massive egos were about to clash.

John Lydon didn't have a conciliatory bone in his body. He was overdosed with spite, wit and aggression. He and the Pistols had a reputation to maintain. "I hear you've not even gigged yet. Rumours going around that you joined The Clash because you heard us play early April."

Joe Strummer stood his ground. They were like two gunslingers face to face. Punks around them closed in realizing two big alpha names were playing out a pitch for supremacy. This could be a defining moment for the punk order.

Joe Strummer moved in for the kill. "We're where punk is at now. We're not arty bohemians from the King's Road. Who is that wanker Mclaren that manages you? Come to the Westway and you'll learn something." A London turf war was being played out.

"It'll always be satisfying to know that the Pistols are your main inspiration." John Lydon smiled at Joe Strummer, adding "We converted you from some middle of the road covers band. Who the fuck were the 101ers? You're a public schoolboy, Strummer. No punk credibility at all."

Those last comments had hurt Joe, though he was too combative to let it show. Lydon had struck his achilles heel. He was reeling on the ropes and needed to respond.

"We're talking about life and our generation. We're relevant. We mean something." Joe had recovered and was back on a roll.

"You're a bunch of pretentious pricks." Lydon was snarling now for his punk credibility and the knockout blow.

"You lot wear swastikas. What does that mean? Are you fucking nazis?" Joe Strummer had landed a heavy blow on John Lydon.

John Lydon strutted pompously over to Joe Strummer. They were inches away from each other now.

"You're too fucking thick to get the joke, Strummer. No working class solidarity here."

At this point, Siousxie Sioux walked up to John Lydon and knocked him out. Just one blow and Lydon was sprawling on the floor of the Roundhouse. The Queen had decreed. Her judgement was everything and the argument was over. Patti Smith would have saluted Siouxsie.

WG and Gene Vincent had ringside seats to this fight. They had never seen anything like it in their lives.

"Rock n'Roll was never quite like this, WG. What a shame."

"I'd imagine not."

Billy Idol was busy talking with Siouxsie as John Lydon was helped off the floor with the assistance of Glen Matlock and Steve Jones.

All the punks looked wired waiting for the next move. The atmosphere was electric. More fists were clenched. WG looked traumatized but alive. Gene Vincent looked ecstatic.

Then Patti Smith arrived on stage to unconsciously broker the piece. This argument still had legs. There was a strange anticlimax amongst the punks. Patti Smith looked over to Siouxsie as if to ask, "What's the matter with you lot?" Siouxsie clenched her fist and that was the cue for Patti to rock.

Patti was the boss, donning the 'Queen of Rock n' Roll' mantle and looking like the blood relative of Keith Richard. She'd clench a fist and the whole audience flashed one straight back as if at attending a North Korean May Day rally. A couple of right hooks and a sea of arms jolted everyone's beer. The atmosphere was not for the faint hearted. 2000 sweaty pits were pumping out pheromones in the pre-deodorant era for 99% of the male population. Mood, music and artiste created an intoxicating cocktail, but you had to be there, living it with smells, warts and all to appreciate it fully.

This was music to be heard live and not something that could be savoured whilst resting in a comfy armchair with a drink after a hard day at work. You couldn't be nonchalant and mellow listening to this music. You had to be wired and engaged. Easy listening music it wasn't. This wasn't Doris Day or Norah Jones.

The Roundhouse heat was building up and Patti threw off a couple of shirts, getting down to minimalist T-shirt and jeans. She punched herself playfully to the music setting the physical mood. She's suffering from travel fatigue (having just played Copenhagen, Paris, Brussels and Amsterdam), time-warp, orientation-stress and lack of sleep. The lights are beating down on her, everyone's sweating like pigs and worse. The low ceilings and brick exterior of the Roundhouse seem to be closing in on the crowd, increasing the intensity. Patti performs a few push-ups, maintaining the physical edge to the evening.

She's pure energy and intensity. This matters and her energy tells you that.

Patti is ready to talk and lecture now. The earlier minimalism is replaced with a more open and gregarious attitude. "Right now, we are here in this room together, I don't think I'm too fucking cool to relate to you!"

She is in preaching mode. Life's deep story is explored as the twisting path of human relations, through the grit and humiliation, the alienation and competition. The lady has suffered and it shows in the lyrics. She's about real life and not Hollywood fantasy. She cuts through the hallucinatory vapours of the American Dream, growing ever more fragile and more and more realizing that no-matter how much more they buy and consume they're not any happier.

Patti is showing them an alternative. The London punk families are on a mission, sucking in every pearl of wisdom, every nugget of truth, enlightened to the possibility of a new world. Earlier tensions between John Lydon and Joe Strummer are forgotten. Something deeper and more powerful is on view. The 'Road to Damascus' has been shown to all of them. A true evangelical conversion to punk is reached. The families now know the conversion is real. Well, for most of them it was, John Lydon apart.

"Do you feel frustrated? Do you feel like a loser?" Heads actually nod in agreement, thinking, "Yes, yes, she's talking to me. She understands." Patti reaches into their souls. She connects intimately.

The audiences have their eyes riveted on her now. They want her for their friend because many of them haven't got any real friends, at least not any that they can talk with about that kind of thing. Patti is friend, mentor, soul mate and visionary.

Patti had relaxed for a while, lowering the intensity so that everyone could last and not hit the physical and emotional wall. But now, she's more intense, similar to the first impressions as the conclusion arrives. She launches into 'Horses' and the Coup de grace has been delivered to all. The punk families were already there, but now, it's got even better, as if to further confirm that special moment. An appreciative crowd of outsiders has joined them. The band was producing a rush. All good things come to an end though and Patti signed off for the night, supposedly.

Patti returned and encored with *My Generation*. The crowd made her return again and she ended with the appropriate Stones number *Time is on My Side*.

Even later at the Hard Rock Café, Patti was still jumping, cruising the aisles, talking to fans, waiters, and friends. But she was coming closer to fade out and as the limo headed back to the Portobello Hotel, Lenny Kaye, flopped out in the seat and muttered, "I can see my little bed and it has a little pillow on it and I'm pulling the cover up round me…"

Patti was asleep.

The scene back at the Roundhouse was not so serene after the concert. Billy Idol had come over to Gene and WG. "It's going to kick off between Joe Strummer and John Lydon. Siouxsie has just told me."

"We heard it. We were next to them. They should both be in prison or sent to Australia," suggested WG.

"We're spirit guides, WG. They can't harm us. That's rock n'roll." Gene Vincent was ecstatic.

"That's your answer for everything. That's all you keep saying."

"You're going to have to do something, Gene. You can't freeze like you did the other night at Shepherd's Bush," explained Billy.

Gene looked worried. "We can't do anything about it."

WG turned to Gene Vincent. "Believe in yourself, Gene. That's what it's about. Belief."

"I can't. I'm a fraud." Gene's mood had changed.

At that moment, Gene Vincent looked the anthesis of rock n'roll rebellion.

"We're going to have separate them. Something terrible is going to happen. Get Joe out of here. John is tooled up," Billy Idol seemed agitated. He was shouting the order.

The 'Bromley Contingent' had strength in numbers. The crowd were barging their way out of the Roundhouse so confusion was everywhere. Thankfully, the argument between Joe Strummer and John Lydon never happened. Siouxsie Sioux and the 'Bromley Contingent' whisked the members of The Clash away as the crowd melted away into the Camden night. There was another massive feeling of anticlimax. The ups and downs of punk rock and youthful rebellion were playing their hand. Everyone had shot their bolt physically and mentally. The night had been intense and all the players were played out. The walls of the Roundhouse had been hit one too many times. John Lydon would have his say a little later on the night.

Two days later, The Clash split. A furious row took place between their manager Bernie Rhodes and Mick Jones at the Camden Railway Depot. Word had got back from the punk grapevine that The Clash did a runner from the Pistols after the Patti Smith concert in Camden. Bernie Rhodes loved controversy, chaos and front-up aggression. He was an anarchist at heart. Harmony was his enemy and made him feel uneasy.

In his words, "The Clash runs from nobody."

Mick Jones's explanation, "That they had lost each other in the crowd and Siouxsie insisted," didn't cut with Bernie.

Bernie Rhodes was clear. "You're a bunch of fucking pussies." Adding succinctly, "Call yourself rock n'roll. Fucking no way! Now fuck off."

Mick Jones declared it, "I want nothing to do with a wanker like you Bernie. I'm out of here."

Bernie Rhodes was in no mood for reconciliation. "Good. I'm wasting my time with you ponces. At least the Pistols have some bollocks."

Joe Strummer moved close to Bernie Rhodes, "Never mind the bollocks, Bernie. We're The Clash."

"No, you're not. Get the fuck out of here."

Paul Simonon left the band also, as he sided with Mick Jones and Joe Strummer. Keith Levene and Terry Chimes weren't in Camden and periphery members of the band, whose heart and soul were elsewhere. Joe Strummer fainted. The Clash, furious and wonderful, was finished.

On stage with the Pistols at the 100 Club a couple of days later, Johnny Rotten launched into a rant about the Patti Smith gig, "In we go to the Roundhouse the other night, see the hippy shaking the tambourines. Horses, horses, horse-shit!" Awkwardly, two of the Patti Smith Band stood in the audience.

On May 22nd–25th, the West Indies were playing the MCC at Lord's cricket ground, staying at a nearby hotel in Maida Vale. They were in walking distance of Lord's and travelled on foot to and from the ground, mingling with their supporters. They batted first and score 251-9 declared. Viv

Richards was out for 5, caught Randall bowled Hendrick. Gordon Greenidge and Clive Lloyd shared a third wicket partnership of 115 scoring 82 and 60 respectively. Michael Holding scored a brisk 42 to bring some respectability to the score. Before the end of play, the tourists were able to take a couple of wickets. Holding hit Dennis Amiss hard on the back of the head. With Andy Roberts, they were a hostile opening attack and you could see the MCC batsmen were uncomfortable. Mike Brearley survived this testing passage of play with a fair amount of skill and courage.

WG was at the ground to watch the first days play. He enjoyed being back at the home of cricket and mingled anonymously with a small crowd on a warm day. References to him were everywhere. He couldn't help but blush at his fame, in a spirit sense. He had meant to hook up with Viv the night before the game but had to help Gene Vincent in putting The Clash back together. The Clash had split up less than a week ago. Patti Smith's performance at the Roundhouse had unleashed a sequence of events culminating in their demise. Word of the split had got to Gene Vincent the day after the split, and since then, they had done the usual trekking around the Westway and Camden to no avail. WG thought there was no point in trying to find The Clash as The Clash didn't exist. Gene Vincent thought he could get them back together with his eternal American optimism.

WG was glad of the rest and to be back in his environment. The life of rock n'roll was exhausting, even for a spirit guide. There was nothing but drama with these punk rockers. He was back in his comfort zone. Cricket was his nirvana.

After his dismissal for 5, Viv had all day to think about WG and if he would ever see him again. He knew WG would be annoyed at his batting. Mike Hendrick, he of the nagging accuracy and decent line and length, had tied him down, and his impatience had seen flash wildly at a decent length ball. Randall, a truly brilliant fielder, had needed to take a very good catch, but that didn't hide the fact it was a poor shot borne out of mental weakness, when not scoring freely, and lack of discipline. He had to do better.

After play had ended on day one; the tourists had walked back to their hotel, enjoyed a meal and then relaxed for the night. Some of the players had friends and family to visit in London. Viv had invitations to meet friends, but decided to stay put, should WG try and find him. Near to midnight, Viv had enough of waiting in his hotel room. He walked out of the hotel to clear his head passing Kilburn High Road tube station. He passed, unknowingly, a fez wearing musician called Ian Dury, walking out of the Dog and Duck pub on the Kilburn High Road. Ian Dury was engaging violently with a musician calling himself Chaz Jankel. Ian Dury was the lead singer of the Kilburn & the High Roads.

A friend of Ian Dury had suggested he give an interview to an up and coming musician called Chaz Jankel who was more than useful as a saxophonist. Chaz had turned up to the Dog and Duck to introduce himself. Ian had told him, "To fuck off." Chaz refused to leave. He was going to tell Ian about jazz heroes. He loved EllaFitzgerald, Miles Davis, Buddy Rich and Louis Armstrong. Ian was impressed but still in a belligerent mood. He had his dark moments when nothing was right in the world. He wasn't going to let Chaz get away without a lesson.

"They're all good. But they're nothing compared to compared to Gene Vincent. That's someone you should be listening to. He is the king of rock n'roll. I love him. He's a good man."

Chaz didn't seem too impressed, "I don't know too much about him."

"You're a fucking idiot then. You're of no use to me unless you appreciate Gene Vincent," Ian got up to leave.

The argument spilled out onto the pavement.

Ian was getting violent and unreasonable with Chaz.

Viv went over to calm the situation.

"Calm down, man. What's your problem?"

Ian Dury looked at Viv Richards. He decided against continuing his argument with Chaz Jankel. Something in Viv's demeanor dissuaded him.

Instead, he pleaded with Viv. "I don't know who you are mate, but tell this wanker he isn't Chaz Jankel."

"But I am Chaz Jankel. Honest," pleaded Chaz Jankel.

"How do you know he's not?" asked Viv.

"He doesn't like Gene Vincent. How can you not like Gene Vincent? He's my hero."

Viv looked totally bemused at this point. "Is this bloke Gene Vincent the cause of the argument?"

Ian Dury felt a little silly and contrite once he realized how stupid the dispute was. This was more an argument for the school playground and not between two grown men. He felt like a stupid, spoilt 8-year-old, riding through Upminster in a Roller with his dad. His dad was a chauffeur to a rich, successful man.

"Look guys. You can disagree. You don't have to like the same people to get on."

The initial argument seemed even sillier the more Viv rationalized the situation.

Viv continued to defuse the argument. "Have you anything in common? That's a good start for a friendship."

Ian Dury had calmed down completely. "You have a point, mate."

"Are you musicians?" asked Viv. Ian Dury had a guitar in his right hand. Chaz Jankel was holding a saxophone.

Chaz and Ian answered together "We are. It's a little obvious mate isn't it?"

"You might have nicked them."

"That's funny, mate. I like that. I like you." Ian Dury laughed. Chaz Jankel smiled nervously.

"Who are you?" asked Ian Dury.

"I'm Viv Richards. I'm here playing for the West Indies."

"Cricketer?"

"Yes. I play a little."

"It's a funny old game. Cricket don't make sense, mate." Ian Dury was right in Viv's face, but more in mischief than aggression. "I couldn't play, anyway. Fucking polio took away my chance. I like that Fred Titmus."

"Fred is a good bowler. What band are you in?"

"Kilburn and the High Roads. Best fucking band in the world. I'm Ian Dury," added Ian.

"You should be mates then."

"I like Bob Marley. Reggae and ska is my thing."

"Nice one, mate."

"Be mates."

That was it. Viv Richards was off into the night thinking if he would ever meet WG again.

"Hope to see you again, mate. You're a good geezer." Ian Dury, as always, had the last word.

Ian Dury turned to Chaz Jankel and offered his hand. "Sorry, Chaz, let's write music together. That geezer bought us together."

Ian Dury and Chaz Jankel would go on and form a magnificent musical partnership. They would leave the High Roads soon to form Ian Dury and the Blockheads. The Blockheads were an inspiration to punks everywhere. The Clash, Damned and Pistols were big fans. Their inspirations were eclectic. Dury was a cocktail of Max Wall, Little Tich, Gene Vincent, Tommy Cooper and London Music Hall with a dark side. One newspaper said he looked like 'a cockney update of a Dickensian villain'. Jankel was jazz, funk, soul and synthesizers. The music and lyrics would be unique and wonderful.

Viv returned to his room at 2am. WG was waiting for him.

Viv felt relieved. "Am I pleased to see you. Where have you been?"

"I've been called into to help other people. It's complicated."

Viv shrugged his shoulders and said randomly, "I've just had a walk as I couldn't sleep. I broke up a fight between two musicians. One of the blokes liked Gene Vincent and the other didn't. Something like that. It's all very strange. The musician was Ian Dury."

"You what? Ian Dury?"

Viv repeated himself then added, "Who is Gene Vincent? I've never heard of him. And Ian Dury?"

WG searched for clarity. "He mentioned someone called Gene Vincent then."

"Yes, WG, I've said it a few times now."

"Sorry, Viv, that name means something to me. I'm just a little shocked."

"Do you know him?"

"I know Gene Vincent. Well, at least, his spirit."

"You spirits are everywhere. Do you all meet up every night for a party?"

"I wish we did. Life gets very lonely." WG got serious. "Has this Ian Dury modelled himself on Gene Vincent?"

"Of course. Gene Vincent is his hero. He loves him."

For a minute or so, they sat in silent contemplation. WG decided he would come back to this Ian Dury and Gene Vincent story later. Cricket was more important.

"What happened out there today?"

"I got impatient. The wicket was doing some naughty stuff," Viv shrugged his shoulders again.

WG didn't look impressed. "It wasn't that bad. There was a little bit of nibble early on and Hendrick bowled well. But it wasn't a minefield."

"You thought it was a bad shot then?"

"Bloody awful. Hobbs would never have played such a shot though, to be fair; Trumper would have done. You never got to the pitch."

"I just like to score fast. I don't want to defend. I don't want no bowler dictating to me."

"Play the ball late then. Let it come onto you. Don't go searching for it. Not in England where the ball moves around."

WG smiled at Viv's explanation. He liked the young man's enthusiasm and self-belief. They were kindred spirits. He had been just like Viv when he was younger.

"You'll get another chance tomorrow. This lot won't last long against Holding and Roberts. They're quick and fairly decent. Faster than Spofforth though not as good as Sydney Barnes. They bowl too short. Holding needs to pitch it up a yard or so and then he'd be unplayable." This was praise indeed.

Viv had never heard of these bowlers. He looked on respectfully.

"Our bowlers sure are hostile. It's hard enough facing them in the nets and at home."

"The England boys are a little gentler, though don't underestimate them in English conditions. If it's a hot dry summer, they'll struggle though."

"Thanks for the advice, WG."

"Just make sure you listen this time." WG said it playfully enough so not to sound too severe, but it had an edge to it as well.

WG got up to leave. "I'll try and see you tomorrow. I should have congratulated you on scoring 176 against Hampshire. The Times said you played well."

"Thanks, WG."

"Just watch out for Hendrick. He's decent and a proper English seamer. Give him some respect."

WG chuckled to himself as he left the Hotel. He knew Viv wasn't going to respect any bowler. No warrior could show that weakness. Viv Richards could make Rome's finest Gladiators look self-doubting.

The next day, the West Indies bowling attack bowled out the MCC for 197. Holding took 4-44 and Roberts returned 3-33.

In the West Indies second innings Fredericks and Greenidge fell cheaply to leave the tourists 15-2 and in trouble. However, this time, Viv made no mistakes. He added 199 with the dependable Larry Gomes, scoring a sparkling 113 before being stumped off Butcher, going for quick runs to facilitate a declaration. Butcher had taken his wicket again, but had felt the full force of Viv's blade first. Gomes scored 101 not out.

WG had not visited after the second day's play when Viv had been undefeated on 42.

The next day, WG explained to Billy Idol and Gene Vincent his encounter with Viv Richards. They met on Bromley Common. They had prepared themselves for another boring cricket story. Instead, what WG said blew them apart.

"Viv Richards bumped into the biggest fan of Gene Vincent," The statement seemed improbable. WG didn't really feel this would lead anywhere.

"Tell me more WG and don't take the piss. Why didn't you tell me earlier? I need a few fans to boost my confidence." Gene Vincent was almost ecstatic.

"He bumped into a bloke called Ian Dury."

"Crikey. I know Ian Dury?" Billy was more enthusiastic now.

"It's on the tip of my tongue. I saw him play about 2 years ago, somewhere in North London."

WG explained, "Viv saw him in Kilburn. It was close to Lord's cricket ground."

"Kilburn and the High Roads. That's Ian's band." Billy Idol punched the air. "This is my destiny. This is fate. It's all written in the stars."

"So how do we find them?" Gene Vincent didn't seem too confident. "Why do you think that's going to make a difference?"

"He can inspire you Gene, It's worth a gamble." Billy was pumped now.

"Don't you want to meet your biggest fan?" asked WG.

"It's another person to find. We're looking for Ian Dury now as well as The Clash." Gene Vincent smiled. "It would be nice to meet Ian Dury even if he can't help. And, perhaps, we should be looking for Ray Davies of the Kinks."

Chapter 5

Trent Bridge (first test)
June 3rd

"Some folks will say, 'Oh, Winning ain't all!" But I know it is all. At the end of the day, no one looks at the loser. So that is why we play to win." – Viv Richards

For the 2 weeks after Patti Smith's concert at the Roundhouse, life was quiet for WG and Gene Vincent. WG had seen Viv Richards at the West Indies match against the MCC where Viv had bumped into Ian Dury, which started another quest. They had extended their search into Kensal Rise, White City and Harlesden for Joe Strummer, though The Clash had disbanded. They'd gone to the Roxy in Harlesden to see The Pistols practice, by accident. Gene Vincent disliked John Lydon though he was starting to really warm to Steve Jones and Paul Cook, who he thought had a real rock n'roll spirit about them. Gene Vincent thought that Glen Matlock was a fake. For him, John Lydon was a mystery, a great enigma. At times, Lydon seemed to be in it just for the fame, and the ability to annoy and shock an audience. At other times, he captured the spirit of punk and was its spiritual leader. Gene Vincent guessed that's what Lydon wanted. He was the ultimate contrarian. Maybe he did understand the spirit of rock n'roll, but he'd never admit to it. The Pistols had something with Paul Cook and Steve Jones though.

They met Billy Idol regularly at the George and Dragon in Bromley. Every day, Gene Vincent's morale seemed to worsen. Billy Idol and WG were anxious to boost his mood.

On June 1st, two days before the start of the first test, Gene Vincent and WG gad gone over to the King's Road, Chelsea in their quest for Joe Strummer. This was more Pistols territory than Clash territory. It felt as if they were walking into the enemy's lair. They walked into the Roebuck and the Pistols were there with Malcolm McLaren. They were bumping into the Pistols, almost daily, but Joe Strummer was the invisible man. They had resigned themselves to another day of failure.

The highlight of their day was visiting Acme Attractions. Don Letts was blasting out some heavy Jamaican base. Billy Idol had joined them after recovering from a hangover. Don Letts was moving around Acme in perfect time to the music.

"I've never heard anything like this before. I love this music." WG was in the zone.

Gene Vincent agreed. "Me too. I love it."

"What is this music Billy?"

"It's heavy Jamaican base, WG."

"I don't know it."

A crowd of about 30 were outside Acme taking in the music.

"It's a little different to punk and rock n'roll," explained Billy.

WG and Gene Vincent were moving in time to the music.

Billy Idol was laughing hysterically. Once he recovered, he said out loud, "This is a sight I'd thought I'd never see. A

1950s American rock n'roll legend and a Victorian English cricketer dancing to some heavy Jamaican base."

"Let me go and have a chat with Don. This is too much." Billy was still trying to control his laughter.

Don Letts and Billy Idol spoke for nearly 20 minutes. Billy Idol and Gene Vincent carried on moving.

Billy Idol went to leave Acme.

"Billy! Tell your two mates to come in. They look interesting. I like what they're wearing."

"They're looking for Joe Strummer."

"I don't know him."

Billy Idol had failed to pick up that Don Letts could see them.

The West Indies were at Trent Bridge, Nottingham. Tony Greig's comments about making the West Indies 'grovel' have created greater media interest in the series.

Viv Richards is determined to make Tony Greig eat his words. Some West Indies players were slightly ambivalent to Tony Grieg's words. Not Viv Richards. He was representing his country, race and people. He was a man who was proud of his African roots. Years of slavery and oppression, the apartheid war in South Africa, couldn't be ignored. This was personal with Tony Greig. The best way of getting back at Greig was to beat his team and make him feel the heat of his blade. He was also going to smell the leather. The West Indies fast bowlers were going to bowl aggressively and fast at him. The West Indians in the crowd were going to remind him every time he crossed the whitewash as to their superior talents and that he would be the only one grovelling. Tony Greig was going to feel the heat in every way.

England had gone for experience. John Edrich, Brian Close and Mike Brearley had a combined age of 118. The West Indies team was much younger. They looked fitter and were rich in talent. The England team would be no pushovers though. Edrich was a seasoned test batsman with an average over 40 and a highest test score of 310 not out. He was a world class player. Brian Close was the toughest man to ever play cricket. He could have got in the boxing ring with Muhammed Ali and wouldn't be afraid. Alan Knott was arguably the greatest wicketkeeper to play the game. Tony Greig had an impressive record as an all-rounder. The bowling quartet of Snow, Hendrick, Old and Underwood were very decent, especially in English conditions.

The West Indies batted first after winning the toss. WG was at the Hawley Arms in Camden watching the test match on the TV. TV was something new to him, but Gene Vincent had explained to him how it worked. He had seen the BBC advertising the game for the past week. WG thought it was like a form of magic. He'd been in two minds about travelling to Trent Bridge, but decided to stay nearer to home to help Gene Vincent find The Clash. The last time WG and Viv had spoken was at the MCC match nearly 2 weeks earlier.

Greenidge and Fredericks opened the batting. Snow and Hendrick opened the bowling for England. The weather was warm. Greenidge scored quickly from the start cutting viciously anything short, particularly off John Snow. He'd got to 22 very easily before Hendrick had him caught by Edrich. Viv Richards walked out to the crease, with the swagger of a gunslinger, chewing gum furiously and looking as if the England bowlers were just mere cannon fodder. He hadn't spoken with WG since the game against the MCC, but he had

WG's words ringing in his head. He had 'to play straight', 'respect Hendrick', 'play in the V' and 'play late'.

WG felt a sense of pride as Viv took guard. Snow bowled short and aggressively to him, but he was second best. This kind of bowling was food and drink for Viv. He liked pace onto the bat and was prepared to take on short fast bowling. Snow was good, but he didn't have the pace of Lillee and Thomson on fast, bouncy Australian pitches. The slower pitches in England meant Viv had even more time to cut and hook the England bowlers to pieces. Eventually, the English bowlers pitched the ball up and Viv hit them with cover drives and flicks to mid-wicket playing across the line. WG was apoplectic when he drove a ball 2 feet outside off stump to the leg side boundary. Viv smiled at the audacity of the shot, knowing that it was risky, and against the way he said he would play. He knew WG would be annoyed.

At the end of day one, Viv was undefeated on 143. His century had come off just 144 deliveries. His partner in a stand of over 100 was Alvin Kallicharran, the stylish Guyanese left hander, who was undefeated on 52. The England bowlers looked as if they were hiding. Viv Richards did that to opposing bowlers, putting them out of their comfort zones. He wasn't looking to slowly accumulate allowing the bowlers the comfort of economy if nothing else, like a Geoff Boycott. Viv Richards made bowlers look stupid and powerless. This wasn't death by a thousand cuts, but the brutality of the guillotine.

The next morning took the attack to Underwood lifting him into the crowd for several sixes. With the West Indies score on 408-2 after lunch, Viv tried to hit Underwood for another 6, but this time his timing deserted him and he was caught by Greig at long off for a masterly 232. He had truly announced himself onto the world stage. He had surpassed WG's highest test score of 170. The West Indians in the crowd were ecstatic, blowing their horns and conch shells. Kallicharran fell to the same bowler shortly afterwards, just three runs short of a century of his own. The third wicket stand between the pair had added 303 runs. England did reasonably well to take the last eight wickets for just 86 as the West Indies closed on 494. One over from Andy Roberts was safely negotiated by Edrich and Brearley at the end of the second day.

WG was sitting in the Hawley Arms in Camden watching the action on a small TV in a dark corner. The sounds of rock n'roll could be heard at the other end of the pub. He felt so happy for Viv. Sadly, he had nobody to celebrate with. The life of a spirit guide was lonely. He had watched his protégé announce himself as a great and he couldn't speak with him or anyone else to reference and celebrate the moment. At least he could sit back in satisfaction of a job done. His mission there was almost complete. Gene Vincent was absent trying, once again, to save The Clash. Gene Vincent was always trying to save The Clash, and now, to find Ian Dury. WG contemplated the chance of meeting any other spirit guides whilst he was back. He'd like some female company. Maybe hanging around Gene Vincent was putting them off. You were always on the outside. It was like still living after all your friends had died. He could sense them everywhere, but none were speaking with him.

WG would try and make conversation with women, but they weren't hearing him. On the second day of the first test, Gene Vincent joined WG as England came out to bat for that one over.

"Hi, WG, who are the old guys batting for England?"

"Have some respect please, Gene. They're Mike Brearley and John Edrich. I've just read that Mike Brearley has a double first from Cambridge."

"What's that mean? They should be collecting their pensions."

"You're a peasant, Gene. This is the game of the Gods."

"The English guys look like they're on valium." Gene Vincent moved his face closer to WG and lowered his voice. "I might have a met a lady WG."

"You had 4 wives, Gene. Aren't you done with all that? Didn't you try and shoot one?"

"I never went that far. We just argued a lot."

"That's an understatement. So who is she?"

"She lives on a canal boat at Kensal Rise and plays a guitar. She's an artist."

"What's her name then?" asked WG.

"We haven't got that far yet."

"Crikey, Gene, with 4 wives and being American, I thought you'd move a little quicker than that."

"She's a spirit also. Died in the '60s "

"Does she have a sister?"

"You old rogue, WG. I'm sure there's one of your old music hall ladies that's come back in spirit."

"Most of the old music halls are gone. I've checked them out already. No luck there, apart from Wilton's."

"Are you going to tell me your history with the ladies?"

"Not to a man who had 4 wives."

"You're jealous."

"Shut up. You're ruining my day. My man scored 232 and you still haven't found Joe Strummer."

At least WG had cricket. Cricket was complex, meaningful, wonderful and spiritual to him. WG never understood that people could never 'get' the game. To him every ball was an event, a physical and psychological contest between batsmen and bowler with a supporting cast of fielders. The game was strategy, chess and intellect. It was also muscular, effort and patience. The ebbs and flows of a five day test match could not be bettered. The moments of maximum intensity with periods of calm shaped cricket's mindset. The anticipation before the start of each days play never left him. The game lent itself for time to think, appreciate and savour. Football was too frantic and Rugby was too brutal. Viv's 232 had been masterful and had been enjoyed over nearly 2 days. What other sport could offer that amount of enjoyment for so long? He had lived every moment of Viv's innings. In fact, he played every stroke, even the shots he disapproved of. He studied his footwork, his trigger movements and reactions. He could sense his mood. Cricket with its generosity of time allowed you do that. The revelers in the Hawley Arms had no idea greatness was happening before their very eyes. The moment when 'stumps' was called at the end of play was particularly poignant and magical. Batsman, bowlers and fielders leaving the field of play with the sun lowering in the sky with lengthening shadows had its own special atmosphere. Bowlers and fielders were happy for a well-earned rest. Batsmen were not out and happy to come back tomorrow. WG never tired of cricket's unique rhythms. No other sport could match it. The breaks for tea and lunch delighted him. This was the height of civilisation.

Back home in Antigua and the Caribbean cricket lovers were jubilant. The bars in St Johns Antigua were full even though it was mid-morning. Not much work was going on. Gravy was wearing his favourite pink suit and wasn't taking any taxi rides that day. Up to this point, Antigua and the Leeward Isles had been the poor relations of West Indies cricket. Viv was just the second Antiguan after Andy Roberts to play for the West Indies and the third Leewarder. Up to this point, West Indies cricket had been dominated by Barbados, Jamaica, Trinidad and Guyana. Now Antigua could stand up and be proud. They had announced themselves on the world stage. Success against the old colonial masters was everything for West Indians. Centuries against Australia and India were special, but 232 against England in England was unsurpassed. It was better than special. He had made it now. He was a name in the pantheon and exclusive club of cricket greats. The membership form had been delivered to and signed in Nottingham, England. June 4th 1976 was a memorable cricket day. On the same day, the Pistols were playing a gig in Manchester.

The third morning brought an immediate breakthrough, with Brearley falling for nought on debut, edging his fourth delivery, from Julien, to Richards at slip. Close also failed but Edrich batted for three hours in making 37 and then Steele and Woolmer put on 121 together for the fourth wicket as they took England to 221-3 at the close of the third day. The pace attack of Roberts, Julien, Holder and Daniels were going for just 2 an over as the English batsmen aimed to grind the West Indies attack down. This was typical English batting. To criticize England's scoring would be unfair as the bowling was high class and scoring was difficult. David Steele played really well in defying a hostile and talented attack.

Refreshed after the rest day, the West Indies' attack immediately gained the upper hand on the Monday morning. Steele hooked a short delivery from Daniel straight into the hands of long leg after scoring his maiden test century. Tony Greig walked to the crease passing Steele as he walked back to the pavilion. There was a buzz around the ground. You could sense every West Indies player steeping up the intensity. This was the moment. The heat and pressure was being turned up a notch. Roberts was at the end of his run up staring at Greig. Then came a moment that the noisy Caribbean supporters celebrated with pure relish. Tony Greig, under intense pressure and scrutiny after his pre-match comments, was beaten for pace and clean bowled without scoring after a hostile delivery from Roberts. The West Indies team celebrated wildly. They didn't sledge Greig as an Australian team would do. They didn't need to. They'd beaten him with skill. Grieg looked chastened. The heat had begun.

England had the satisfaction of seeing David Steele scored his first test century with a 106. You could not fault his courage and fight. Woolmer made a patient 82 and useful contributions of 33 and 20 from Chris Old and John Snow ensured that the follow-on had been saved with England all out for 332. However, the West Indies began their second innings 162 ahead. Wayne Daniel with 4-53 had been the West Indies most successful bowler.

Greenidge had an injured leg and was allowed to bat with a runner, although umpires Dickie Bird and Tom Spencer intervened when Collis King came out to do the job. Collis King wasn't even playing in the match. Larry Gomes took over instead. Pushing for quick runs, the West Indies reached 176-5, scoring at 5 an over. Richards was dominant in making 63 off 84 deliveries with eight 4s. Lloyd and Kallicharran hit two 6's each, being particularly severe on Chris Old and John Snow, before Lloyd declared. Snow had some consolation taking 4-53, including the prized wicket of Richards.

Set 339 to win in five and quarter hours, England were content to bat sensibly and safely to ensure the series would remain level going into the next match. Edrich finished 78 not out. Brian Close scored a patient 36 not out in just under 3 hours. England had done well again against excellent bowling, albeit, they weren't taking the attack to the opposition. It was impossible to escape the feeling that England were hanging on against superior opposition and that soon or later, the dam would be breached, and they would be well beaten. Earnest and stubborn resistance would not be able to resist the superior force forever. The cavalry was warming up to strike. The English had pitchforks and honest endeavour. The West Indies had a nuclear arsenal.

The Pistols turned up to a gig in Manchester on June 4th 1976. The gig has been called many things over the years. It's been called 'the gig that changed the world'. The crowd was barely 50, but according to legend, just about every punk band from the north was there and inspired from that moment to form a band. The gig has attained mythical status. It's become one of punk's 'I was there' moments. There are quite a few of those.

Peter Hook from Joy Division, and latterly, New Order spoke of the gig. "I walked out of that gig as a musician. I came home with a guitar and told my dad, 'I'm a punk musician now', and my father said, 'You won't last a week'. Here I am, 40 years later.

Peter Hook continued, "Ever since a young age, I've been an avid reader of the music papers and my escape during work was reading them. I was reading about all these heavy metal bands, Led Zeppelin and Deep Purple, but I never felt inspired by it – it seemed so untouchable."

Punk had that magic pull. You could feel part of it from day one. The punk bands were accessible and its lead singer could have been your next door neighbour. You were on the inside and not the outside from day one. You were on the same level. Their frustrations, anger and alienations were the same as yours. They spoke your language. They had faults and the same inadequacies. They weren't mystical, untouchable superhuman musicians with rich and wonderful lifestyles, adored and idolized by the many. They were as fucked up and useless as you were.

You'd come home. The Zeppelins and Rolling Stones of this world felt they were from another world. They had become boring and elitist. Once a stretch limousine is taking you to and from a stadium to perform then it's 'over' in terms of credibility. You're all 'Hollywood' and no interest to me.

"I kept reading snippets about this group called Sex Pistols and all they seemed to do was fight at their gigs. I saw the advert in the NME and said to Barney, 'We've got to go and see this band, and they do nothing but fight'. There was a lot of football violence then, it felt like the working class world I was used to as a lad from Ordsall and Salford." Punk was another outlet for the young with attitude and aggression. The fast pace of its chords and vocal aggression added to the gobbing and spitting from the moosh pit was nirvana to some. Punk allowed you to express yourself. There was none of the fluffiness and wooliness of the Hippy flower power generation of the '60s that had no direction and ended up navel gazing and little else. Punk allowed the young to shock their neighbours and families and that was liberating. It empowered the young to see people in the street recoil with horror at your attitude and clothes. That feeling of liberation would never leave you.

Peter Hook went on to describe the Pistols performance that night. "The Pistols came on, John Lydon told us all to 'Fuck off'! It sounded awful; their attitude was like they were messing about on stage. They seemed to be taking it not very seriously – laughing at us. I literally thought, 'I could do that'.

"For a lot of people, it demystified music and brought it down to our level. The energy of it was so genuine; punk was very genuine. Bands were forming and playing a gig the next day with no songs, buying instruments and making a racket. It was like being a child in Toys R Us."

The gig wasn't one that Pistols John Lydon, recalls the details of that well. But he does remember that, "If we were going to play outside London, Manchester had to be the place."

"They say everyone who was at those gigs went out and formed a band, but that wasn't our plan – or our fault!"

It wasn't just bands either. Celebrated photographer Kevin Cummins was there, then a photography student at Salford, as was writer and journalist Paul Morley. Facts remain vague on whether Anthony Wilson was there, but the Granada TV broadcaster – who would go on to mastermind Factory Records and co-found The Hacienda nightclub – saw the Pistols at the venue at some point.

Steven Morrissey was at the gig and, six years later, would go on to form The Smiths with Johnny Marr, Andy Rourke, and Mike Joyce. The band remain one of the most acclaimed groups to emerge from Manchester, particularly for their 1986 album The Queen Is Dead – a record still hailed as one of the greatest British albums of all time.

A bank called the Buzzcocks announced the coming of the Pistols. "Hi, we're the Buzzcocks but we're not ready yet, so we're not playing tonight, but this is the Pistols." The attitude was so punk, so refreshing and honest. A revolution was starting and it was DIY and moving on day to day. At the same time, the Rolling Stones were on a world tour playing their stale stadium rock to large audiences at inflated ticket prices. The attitude of the Buzzcocks made you want to love them on top of the music.

Lacking a regular bassist and a drummer, Buzzcocks were unable to perform at the Lesser Free Trade Hall on 4 June, and instead drafted in a local heavy rock group called Solstice to open for the visiting Pistols. I salute you, Buzzcocks.

The NME described it succinctly, "A band emerged, unknown at that point. Who knows what the drummer, bass player and guitarist looked like? The guy who took centre stage took the mike, took your mind. A swagger to make John Wayne look a pussy. A sneer so dismissive of everyone and everything, of God and civilization, in just one pair of twisted lips. And then they started playing…"

"They stared, open-mouthed, transported to a place where you didn't need to pogo (it wasn't invented till three months later). That place was real life; that place was the clearing in the undergrowth where meaning and elucidation live, that place where the music came from and the place it would take you back to."

"But they knew nothing, these forty-odd strangers, gathered by chance and chat, they just knew their world would never be the same again. A past obliterated and No Future."

"There to greet us was Malcolm McLaren, dressed head to toe in black leather – leather jacket, leather trousers and leather boots – with a shock of bright-orange hair, a manic grin and the air of a circus ringmaster; though there was hardly anyone else around... Look at the photographs of the gig and you can see that everybody in the audience was dressed the same way, like a Top of the Pops audience. There were no punks yet. So, Malcolm, he looked like an alien to us..."

"The Sex Pistols' gear was set up and then, without further ceremony, they come on: Johnny Rotten, Glen Matlock, Steve Jones and Paul Cook. Steve Jones was wearing a boiler suit and the rest of them looked like they'd vandalized an Oxfam shop. Rotten had on this torn-open yellow sweater and he glared out into the audience like he wanted to kill each and every one of us, one at a time, before the band struck up into something that might have been *Did You No Wrong*, but you couldn't tell because it was so loud and distorted..."

Morrissey also wrote a 'review' of the gig as a letter to NME. Review by Steven Morrissey of a Sex Pistols concert: "I pen this epistle after witnessing the infamous Sex Pistols in concert at the Manchester Lesser Free Trade Hall. The bumptious Pistols in jumble sale attire had those few that attended dancing in the aisles despite their discordant music and barely audible lyrics. The Pistols boast having no inspiration from the New York / Manhattan rock scene, yet their set includes, *I'm Not Your Stepping Stone*, a number believed to be done almost to perfection by the Heartbreakers on any sleazy New York night and the Pistols' vocalist / exhibitionist Johnny Rotten's attitude and self-asserted 'love us or leave us' approach can be compared to both Iggy Pop and David JoHansen in their heyday. The Sex Pistols are very New York and it's nice to see that the British have produced a band capable of producing atmosphere created by The New York Dolls and their many imitators, even though it may be too late. I'd love to see the Pistols make it. Maybe they will be able to afford some clothes which don't look as though they've been slept in."

Punk had multiple beginnings. Some would say more beginnings than Frank Sinatra had comebacks. Perhaps this was one of the most famous. The contrariness of punk meant that there'd never be an answer to that conundrum. Punk was never an exact science. Punk showed itself to all of us differently. We all had a different story.

If the Pistols had one epitaph it may have read like the famous quote of Mehmat Murat Ildan: "The beginning is the best time to think about the end!" Even John Lydon could see something in that quote.

Chapter 6

Louise's Nightclub
Near Oxford Street, June 10th 1976

"I think London's sexy because it's so full of eccentrics." –
Rachel Weisz

*"My dad says that being a Londoner has nothing to do with
where you're born. He says that there are people who get off a
jumbo jet at Heathrow, go through immigration waving any
kind of passport, hop on the tube and by the time the train's
pulled into Piccadilly Circus, they've become a Londoner."* –
Ben Aarononvitch

After the first test, the West Indies had two games before the
next test match at Lords which would start on June 17th. These
were against the Combined Universities at Fenners,
Cambridge and then Lancashire at Old Trafford. These were
gentle warm up games for the West Indies and gave them the
opportunity to give fringe players some practise. The games
were useful for those players who had underperformed in the
first test match. They could find some form against weaker
opposition, especially against the universities. Fenners was a
beautiful ground in wonderful Cambridge.

Now the first test match at Nottingham had finished, WG was back helping Gene Vincent find The Clash and save rock n'roll. The Clash broke up on May 18th, 2 days after the Patti Smith concert. Since then, Bernie Rhodes had been unattainable. Rumour was that he was hiding away in the south of France. Mick Jones, Paul Simonon and Joe Strummer were still practising daily. Terry Chimes and Keith Levene were non-committal about continuing with The Clash. Joe thought they'd be able to manage themselves, but wasn't too confident. All three wanted just to write and play. Bernie Rhodes was the person with the contacts and who could fix them up with gigs and sort out equipment, the road crew and all the boring admin stuff.

Billy Idol, WG and Gene Vincent met up almost daily in Bromley. They were getting nowhere. It was like a broken record. They were getting to be crisis meetings. Everything was going well for WG. For Gene Vincent, it was anything but well. His morale was falling apart. Was there another way to save rock n'roll?

Billy spoke. "I think Joe Strummer is the only person to reform the Clash."

"But we can't find him anywhere. He's like the scarlet pimpernel," explained WG, adding,

"What about Bernie Rhodes?"

"He's disappeared hasn't he? replied WG.

Billy was no fan. "Yeah, he's gone as well. Bernie Rhodes is a complete wanker," adding, "He's fucking mental. There'd be better off without him."

Gene Vincent gave his thoughts, "The person has to be Joe Strummer. Strummer is the front man. It's all about him.

Strummer was born to play rock n'roll. He's got the whole package. He's the fucking best."

Billy agreed, "You'd know, Gene."

"Joe Strummer has the X-factor. His time with the 101ers, his charisma and energy. Nobody comes close. The man is dynamite." Gene Vincent was rambling like a fan.

"What about Ian Dury?" WG came in with a left field question. "He's a fan. And we've been looking for him."

"I don't know too much about him." Billy Idol had never been that confident about Ian Dury and him being the saviour. "And he's got his own band already."

Billy's friends in the 'Bromley Contingent' were vital in giving out the latest news on the 'punk explosion'. The 'Bromley Contingent' was like a spy network for punks. Even though it was 'over the water' in south London, the messages and stories still got across. For WG, it had been a whirlwind. A few weeks trawling around Camden, Bromley and the Westway were getting Gene Vincent and WG nowhere. They were getting well versed with Camden pubs, its music scene and the geography of the Westway. The gritty delights of Shepherd's Bush, Kilburn, Kensal Rise and Harlesden were character forming. But none of it had been any use in helping Gene Vincent find his confidence or even The Clash. They felt like 'Proper Londoner's' now. They'd seen Chas n'Dave at the Goldhawk in early June to confirm their membership. Also, they had stood next to the mausoleum in Brompton cemetery in an attempt at time travel.

On their travels around London, they got to know each other really well. WG continued to speak of cricket and the Victorian music hall scene in London. He had spent a lot of time in music halls during his time as a player and then in retirement, when he settled in London. WG couldn't get over the fact that the London music hall scene was finished. However, he'd still visit Wilton's Hall close to Cable Street in Whitechapel. He had happy memories of the place. When cricket wasn't being played, and in breaks whilst searching for The Clash, WG would walk around Wilton's reminiscing. The place still spoke to him. The walls had a thousand stories to tell and more. Spirits were everywhere but he couldn't get personal with any of them. He yearned for his lady friends of yesteryear. The temptresses were there, still around and still teasing him. However, the entertainer Roy Hudd was always there to speak with him. Roy seemed to live there, though he was no spirit. WG and Roy became friends. Roy couldn't get enough of WG's story about the Victorian music hall scene in London. Roy had rhe gift to see WG and was a sponge that held onto every word. He wasn't so interested in WG's cricketing exploits.

Gene Vincent came with him several times in the late May/early June weeks. Gene Vincent was fascinated about the stories of Victorian London music halls. The mixture of entertainment, elaborate surroundings, salacious behaviour, seediness and music excited him. He connected with Roy Hudd as well. Together they'd sing 'be pop a lula' Wilton's had not heard anything like it for over 50 years. Roy Hudd was adamant that with Gene Vincent the London music hall scene could have a comeback. Even WG was feeling it. Gene Vincent was happy again. However, he had to limit conversations around cricket. The game continued to be a mystery to him. He'd never 'get' the game. The great

American comic and actor Robin Williams spoke of 'cricket being a game like baseball but with the players on valium', Gene Vincent agreed and would go further. For him they looked like corpses on strings. They were the walking dead playing out their own strange torture in front of a crowd who were really dead. He wouldn't go in a cricket ground.

Gene Vincent spoke much about his relationship with Eddie Cochran. He was still devastated over Eddie's death. The rock n'roll story was everything for him. As to the relationship with his 'artist' friend in Kensal Rise nothing more was said.

WG faced many challenges. The transition was more difficult for him than Gene Vincent. He had to get accustomed to late 20th century living. Cars, television, radio, post-war concrete tower blocks and punks were all new to him. Every day was a voyage of discovery. Billy Idol was challenging. However, both Gene Vincent and WG really liked him. WG loved his spirit and humanity. He was a wild, fantasy driven, unruly youth, but his humour and inner gentleness won WG over. There was something in Billy that made him incredibly likeable. You wanted to write him off, but you couldn't. His snarling, pouting punk image was a front for the real William Michael Albert Broad, trying to hide an appealing inner vulnerability.

Billy Idol was going to play his trump card in trying to resolve Gene Vincent's crisis of confidence. He knew a lady called Linda. She might be able to help.

The 'Bromley contingent' were a group that included Siouxsie Sioux, Steven Severin, Billy Idol, Soo Catwoman, Simon 'Boy' Barker, Debbie Juvenile, Linda Ashby, Philip Sallon, Simone Thomas, Bertie 'Berlin' Marshall, Tracie

O'Keefe and Sharon Hayman as its members. They were frequent visitors to the nightclubs and hotspots of London's West End. One explanation for the rise of the 'Bromley Contingent' was its fast direct train link to London's Victoria and quick access to the West End and City. That was underselling the magic of Bromley. Bromley was a conduit for some of the greatest human talent ever produced. David Bowie, Charles Darwin, H.G Wells, Derek Underwood and Enid Blyton had all lived there. The Ravensbourne was the river that ran through Bromley with some magical properties.

Their clothes and make up were different to the norms of '70s Britain, an era defined by a mixture of grey boring austerity, flared trousers, awful haircuts, disco and drag queen glam rock. They stood out and enraged conservative England's sensibilities. Ladies in twinsets and pearls with men in bowler hat and pinstripes sat uneasily with punks. People took one look at the 'Bromley contingent' and muttered 'Britain's finished'. All norms and sensibilities had been destroyed. The 'Bromley contingent' dressed like they were a different species. The fashion was as much of an attraction as the music. For the first time, people could dress in a way to really enrage and disturb. Mods and Rockers shocked a decade or so earlier, but sartorially, the shift was manageable if challenging. Mods were the height of smart fashion with their mohair jumpers, Italian suits and leather or suede loafers. Style counted. Rockers were less sartorial, but leather jackets, weren't a quantum leap for the imagination. Many of the Bromley's clothes were from SEX, Malcolm Mclaren and Vivienne Westwood's shop on the King's Road. There was a significant DIY customised element to the outfits also. The outcome was often sex and bondage with a twist. Heavy makeup, multiple piercings and spiked dyed hair completed the look for men and women. Middle England was outraged. Very few people 'got the look'. For a while, it was classless, genderless and liberating. For so long, Britain's uniform had been defined by gender, convention, money and class. Wonderfully, this was different.

The 'Bromley Contingent' would regularly meet up at Louise's nightclub just off Oxford Street. Billy was often with them. Louise's was a place where 'punk gossip' was rife. The Pistols were often there as were members of the Slits and the Damned. It's the place where Steve Jones was meant to have uttered the famous phrase 'never mind the bollocks'. A few wannabee punks would go there hoping to become associate members of one of the new punk bands setting up all over London and surburbia.

Louise's place was a lesbian club. It was one place where the Bromley Contingent felt safe. Louise's became a midnight meeting place… a sanctuary for the disenfranchised. The words of The Who, 'We're all wasted', would describe its atmosphere. The punks would offend when visiting many other places, resulting usually in verbal and physical abuse. There was no prejudice at Louise's, a haven of civility, peace and respect. WG and Gene Vincent walked into Louise's with Billy Idol, a place unlike any other they had visited. The Pistols weren't there this night.

The 'Bromley Contingent' was there with nearly all its membership. WG and Gene Vincent were sitting near to Billy Idol taking in the unique atmosphere of Louise's. Up until then, they had no connections with any other spirit guides. Gene Vincent had connected with Billy idol and Bernie

Rhodes's mate in Camden. WG had his relationship with Viv Richards.

The DJ was playing his favourite track at the time, Lou Rawls' *You'll Never Find a Love Like Mine*. The dancefloor was full.

Then out of the shadows, Bessie Bellwood came over to WG. They were old friends.

"Hello, WG. How are you? It's a long time no see." They hadn't seen each other for almost a century. WG was surprised to his core but relieved. They were comfortable with each other.

"Bessie, what are you doing here?"

"The same as you. I'm helping out poor souls who need guidance and inspiration. The usual spirit guide stuff."

"This is my friend, Gene Vincent."

Gene Vincent could see Bessie as well. It was a hallelujah moment. He made a breakthrough. Gene went over to Bessie and hugged her.

"I can see. I can see. I love you, Bessie."

"Calm down. Calm down. Your friend WG is a wild one."

Bessie was ecstatic. "Crikey. Who would have thought we'd hook up again? What bought you back, WG?"

"I'm looking after a young cricketer called Viv Richards. He's something special."

"I knew it'd be about cricket. You were always mad about it. It's all you ever talked about."

"Who did you come back for? How long have you been back?"

"She's not a star yet, though she will be. A young girl called Kate. I'm working with her and she has an incredible voice. I've been back for 2 years now."

"Is she performing yet?"

"Not yet WG! She's a Bromley girl, but not one of the punks or the 'contingent'. She's a voice like no other. She's mystical and magic. You'd think she was from another world."

"Good. At least you've got a proper purpose. Are you working here?"

"In a manner of speaking I do. I help out Linda." Bess went on. "If you've come back for cricket then why are you in a place like this? I know you've visited some dodgy haunts in your time."

"Gene Vincent." Louise's went quiet for a moment. The world stopped.

WG looked at Gene Vincent and then turned to Bessie. "This man is Gene Vincent. He was famous in the '60s. He's a rock n'roll star. Have you heard of him?"

"Of course I have. Everyone knows Gene Vincent."

"Really?"

"How are you involved with Gene Vincent?"

"We were introduced to each other at Beckenham Cemetery. It was during a massive thunderstorm. Siouxsie was involved."

"Nice place to meet. There's nothing like a bit of posh suburbia."

"Do you mind not talking about me while I'm here. I know we're spirits but it still counts."

"WG doesn't believe I was a star." Gene Vincent looked indignant.

"You don't act like one, Gene. That's the problem. Sadly, I'm more rock n'roll than you. And I've a long beard and tweed suit." WG was on his case again and on vogue with rock n'roll fashion. He was a quick learner.

"You're like a broken record. I know I'm the fucking problem."

Billy came over, unconsciously smoothing over the tension between WG and Gene Vincent. "What are you there talking about? Hello, Bessie, I see you've met these fellows then."

"I have. I already know, WG."

"You're kidding me!"

"WG and I knew each other when I was performing in the music halls. Camden, Shoreditch, Blackfriars, Borough, Oxford Street, I performed all over London."

"I saw Bess perform numerous times. It was the entertainment of the day. You didn't have this TV thing. After a hard day out on the cricket field, there was nothing better than a night out at the music hall."

"So you're a music hall Queen then, Bess? WG has dragging me over to Wilton's almost daily for the last few weeks. He loves the place." Gene Vincent was excited.

"Yes. I performed at Wilton's. I loved the place as well. I must go back there."

"Were you a groupie of Bess?" asked Billy, smirking at the same time at WG.

"What are you on about you idiot?" WG wasn't impressed.

Billy explained. "Fan. You liked her. Followed her around. All that sort of stuff. Do you know what I mean?"

"You make it sound seedy and rather inappropriate."

"I'm only kidding you. I didn't mean to upset you WG. I'm ripping you mate."

"Cricket is a hard game. I bowled, batted and captained. It's not easy you know. Much tougher than this rock n'roll rubbish. We needed entertainment at night, as I've just said."

"I can imagine. Who wouldn't want a night out?" Billy sounded philosophical.

"How well did you know each other?" both Billy and Gene Vincent smelt some juicy gossip.

Neither Bess nor WG seemed too keen to answer. They were hesitant and looked at each other. There was chemistry and history there.

Billy Idol started laughing, adding "

Did you two have any… you know what I mean? I bet you were an item?"

Bess and WG looked even more awkward. Neither could utter a word. Their saviour came in the form of the Club's DJ.

The DJ started playing *Dreamy Lady* by Marc Bolan and the mood was broken for the moment as people took to the dancefloor. WG wondered if he should ask Bess for a dance. She could read his thoughts.

"No. I'm not dancing with you, WG. You could never dance."

Bess was keen to divert attention away from her and WG. Once Marc Bolan had sung his masterpiece. "So what's the story with you Gene? Billy's getting desperate with you?"

"I haven't any confidence."

"You need a session with Linda. She'll sort you out."

Billy Idol and Bess laughed together. Linda was a dominatrix. Many of her clients were there that night. She was particularly savage.

Gene Vincent looked worried, "I'm a spirit guide. Is that possible?"

"Anything is possible with Linda. She'll take you to places you could only dream about."

"Linda and Bess make a great double act," Billy tried to sound earnest. He was struggling to keep a straight face.

"You won't worry about facing anyone after Linda and Bess. Joe Strummer and The Clash will be easy after those two."

"You'll be straight up to Shepherd's Bush to have a picnic with them on the Green."

"They're that good?" Gene Vincent didn't know if to laugh or cry.

"Don't worry, Gene. You can still save rock n'roll."

Billy Idol was running around the floor singing *Be Bop a Lula*, Gene Vincent's finest hit.

All of the Bromley Contingent joined in a very soon the whole of Louise's was singing *Be Bop a Lula*.

Gene Vincent then got onto the stage and performed his most famous song. He was ecstatic and couldn't help himself. People flocked around him. They could see him, but in the words of the Who, 'they were all wasted'. For a moment, he was on stage performing in front of a crowd, like it was the 1960s and his heyday again. The moment was soon gone, and he was back to anonymity to most of them. However, there had been a moment. Maybe that moment and Linda would give him hope.

"I'm sure I've just seen Ray Davies of the Kinks. Did you see him Billy?"

"Leave it out Gene. Just enjoy the moment. You're here to find Joe Strummer not Ray Davies."

"Bess was delighted to be reunited with WG. She hadn't met too many people from her past.

She connected with Billy Idol, Linda and Siouxsie Sioux from the present and was excited about the punk explosion. Punk was dangerous, rebellious and liberating. The new punk order was music to her ears. Punk fed her spirit. Then there was Bromley Kate. She'd never known anyone like Kate. Then again, nobody knew anyone like Kate. Her voice could smash glass and she looked elfin like, like a magical woodland creature with the same magical spirit. Much like WG, she was lonely, feeling she's left all her friends behind.

Bess's story was inspiring. In 1876, aged 20, Catherine 'Kate' Mahoney assumed the stage name Bessie Bellwood and made her music hall debut at Bermondsey in London, where she had been a rabbit puller, or skin-dresser, in a local factory. Although she lacked the versatility of her rivals, Marie Lloyd and Jenny Hill, she nevertheless became a popular performer noted for her 'saucy' stage manner and her ability to argue down even the toughest of hecklers, including a 15 stone coal-heaver who left the music hall where she was appearing after a five-minute dispute during her act. Her volatile, unpredictable nature was such that within four hours of having a devout conversation with Cardinal Manning about a Catholic charity she was shortly afterwards arrested in the Tottenham Court Road for knocking down a cabman because she believed he had insulted the man she loved. She was tough and might be the person to help Gene Vincent.

A devout Roman Catholic, she was admired by her public for her many acts of kindness to the poor, which included paying for Masses for the dead and dying, giving away her own money and possessions, taking in laundry, cleaning homes and looking after children. She had heart, compassion and punk energy with a sprinkling of danger. She was a diamond. A rough diamond but 24 carat.

Chapter 7

Catshit Mansions and Ian Dury
June 11th

"Sex, drugs, and rock and roll is all my brain and body need. Sex, drugs, and rock and roll is very good indeed." – Ian Dury
"One thing about London is that when you step out into the night, it swallows you." – Sebastian Faulks

The search was still going on. Not only were they searching for The Clash, but now, they were looking for Ian Dury. This was becoming a farce. Both felt they'd be equipped to write a tourist's guide to London. They felt as if they were on a spirit traveller's tour of London.

At least they were looking around Kilburn and not Camden or the Westway. That made a pleasant change. Billy Idol was struggling to help as the Bromley Contingent didn't move in the same circles. The Kilburn and the High Roads were on the periphery of punks. They were a little more pub rock with a rebel twist. Only Ian Dury gave them some punk credentials. They didn't really fit into the new punk world in terms of attitude and fashion. And they were on their last legs. They were yesterday's papers, to coin a Joe Strummer phrase.

Viv Richards had explained Ian Dury's appearance. He would be difficult to miss. However, after their night at Louise's they had a spring in their step. WG was delighted to have met Bess. Gene Vincent was a changed man. His brief appearance to the crowd at Louise's had given him his confidence back as well. The evening had been the highlight of his spirit comeback. The crowd was so wonderful. He couldn't remember enjoying himself as much.

Later in the evening Linda had whipped him into shape. Gene Vincent had no problems appearing to her. She was strict and sensational. Gene Vincent felt that he could conquer anything after a session with her. Linda could do anything. Apparently, he wasn't the first spirit guide Linda had performed on.

WG and Gene Vincent started early walking the length of the Kilburn High Road, more in hope than expectation. In their minds, they were on the road to nowhere. However, Billy Idol was on their tails with news to change everything.

"This is madness. I've spent the last month just walking up and down the streets of London." Gene Vincent said it more in gallows humour than anything else.

Billy Idol had just caught up with them and had heard the last comment. "Nothing wrong walking the streets of London."

This was the cue for Billy Idol to go into song, *Streets of London*, something he did regularly.

Gene Vincent looked impressed, "You're really are a frustrated performer, Billy. We need to get you on stage."

"That was Streets of London by Ralph McTell."

"Ralph who?" asked WG.

They all looked at each other.

"I know where Ian Dury lives," Billy Idol was joyous. He was like a kid telling his mum that he had found what he wanted for Christmas and knew just where to get it.

"Don't tell me its miles away from here," said WG resigning himself to another day of futility and walking.

"Well, yes, but not too far. It's catshit mansions."

WG looked perplexed, then exasperated, as if he were dealing with imbeciles. "Is there such a place?"

"You know it, WG," Billy was still very excited.

"I'm not sure I do," WG was at his condescending best.

"It's next to the Oval. Catshit is 10 yards away from the gasometer."

WG didn't know if to laugh or cry. Gene Vincent was smiling away still in his own post Linda euphoria.

Billy Idol explained, "Ian lives in a squat. Lambeth Council are too lazy to close it down."

"Let's find it, WG. It always comes back to cricket." Gene Vincent was excited.

WG and Gene Vincent made their way via the Northern Line to the Oval. Nearly a month had passed since WG had seen the West Indies v Surrey match where he had first met Viv Richards. How strange that they were back at the Oval.

The squat was officially called Oval Mansions. With 60 flats and its own thriving art gallery, it was one of London's most notorious squatted buildings, long abandoned by Lambeth council. Ian Dury dubbed the building Catshit Mansions and wrote most of his best songs there. The experimental electro duo Pan Sonic were also in residence, alongside teachers, social workers and many others.

The tenants maintained the building for nearly three decades – doing what the council should have been doing –

until someone at Lambeth realised they were sitting on a property goldmine. In 2001, the squatters were evicted, the building sold to developers and a two-bedroom, cat-shit free flat will now cost more than half a million pounds. Residents would watch the cricket from the rooftops, and were often picked up by the TV cameras, becoming a part of the test match scene at the Oval. Nowadays, there is a luxury terrace where people Bar-B-Q, drink Prosecco and Champagne, look good for the TV and pay a passing interest in the cricket.

WG and Gene Vincent ventured south of the river, avoiding the attraction of the Hanover Arms after coming out of the Oval tube station. The Oval cricket ground stood before them. How ironic that WG was probably sitting just yards away from Ian Dury a month earlier at the Surrey game.

They turned to the right of the main pavilion, past the Peter May Stand. There stood the gasometer, one of English cricket's most iconic landmarks with Catshit Mansion nestling in its shadows.

"This is it, Gene. You're about to meet your greatest fan. He loves you. You can't freeze now."

"I won't. I'm confident. He'll recognise my style. Who else wears a leather glove on just one hand?"

"I won't answer that, Gene."

"Should I sing Be Bop a Lula?"

"No."

They stood outside Catshit mansions, as if by magic, Ian Dury would appear.

"Let's see if anyone can see us," Gene tried to sound confident. He wasn't convincing.

"This is desperate. I'm going to try and talk with someone."

WG went up to over 30 people, but nobody saw him.

Gene Vincent tried the same with a similar result. They'd been outside the Mansions for over 3 hours.

"Do we stay here all night?" WG sounded desperate.

Sweet Gene Vincent.

A song was coming out of Catshit mansions.

"Did he say Gene Vincent?" asked Gene Vincent.

"Come in, boys. Are you going to stand out there all fucking day?" Ian Dury was asking from the second floor window.

"Come on, Gene Vincent. Bring your Virginia whisper."

"How did you know?" Gene Vincent was almost falling down in shock.

"I know it's you. That's why I've been writing this song about you. Nobody else knows you here. Only I can see you. Promise."

"But how did you know?"

"I knew you'd come back. I dreamt about it for years."

"Really?"

"The spirit of sweet Gene Vincent has come back and the whole world is fucking rejoicing. I know it was you straight away. Let me make you a cuppa."

"You're kidding me?" Gene Vincent was starry eyed.

"And I want to know! What took you so fucking long?"

WG and Gene Vincent both looked a little wobbly as if they'd seen a ghost. They were both thinking, 'he can't be this cool'. Ian Dury looked nonchalant, as if he'd just come back from the corner shop with some milk.

"Well, are you fucking coming or what? Mind the fucking catshit. It's everywhere. Welcome to Catshit Mansions," Ian Dury was laughing wickedly.

"We're coming, Ian."

The flat looked messy and rundown. There were two cats sitting on a window ledge. Ian didn't have a talent for cleaning.

The sofa had seen better days. The cats had wrecked it. Ian passed them both a cup of tea. The cups looked dirty.

"We can't take them Ian. We're spirits," WG and Gene Vincent spoke together.

"Of course you are. What a shame. Now, come on, you two. Tell me your story." Ian could have been talking to his neighbour. He seemed totally unfazed. He had more front than Walthamstow high street.

WG and Gene Vincent looked at each other.

Ian Dury was fed up waiting, "I want the geezer with the beard to go first. By the way, are you WG Grace?"

"I am, indeed. How did you know?"

"You're famous, mate. Me mum and dad had a picture of you over the fireplace. Big belly and a big beard. You played a bit of cricket didn't you? That's fucking famous, mate."

WG looked at Ian Dury as if he was a lunatic, and then asked, "Do you perform in a circus or music hall?" WG was being serious.

Ian Dury fell onto the floor laughing, "That's fucking brilliant."

Two minutes later, Ian Dury was rolling about on the floor still laughing. "You're going to have to help me up. I'm a cripple. I had polio when I was young."

"I know how you feel, Ian." There were tears in Gene Vincent's eyes… part sadness… part laughter.

"I know you do, mate." They had connected.

WG managed, with some guilt, "I was a doctor. Let me try and help you." Both Gene Vincent and WG helped Ian back into his armchair. Ian was still chuckling away.

Eventually, Ian composed himself and asked, "What's your story then? Why have you come back then?"

WG went through his history and the night at Beckenham Cemetery on May 10th when he came back as a spirit guide and source of enlightenment to the genius of Viv Richards and Cricket during a massive thunderstorm.

Ian was fascinated. "So this Viv Richards is a West Indian geezer who's a bit special then?"

WG explained, "You met him in Kilburn a few weeks back when you were arguing with Chaz Jankel. He stopped you thumping Chaz."

"Fuck me. I do remember. He was a fit geezer in a big overcoat. I wasn't going to mess with him. This is fate with a capital fucking 'F'."

"Viv told me that you kept going on about Gene Vincent all the time."

Ian Dury blushed in embarrassment, perhaps for the first time in his life. He collected himself after a few moments.

Ian looked at Gene Vincent and then back to WG. "This bloke blew me away the first time I saw him in a Jayne Mansfield film. He helped me fall in love with rock n'roll and get through the polio."

Now it was Gene Vincent's turn to blush.

"You've got to tell Ian your story now, Gene," WG had a serious tone to his voice.

"I came through at the backend of Bromley High Street. A few months back."

"Bromley High Street? You're fucking kidding me?" Ian loved the story.

"Do you know it, Ian?" Gene Vincent was hopeful.

"Of course I do. The Kilburns have played a few gigs over there. A few years ago though."

Gene Vincent continued, "I met a young man there called Billy Idol. He's a punk practising with Siousxie and the Banshees. He's a banshee as well."

"Billy Idol. I've heard Chaz mention him. Young kid with a bit of attitude. He's part of this punk thing."

"Billy said I came back to save rock n'roll. He's got some weird gift. One of his descendants was hung at Tyburn. Another was shot in a duel at Hampstead Heath."

"What?"

"He's gifted. Billy is putting this all together. He said I can save The Clash."

"Who are The Clash?"

"It's Joe Strummer's new band, but they've just broken up."

"What?" Ian Dury was struggling to understand.

"Billy thinks with my reputation I can inspire Joe Strummer and The Clash to save rock n'roll. It needs me or Eddie Cochrane."

"So what's the problem?"

"Billy Idol sees Joe Strummer as the new king of rock n'roll."

"I know Joe Strummer. I've seen him playing for the 101ers over in Fulham and Kilburn. They supported us once."

Gene Vincent looked at Ian, "I need to save The Clash and rock n'roll."

Ian Dury's eyes lit up, "You want to save rock n'roll?"

"Can you help me Ian?"

Ian was hooked. He was unfazed as if born to this sort of madness. "Rock n'roll That's my story. That's my calling as well."

WG came in with his thoughts, "Why can't you be the new king of rock n'roll, Ian?"

"I'm a cripple, mate; fucking ugly and 15 years too old. I ain't no Gene Vincent. You can dream."

Ian Dury was born in 1942 in Harrow Weald, Middlesex. At the age of seven, Ian contracted polio from a swimming pool in Southend-on-Sea during the 1949 polio epidemic.

Ian spent six weeks in a full plaster cast in the Royal Cornwall Infirmary, Truro before he was moved to Black Notley Hospital, Braintree, Essex, where he spent a year and a half before going to Chailey Heritage Craft School, East Sussex, in 1951. The outcome of his illness was the paralysis and withering of his left leg, shoulder and arm.

He left the school at the age of 16 to study painting at the Walthamstow College of Art, having gained GCE O Levels in English Language, English Literature and Art.

From 1964, he studied art at the Royal College of Art under Peter Blake, and in 1967 took part in a group exhibition, *Fantasy and Figuration*, alongside Pat Douthwaite, Herbert Kitchen and Stass Paraskos at the Institute of Contemporary Arts in London.

From 1967, he taught art at various colleges in the south of England and painted commercial illustrations for The Sunday Times in the early 1970s.

Dury formed Kilburn and the High Roads in 1971, and they played their first gig at Croydon School of Art on 5 December 1971.

Ian changed the subject, "I could see nobody was clocking you."

Gene Vincent looked perplexed. "Am I your spirit guide, Ian? Maybe I'm not meant to help Joe Strummer."

Ian Dury threw his arms up, "I don't know, mate. In the long run, we're all fucked up."

After a long silence, Ian carried on with his sermon. "We all need a spiritual guide. You can't get through this shit life without one. Without one you're totally fucked."

Gene Vincent had tears in his eyes, "That's unreal, Ian. You've saved me. You and a lady called Linda. I was getting desperate as I couldn't help anyone. I felt useless."

"You fucking saved me, mate, as well. Who is Linda?"

WG interjected this time, "She's a dominatrix at a lesbian club called Louise's just off Oxford Street."

"That's nice. I hope she treated you bad. I knew it was you. Just bloody knew it was. You deserve it, mate. You died far too young."

Ian was laughing so much that he fell on the floor again.

"Fuck off, you two. I need to do this myself." This time, he managed to get himself back on the settee.

Ian composed himself, and then twisted his face towards Gene Vincent, as if Gene Vincent was going to deliver the most profound message of his life and he wanted every nuance of his delivery. Gene Vincent duly obliged. "Eddie Cochrane died younger. That was a tragedy. I had the '60s and Eddie was ten times better than me."

Ian shrugged his shoulders. "There's no point comparing yourself to Eddie Cochrane. You've had your accidents to contend with. At least you don't have that limp anymore."

Gene Vincent contemplated Ian's last comment, "I never think of it anymore. You've just reminded me."

"You were both great," Ian was struggling for words. He wasn't his normal bellicose self. That's what happens when you meet your hero, and the realization eventually hits you after the initial euphoria.

WG could sense the difficulty of the conversation. He had to say something even it was pathetic and stupid.

"Ian, you look a lot like Gene. You look something... what do you call that look?" WG was intrigued.

"It's a mixture of rock n'roll and rockabilly."

That had been the cue. WG was a genius. Gene Vincent and Ian Dury sat there for hours discussing the history of rock n'roll. WG listened patiently. Then they moved onto the subject of London music hall to include WG.

"Did you know Little Titch, WG? He was knocking around in your day."

Ian went even more 'Essex' in his accent than normal as if he was acting out a character.

"I did. Bess knew him as well," explained WG.

"Who is Bess?" Ian was interested.

"Bessie Bellwood. She was a star in the late 19th century."

"So you knew her and Little Titch?" Ian Dury was impressed.

"I'm surprised you know them," WG was impressed this time.

Gene Vincent intervened, "WG won't tell us about their relationship. They seem pretty close."

Ian Dury got to the point, "Were you knocking her off?"

151

"We're friends, I'll have you know." At that point, all three of them started laughing. Even WG could laugh at his pomposity.

Eventually WG called a halt to the laughter. "Let's get serious again."

"All right. I've got it. I'll do a concert next week. I'll get Joe Strummer along."

"So you know where he is? We think he's disappeared," argued Gene Vincent.

"I'll get him along. I've got contacts. Do you know who I am?" laughed Ian.

"That would be brilliant, Ian," Gene Vincent could see light at the end of the tunnel.

"I'll reform the Kilburns. I'll get us a night at Walthamstow next week. I'm Lord Walthamstow, I'll have you know," sniggered Ian.

"That quickly?" asked WG.

"I know the geezer than runs the assembly rooms. He owes me a favour."

"Shall we come back in two days?" asked Gene Vincent.

"Yeah, mate. Two days. Mind the fucking catshit on the way out." Ian was laughing and he fell off the settee again.

WG and Gene Vincent made their way onto the streets of South London. They could hear the sound of leather upon willow. Surrey were playing a match. They were happy. Gene Vincent had met his greatest fan. WG thought of cricket.

Roy Harper's emotional and evocative 'When an old cricketer leaves the crease' summed up his feelings. He had come back to this song back in May 10th at Beckenham cemetery whilst Siouxsie and the Banshees played.

WG and Gene Vincent walked around the Oval and past another iconic Oval landmark. The Archbishop Tenison's School stood before them. Don Letts, a former pupil, walked out of the school, having shown the pupils a short, much edited film, about the 'King's Road in Chelsea'.

"Is that the bloke who runs that Reggae music shop we liked in the King's Road?" asked Gene Vincent.

Don Letts walked past, "Hi guys. How you doing?"

"Fine, Don, just fine," WG answered for them.

"Good. See you around," Don Letts had clocked them both.

Thomas Tenison, an educational evangelist and later Archbishop of Canterbury, founded several schools in the late 17th and early 18th centuries. A boys' school was founded in 1685 in the crypt of St Martin's in the Fields and relocated by 1895 in Leicester Square on the site previously occupied by the Sabloniere Hotel. The school moved to The Oval in 1928, with the new building being opened by the then Prince of Wales. A girls' school was formally established in 1706 for 12 girls and in 1863 a new school building was erected at 18 Lambeth High Street. The girls school closed in 1961, when it amalgamated with Archbishop Temple's Boys School to form a mixed school.

"Do you feel better now you've met Ian Dury?" asked WG.

"I fucking do. I'm sounding like Ian now."

WG and Gene Vincent made their way onto the Thames path by Vauxhall bridge. The sun had set an hour ago. London was dark with only a faint illumination coming from the bridges that spanned the Thames. London looked as if it were in blackout. Big Ben and the House of Commons stood oppressively in the distance, but weirdly satisfying in a dark way, as to perfectly fit the mood of London. St Pauls and the city were further in the distance. London suited the night better than the day. At night its true spirit came out, making everyone feel the undercard to the main greater event, as if a great opera was being performed. The Thames flowed past. Gene Vincent was sure it was talking to him. A whisper said, "Welcome home." He may have come from Virginia, but London was his home now. London was like that. The Thames was his guide and mentor. Siouxsie Sioux came up to Gene Vincent, "Have you seen Ian Dury?" The Lady of the Thames had spoken.

David Bowie, Marc Bolan and Ray Davies of the Kinks walked onto Vauxhall Bridge. Both WG and Gene Vincent failed to notice them. They were singing 'you really got me now'. And they were heading towards the Chelsea Physic Garden to meet Siouxsie.

Chapter 8

Music galore and second test
Lord's, June 1976

"In London, everyone is different, and that means anyone can fit in." – *Paddington Bear*

The second test match was taking place at the home of cricket; Lord's cricket ground.

England won the toss and batted first. Michael Holding had missed the first test with illness and was back replacing Wayne Daniels. Viv Richards was ill with glandular fever and wouldn't be playing. England breathed a sigh of relief over Viv Richard's absence, but had a sharp intake of breath knowing Michael Holding would be launching his missiles towards their batsmen. They wouldn't be driving off the front for sure. In the words of Michael Holding "If you want to drive, buy a car." There was going to be more jumping and hoping than at a Gene Vincent concert.

After scoring 232 and 63 in the first test, Viv was excited about playing at the home of cricket. He had dreamt of this day ever since he had success as a young cricketer back in Antigua. To play at Lord's was mystical for West Indians. Viv had developed a taste for Lord's 12 month earlier when the West Indies won the 1st One day World Cup. Lord's had an Honours board for those scoring test centuries or taking 5 wickets in an innings. Lords was cricket and to play there, with its history and aura, was to have made it in the game. Every cricketer wanted a Lord's test match on their CV.

Viv knew 2 days before the start of the Test match that he was struggling. He was sitting with WG at the hotel on the borders of Maida Vale and Kilburn. He was feeling low mentally and physically.

"I'm fed up WG. I'm on a run here. A century at Lord's is everything. To play at Lord's is everything."

"You'll soon recover. You're young and fit."

"I know. But this is a Lord's test match. I might not get another chance."

WG felt his pain. Viv was in the form of his life and to light up Lord's would have been the highlight of his career to date. This was like a footballer missing out on a FA cup final at Wembley after scoring a hat-trick in the semi-final.

"You need cheering up. We're going to the Bob Marley gig in Hammersmith tomorrow night. I can get you in and will bring over the ticket tomorrow."

"That would be cool. Bob Marley is a hero to West Indians. I can't tell you enough what this man means to me."

Billy Idol could lay his hand on tickets for most gigs going on in London. He and Siouxsie had contacts all over London. Steve Jones of the Pistols, and a good friend of Billy and Siousxsie, knew a thousand ways of breaking into the Hammersmith Odeon if they couldn't lay their hands on any tickets. Steve Jones, looking down at bands from the rafters of the Odeon in the 1970's, was a famous sight. Failing that, he'd steal them.

WG had become a serial gigger creating his own quantum leap. Bess had bought out his musical side again. London music hall 1880s was now Reggae Hammersmith Odeon 1976. He could barely contain his excitement.

"What time does he come on?"

"It'll be late. 9–10pm I think. There are a few acts on first."

"The team meeting should be finished before 8. I'll get myself over to Hammersmith. Anyway, I'm ill and in quarantine." Viv was happy again.

"Shall we meet outside the Odeon? I might have some friends with me." WG decided against embellishing further so as not to scare Viv off. Viv Richards was in for a surprise. WG just hoped he either had the gift of sight or was off his head on something. Maybe he was on some form of strong medication for his glandular fever. Then he thought again, and realised he'd been really stupid. Of course, Viv had the gift; otherwise, they'd never have met. Though, three spirits and Billy Idol would be a challenge for everyone to get their head around.

The punks weren't fully tuned into reggae yet. The reggae all-nighters with Don Letts and Joe Strummer were to happen later. Up until this point, their only experience had been visiting Acme Attractions in the King's Road, a shop run by Don Letts. At Acme he would play Dub Reggae and the punks were becoming turned onto it. Reggae was against the mainstream and a life saver for many members of the West Indian community. The music rebelled unconsciously against White England sensitivities. Don Letts was getting ready for June 16th and the Bob Marley concert. For a few hours, he could forget the daily nuisance of being searched by the Police and facing the contempt of your fellow citizens.

WG, Bess, Billy Idol and Gene Vincent were at the concert. Viv Richards could see them all. He had never felt so out of his comfort zone in all his life. 3 spirit guides and Billy Idol was not your usual group of friends for a Bob Marley concert. He had the eye for more than a cricket ball. He was experiencing a mixture of emotions; there was the pure joy of being at a Bob Marley concert, then there was the realisation he had the eye and gift of sight for the spirits, which pleased and slightly frightened him at the same time. But, it wasn't normal. Viv didn't feel grounded or in control. This wasn't like facing English medium pacers on a flat wicket in the happiest of comfort zones.

His meetings with WG had seemed something different, and for some reason, he'd never thought of having the gift. The meetings with WG had been so special they transcended any such thoughts. This seemed to conflict with the religious beliefs he had been brought up with but he didn't know why. It was like waking up one morning to find you had developed a weird super power. The gift was something he'd had to live with. He queried why this gift had not made itself known earlier. Did it come on like a virus?

WG was working the introductions as they stood near the front of the Hammersmith Odeon, waiting for Bob Marley to come on. "This is Viv Richards."

"Hi Viv. What do you do?" asked Bess.

"I'm a cricketer. I'm over here touring with the West Indies."

"Is that's how you and WG got together?"

"He's been mentoring me. I'm trying to make my name in the game."

"Cricket or life?"

"Both."

"Make sure he just sticks to the cricket. Don't listen to him about anything else." Bess laughed.

"Don't listen to her Viv. She's a tease. I was always exemplary."

"WG and I were friends back in the day. That day was a long time ago. Nearly a century past," explained Bess.

WG added "We were out there in the day. We were celebrities. The Press were always trying to get a story on us." WG looked reflective. "Fame fucks you up."

You could have heard a stone drop. Billy broke the stunned silence. "Crikey mate. I can feel your pain."

Bess understood as well, and changed the mood, "I had a husband WG. I was good. I wasn't like that Marie Lloyd who could get any man in her day."

"You could as well Bess. You were the original femme fatale." This time WG laughed.

"Maybe. I guess we were." Bess smiled at the memory.

"They liked a cricketer as well. We were more popular than these rock n'roll idiots."

Billy Idol was having none of it. "Fuck off WG. Boring cricket to rock n'roll? Women love rock n'roll not cricket."

"They can like both Billy." Bess was running this show as if she's was back at Wilton's music hall.

"You're out of your mind. Rock n'roll is the best thing that has ever happened and will ever happen." Gene Vincent was having his say now.

Bess laughed. "Calm down boys," adding, "WG was the hero of his day. He loved the music halls. You couldn't get him out of them."

"He's not such a boring old fart then?" asked Gene Vincent.

Bess winked at Gene Vincent. "Only sometimes! He had his wild side. He could be very naughty."

WG was speechless. Bess had put him in his place. But she loved him as well.

"Tell the boys your story Bess." Billy Idol had saved WG further embarrassment.

"Drugs and drink were my downfall," explained Bess. "We were decadent and far worse than people today. These punks don't shock me."

"What do you mean, Bess?" Billy was interested in her views.

"They're just kids. Back in the day, we had gin palaces and opium dens. People were out of their minds all the time on drugs. Even respectable people. Politicians, Police, famous people of good backgrounds."

"Life is terrible. 1970s Britain is shit. We're bored. No, we fucking bored."

"You've got to be joking, Billy. This is paradise to what we had."

Viv Richards looked confused. "I don't understand too much about any of this stuff. All I know is that if you're West Indian, life ain't too much fun here."

Viv Richards had just made the most hard hitting comment of the night. He hadn't said much, but his words had hit home. He had come in to bat, and hit the opponent's fastest bowler first ball deep over the square leg boundary for six.

The 19th century was a crucial period of drug-taking development both in terms of potency and plurality. The Victorians took not just alcohol and opium but cannabis, coca, mescal and, with the invention of the hypodermic needle in the 1840s, morphine and heroin. The 19th century also saw the origins of drug control, and the medicalisation of addiction to these substances. These drugs were portrayed as a liberation, a fight against the boredom of respectability. They were needed to deal with the cruelties and harshness of Victorian London.

Billy Idol and Gene Vincent were fascinated with the history of the London music halls.

Bess was on a roll. "I played both the Alhambra and Empire in Leicester Square. The place was wild. Prostitutes and pimps were everywhere. The atmosphere was salacious."

"What was it like working all these music halls?" Billy was excited.

"Crazy. We performed numerous halls each night, criss-crossing London in horse drawn carriages."

"Did you earn good money?" asked Gene Vincent.

WG was quiet and looked nervous.

"We earnt good money, though we had to work hard for it. We worked hard and lived fast; the stresses of this lifestyle meant that many of us died young."

"Any regrets Bess?" asked Billy.

"Plenty. If I'd kept going another 20 years I might have performed with Charlie Chaplin or Stan Laurel. I might have gone to America with Fred Karno."

"You were better than them Bess."

"No I wasn't WG. I saw Charlie at the Coronet in the Elephant and Castle just before I passed. He was a genius and still so young."

Gene Vincent looked at Bess. "What made the music hall so popular?"

WG answered, "I can tell you. It was Bess's charm, vivaciousness and ability to fascinate. She could work an audience."

Gene Vincent sniggered, "She's got you on a hook, WG."

This time WG was on a roll, "Her saucy looks and beauty won you over. Bess would be dressed in frills, lace and ribbons, twirling a parasol coquettishly whilst giving 'knowing' winks to all in the audience. She was a temptress."

"Music hall was hard work with too many temptations. Sex and drugs were everywhere. No wonder we died young." Bess looked sad, reinforcing her earlier comment.

Gene Vincent agreed, "Just like rock n'roll, Bess."

"That's true, Gene. The rock n'roll of its day. I guess rock n'roll is always changing."

"Where did you like to perform best?" asked Gene.

"Wilton's Music Hall in Whitechapel or Brick Lane Music Hall. The crowd were always rowdy and entertaining. Different crowd in the East End to the West End. I'm a Hoxton girl so that's natural."

"Were they difficult to handle?"

"Men are easy. Look at WG. He's a puppy dog really." Bess winked at WG.

John Davidson's 1891 poem, In a Music Hall, gives some idea of the audience's attraction to the halls:

"I did as my desk fellows did;
With a pipe and a tankard of beer,

In a music hall, rancid and hot,

I lost my soul night after night.

It is better to lose one's soul,

Than to never stake it at all."

Bess was excited about tonight. "I'm so looking forward to seeing Bob Marley."

Gene Vincent was all questions, "Who is this lady you're looking after Bess."

"She's a Bromley girl. She's something ethereal. There's nobody like her."

Billy Idol went up to Viv Richards, "I need to tell you about my own cricketing family. My forefathers played the game. One was hanged at Tyburn for the game. Another was killed in a duel on Hampstead Heath." This was the last thing Viv was expecting. He was lost for something to say. Billy went into fill detail about his cricketing history.

Viv recovered his voice. "So Billy! You could be more cricketer than rock n'roll?" Once gain Viv had hit the sweet spot.

Billy Idol looked nervous. "Possibly! But keep it quiet Viv please. I've a reputation to maintain."

Billy was in full flow talking to Viv Richards when Bob Marley came onto the stage. Don Letts was standing 10 yards away. The crowd were engaged as they sensed something very special was about to take place.

Viv had taken the tube from Maida Vale sneaking out of the bank entrance of the hotel. Viv's team mates imagined him sleeping trying to get over his sickness. The team's doctor would call to check to see how he was doing, but he could always pretend that he'd been asleep. The concert was euphoric and liberating. Bob Marley had played in the UK in 1973 at small venues, but this would be his largest audience in the UK. He was now a world star who was poet, political player and saviour.

A few quotes of Bob Marley sum up the wisdom and greatness of the man.

'One good thing about music, when it hits you, you feel no pain'.

'Emancipate yourselves from mental slavery. None but ourselves can free our minds'.

'Better to die fighting for freedom then be a prisoner all the days of your life'.

'Don't gain the world and lose your soul, wisdom is better than silver or gold'.

For punks, and much more importantly, West Indians living in Britain, this was inspirational.

Only Viv Richards and Billy Idol had heard of Bob Marley before. Gene Vincent, WG and Bess loved the concert though the genre of music was new to them. Bob Marley was charismatic, like a spiritual leader. The music was empowering though there was so much more to him than the music. He had presence. The event was a religious experience with a higher meaning. This was no ordinary man and no ordinary performance.

Don Letts was on a high. He decided that Bob Marley would be his friend. This was going to be his 'sliding doors' moment as was seeing The Clash at the Roxy in Harlesden later in 1976. He followed Bob Marley back to his hotel and introduced himself. At the end of the evening they were friends. A plentiful supply of weed helped cement the friendship. Nobody could ever accuse Don Letts of not seizing the moment. Unconsciously, he had already bought into the DIY culture of punk.

Kilburn and the High Roads played the Assembly Rooms in Walthamstow the next day on June 17th. The Assembly Rooms were an art deco style, 1940s Grade II listed building in the grounds of the town hall. They had only played a couple of gigs in the last 12 months. The Kilburns were played out and on their last legs. The spirit and meaning of the music had deserted them. Like many bands that live in each other's pockets they started hating each other. WG, Bess and Gene Vincent were personal guests of Ian Dury. For almost a week, Gene Vincent and Ian Dury had been inseparable.

Ian Dury had laid on the gig for Gene Vincent after their meeting at catshit mansions, Oval cricket ground on June 11th. This would be the last time the Kilburn's ever played and was a thank you to Gene Vincent. The Assembly Rooms would be the first time Ian Dury had sung *Sweet Gene Vincent* to an audience and the Kilburns. It had been his secret other than liaising with Chaz Jankel as to the arrangement. Ian was in tears of emotion and was struggling to form the words of the song. It wasn't often you saw Ian Dury struggling with verbiage. Usually, Ian had words and then more words for every occasion with some added spice on top. The band was struggling with a song they didn't know. *Sweet Gene Vincent.*

The song finished and you could have heard a pin drop. The crowd didn't know if to cry with Ian or applaud. Something special had happened but nobody quite knew why. Eventually Ian pulled himself together.

In his gruff London accent Ian spoke, "That was for Gene Vincent. Good geezer. Good fella. He's with us tonight."

Ian Dury gestured towards Gene Vincent who was with Bess and WG. "That's where they are."

The crowd looked at Ian as if he'd lost his senses. Ian started to cry again and the crowd sensed something higher was at play, as if the concert was just a prop for the night. They'd never seen Ian's sensitive side before and were more accustomed to Rottweiler Ian than soft, caring Poodle Ian.

Ian Dury recovered himself again, "That's it. We're fucking finished. That's the end."

After 60 minutes of playing, Ian walked off stage and away from Kilburn and the High Roads. He was euphoric and sad at the same time. A chapter in his life had closed and a new one was about to open, He had to get away to the South Coast and be on his own for a few days… a few weeks… a few years. The song had meant so much to him. He had never expected to meet his hero. They say, 'never meet your heroes or you'll be disappointed'. For Ian, the emotions were much more complex. They were wrapped up into his psyche, his illness and disability. Sweet Gene Vincent.

Gene Vincent didn't know what to do. Something in him said to 'leave Ian alone'. He wouldn't chase after him. His job here had been done. There was nothing to add. They had saved each other, even if it didn't seem apparent at the time.`

The crowd was stunned. Chaz Jankel stayed on stage on his own and played jazz on his saxophone for the next 40 minutes, mainly Miles Davis numbers.

They needed a 'come down'. Chaz Jankel and Miles Davis were the perfect combination for the baring of Ian

Dury's soul. Luckily, it wasn't the last time people would be able to enjoy the musical marriage of Chaz Jankel and Ian Dury. Joe Strummer never made it to Walthamstow.

WG and Bess didn't know what to say as Gene Vincent stood in Walthamstow High Street trying to take in the events of the last 2 hours. It was one of those 'did that really happen?' moments in your life. Gene Vincent didn't know or care where he was going. For sure, all the frustrations of the past 6 weeks had disappeared. But melancholy was now hitting him like a Michael Holding bouncer.

Bess spoke first, "Let's get you to Louise's."

"Why not? Let's get out of here. I'm done with Walthamstow," Gene Vincent had spoken.

"You never know, Gene. The Clash might be at Louise's tonight," Bess was hopeful.

We might as well. Who knows what tonight will bring? I can do no more."

"We're with you all the way Gene. We're your friends." As ever Bess was warm, generous and kind.

"Did you see Ray Davies of the Kinks in the crowd tonight?"

WG and Bess shrugged their shoulders. "What does he look like?"

Young aspiring film maker John Rogers walked passed. He looked at Gene Vincent and spoke. "Go west my friend. Bess is right."

"Who the fuck are you? What do you mean?"

"I've just spoken to Siouxsie in the Chelsea Physic Garden. She wasn't alone. Gerard and Culpeper were talking to her." Then John Rogers was gone.

Gene Vincent looked bewildered. "Who the fuck was he? Yes. Let's get to Louise's."

Louise's was warming up. WG, Bess, Billy Idol and Gene Vincent walked in.

They were amazed to see Joe Strummer, Mick Jones and Paul Simonon in the club. Paul Cook and Steve Jones of the Pistols were there also talking to The Clash. Dave Vanian, Captain Sensible and Rat Scabies of the Damned were there as well. The Bromley 'contingent' were also in attendance. Siouxsie Sioux was reputed to be there, but nobody had seen her. This was like a punk convention.

They didn't notice the king of rock n'roll and his entourage making their way to the bar.

"Look, Billy, Joe Strummer is here," Bess was excited.

"That's unusual. I've never seen them here before. That's a result. That's fate, Gene."

"How do you mean?" Gene Vincent seemed confused.

"Tonight is the night. You and Joe Strummer are going to be best mates at the end of the night," Billy didn't seem that excited. It was as if he'd known all along that Joe Strummer would be there.

The DJ was playing his favourite track at the time, Lou Rawls' *You'll Never Find a Love Like Mine*. The dancefloor was full.

Billy Idol looked to Gene Vincent, "Do you want to see Linda?"

"I could do with seeing her. I need that confidence. She's amazing."

Billy laughed, "I'm glad you like her."

"I could have done with her in the '60s. She works wonders with my leg."

"I bet she does."

Bess made the arrangements. Gene Vincent started limbering up.

WG turned to Gene Vincent, "You'll be fine, Tiger."

The punks were holding centre stage and most of the attention. Joe Strummer was still talking with Paul Cook and Steve Jones. Mick Jones was with Viv Albertine and Ari up of the Slits. Paloma Romero, aka Palmolive and fellow Slit, was dancing with Dave Vanian of the Damned. Captain Sensible and Rat Scabies were insulting, playfully, anyone in earshot. Members of the Bromleys were pouting and scowling with attitude. Billy Idol had taught them well.

Linda beckoned Gene Vincent over to her office. He went submissively.

WG spoke first, "I do hope he'll be okay. Bess said she can be rough."

Bess explained, "It did him the power of good last time. That was Billy's most inspired call."

"Without Linda, we would never have met up with Ian Dury," observed WG. "I'm totally convinced."

The DJ started to play *Play that Funky Music* by Wild Cherry.

"Funny old music to be playing with a load of punks here," mused Bess. "I do wonder why all you punks come here. It's a little ironic."

"We get beaten up everywhere else, Bess," Billy was philosophical. "You're right. It is the supreme irony."

"I wonder how Gene is doing with Linda?" asked WG.

169

"Maybe the music is drowning out the screaming. I reckon he'll be rocking when he comes out. Joe Strummer won't stand a chance," Bess was adamant.

You Should be Dancing by the Bee Gees came on after Wild Cherry. This was the cue for Mick Jones to start dancing with Viv Albertine. Mick lacked any rhythm, though Viv managed to get the beat. Clearly, they were on something to be dancing to the Bee Gees.

Gene Vincent came back onto the dancefloor arm in arm with Linda. He was smiling like a Cheshire cat.

The DJ then played *Heaven Must be Missing an Angel* by Tavares.

Linda took him to Billy Idol, "He's all yours now, Billy." Linda gave Gene Vincent a big kiss.

"I'm ready, Billy. I'm like a boxer. Gene Vincent is ready for some rock n'roll. Here I come, Joe Strummer."

Billy had asked the DJ to play *Be Pop a Lula* for when Gene Vincent returned.

The expectation was massive. Nerves were starting to affect Billy Idol, WG and Bess. This was the moment. The last 6 weeks since that night at Beckenham cemetery led to here.

Disco Lady by Johnnie Taylor came through the speakers. Louise's was packed. The atmosphere was vibrant and electric.

Gene Vincent looked at Billy Idol, "I thought *Be Pop a Lula* was coming on."

"It must be on next, Gene. I promise you."

Gene Vincent was starting to fidget. Bess went over to Gene and gave him a big hug.

"Thanks, Bess, I'm okay. I promise."

After what seemed an eternity, the DJ played *Dancing Queen* by Abba.

Joe Strummer came over to Billy Idol, "On your own again, Billy, talking with yourself? Where's your Queen Siousxsie? I hear you don't go anyway unless she gives you permission."

"She has something you'll never have, Joe."

"What's that?" Joe Strummer jumped straight in. He was inches away from Billy Idol, eyeballing him furiously.

"Class and presence. You shout a lot Joe. But you're nothing. You don't even have a band now."

"I bet that pleases you, Billy?"

"In a way, it does, Joe. You're a fucking poseur."

"Fuck off, Billy. You're a loser," then Joe Strummer struck Billy Idol with a fierce right hook.

WG, Bess and Gene Vincent had witnessed it all. Billy got to his feet slowly.

Captain Sensible and Dave Vanian helped him.

"Fuck off Strummer. You're a wanker." Captain Sensible was ready for a fight.

"Thanks Captain. But leave it. It's Gene Vincent here who needs help. Not me." Billy rubbed his jaw.

Dave Vanian and Captain Sensible both spoke. "Gene Vincent. I want to meet him. Where is he?"

"He's here Captain." Billy was struggling to speak.

"I can't see him. Where the fuck is he?" Captain Sensible was despairing.

"He's next to me Captain."

"He's a spirit then? Pass on my regards. I love Gene Vincent. Tell him to pat me on the head."

"I love Gene Vincent as well." Dave Vanian was another member of the Gene Vincent appreciation society.

"I'm sure he'll be delighted Dave." Billy was still struggling to speak.

Then another blow came his way, "Billy! It's over. He didn't even notice me," Gene Vincent was distraught. "It's not going to happen."

"Of course it is. He was just looking at me," Billy was less than convincing. Billy was struggling to think straight.

Could it be Magic by Donna Summers came on. "Is *Be Pop a Lula* ever going to be played?" Gene Vincent was losing hope. It was almost tangible. Bess, WG and Billy could feel it.

Then it happened. The DJ had kept his word. *Be Pop a Lula* was belting out of the speakers. Billy Idol and WG pushed Gene Vincent onto the stage. He was reluctant.

Gene Vincent started slowly, but the song he loved the most, soon gave him back his spirit. He thought, 'I'm still a performer even if Joe Strummer can't see me'.

Then the magic happened. Donna Summers' *Could it be Magic* had been right. The crowd saluted him and joined in singing *Be Pop a Lula*. Mick Jones was coming straight for him. There was eye contact. It was going to happen, but it was the wrong person. The crowd were going wild. They could see him again. *Be Pop a Lula* always did it. The song was like magic.

Mick Jones got up onto the stage and hugged him. He was now playing air guitar next to him as he sang. Mick moved closer to speak with him. "It's great to see you, Gene. Welcome back," they were the most beautiful words that he

had ever heard. He couldn't believe the earlier experience with
Ian Dury at Walthamstow could be trumped.

"Did you know this would happen, Mick?"

"Siouxsie told me something. It's turned out a little
different, but this is better."

"Did she? That's interesting."

"I'll come over for a chat. Give me a minute." They were
still singing *Be Pop a Lula*. The crowd had taken over. Captain
Sensible was orchestrating them. Steve Jones and Paul Cook
were playing air guitar. Dave Vanian was singing every word
as if life depended on it. Joe Strummer and Paul Simonon had
been encouraging Mick Jones. Viv Albertine and Chrissie
Hynde were rocking to their core. The moment was seminal
and magical.

Gene Vincent came back to WG, Bess and Billy Idol. They all
hugged him. The DJ started applauding. It had been 3 minutes
of fame. Then it was over. Did it really happen?

A pre-released song came on. *Car Wash* by Rose Royce
was enchanting the audience.

There was shock on all their faces.

"Fuck me. I didn't see that coming," Gene Vincent was
stunned.

"It's Mick Jones then and not Joe Strummer. From despair
to glory all in 5 minutes," WG summarised it perfectly.

Bess gave him a big kiss. Then Linda kissed him.

Gene Vincent sat down. Relief was the overriding
emotion. This was his moment of triumph. The last 6 weeks
had been painful, but the misery was now forgotten. He had
felt inferior to WG. WG had been so successful with Viv

Richards. Viv Richards was having the season of his life. He was the greatest batsman in the world and WG had help make him that. In comparison, he had achieved nothing. There'd been 6 weeks of walking around London, getting nowhere, and freezing in moments when he could have made a difference. Now he could walk tall.

His evening went from strength to strength when Mick Jones came over with Viv Albertine for that chat.

"Hi, Gene, this is a privilege."

"The privilege is mine, Mick. It's nice to meet you, Viv."

The DJ played *Midnight Love Affair* by Carol Douglas.

"What did Siousxsie tell you?" Gene had to know.

Viv replied, "Nothing too much. Just that a rock n'roll legend was going to help reform and save The Clash. We thought he'd been still alive and not a spirit. I thought it might be Pete Townsend of The Who. Joe thought it was bollocks."

"Never mind the bollocks; I've heard that before. Where's Steve Jones?" They all fell about laughing.

Tina Charles' *I Love to Love* was being played.

Mick Jones was starstruck, "You're Gene Vincent. You're a rock n'roll superstar, mate."

"Thanks, Mick. That's what I've been telling this lot for the last 6 weeks. Some people never believed me."

Viv spoke next. "What's the score then, Gene? Are you going to help The Clash become a half decent band? They need help."

Mick just nodded. He was still starstruck.

Viv was on a mission to help her boyfriend, "They're hopeless, Gene. You'll have your work cut out."

"I'm ready, Viv. This is why I came back."

I Love to Boogie by T Rex was playing as they left Louise's. The night had been intense.

The night belonged to Gene Vincent. Linda followed him out into the London night. London belonged to sweet Gene Vincent. He felt ten foot tall. "London is fucking brilliant. The best place on God's earth." Gene Vincent was a Londoner now.

Dawn was about to break over Oxford Street. Night time London and some of its decadence excesses was about to end. Business London would soon be awakening. Gene Vincent was breathing in the London air. Life felt good. Billy Idol, Bess, WG, Linda and Gene Vincent walked along Oxford Street towards Bond Street and Marble Arch.

Billy Idol turned to his friends. "Just over there is the Tyburn Tree. To the right is Hampstead Heath. That's what this is fucking all about. Redemption for my family. Thank you, WG, and thank you, Gene," Billy Idol was crying.

"Are you okay, Billy?" asked WG.

Billy Idol's reaction had surprised them, but it was Billy Idol who had got the Gene Vincent and WG show on the road, and was fighting to make a name for himself and his family. Their successes impacted on him. He felt responsible for them both.

Siouxsie came over to Billy Idol. "Well done, Billy. Go and have a look at Tyburn." Then she disappeared. The evening felt it had lasted 100 days. Momentous would not do it justice. Walthamstow to the Tyburn Tree felt like Chairman Mao's Long March on an ecstasy tablet. The only problem was The Clash. They had broken up and Bernie Rhodes was still like the Scarlet Pimpernel. Nobody had seen him.

Siouxsie then elaborated, reappearing as they approcahed Tyburn, as if she'd read everyone's minds. "The Clash will reform today. Don't worry." Then she was gone again.

England was batting on the first morning of the Lord's test match. They opened with Barry Wood, replacing the injured John Edrich, and Mike Brearley. Barry Wood and David Steele went early. Brian Close strode to the crease at the ripe old age of 45. He could have been 95 and he'd still feel confident enough to head butt a Michael Holding 90 mph bouncer to the boundary minus a helmet. That sense of Yorkshire indomitability and self-certainty had never left him. Hundreds of stories about Brian Close would circulate around the county cricket grapevine. His antics had been a topic for many after dinner speeches.

Vic Marks, an England spin bowler and now excellent journalist and commentator, who played under Brian Close at Somerset, remembers when he was the third victim in a hat-trick by Nottinghamshire's Barry Stead, a left-arm swing bowler. Brian Close, who was caught in the slips, marched into the dressing-room at Trent Bridge and immediately began upbraiding the second man in the sequence, Richard Cooper, who was making his county debut. "You bloody idiot," shouted Closey. "You told me he was swinging it, but you didn't tell me he was seaming it as well. No wonder I bloody nicked it."

The sense that he felt nothing was impossible often left his teammates either gobsmacked or sniggering in disbelief. Ray East, Essex cricketing legend of the 1970s and '80s, had many stories about Brian. "I was travelling with him in a car somewhere when news came that Muhammad Ali had defeated George Foreman in the 'Rumble in the Jungle'."

"I could beat him," said Brian Close.

"Who, the announcer?" asked Ray East.

"No, Muhammad bloody Ali. He'd never knock me down and in 15 rounds all I'd need was one lucky punch. One lucky punch to be champion of the world."

"The scary thing was," recalled Ray, "that he believed it."

Brian Close batted for 3 ½ half hours for his 60 runs. He was stoic, gritty and pugnacious rather than flowing and graceful. You felt he'd rather break an arm than give away his wicket. Eventually, the spinner Raphick Jumadeen snared him. At least, he had blunted the fast bowling attack of Roberts, Holding, Julien and Holder. Woolmer added 38 with a useful knock of 31 coming from the tail-ender Derek Underwood. England had managed 250. This was an in-between score on most wickets. It wasn't high enough to intimidate a team batting second, but could be half decent on a sporting bowler's wicket. Andy Roberts finished with 5–60 and was the pick of the bowlers. He had been accurate and hostile, an ever present threat to the batsmen. Holder with 3–35 supported admirably with a nagging accuracy and some decent seam movement.

Chris Old and John Snow opened the bowling for England and soon struck. Roy Fredericks went for a second ball duck. Larry Gomes and Alvin Kallicharran went for 11 and 0 respectively. The West Indies were struggling at 40–3 and missing Viv Richards. Greenidge and Captain Clive Lloyd steadied the ship and added 99 for the fourth wicket. Greenidge went for 84 off 119 deliveries and had been particularly severe on Chris Old. A collapse of 4 wickets for 14 runs then happened with Clive Lloyd for a well struck 50 the last of the victims. The classic Kent combination of caught Knott bowled Underwood had done for Lloyd. The Friday afternoon crowd of English supporters in the Tavern stand were dinking and celebrating England's dominance. They were singing, fuelled with alcohol and hope. Alcohol and hope – that deadly combination. Was England really going to beat the West Indies? For a brief moment on that Friday afternoon, and with a few pints inside, English people dared to dream. Were the stoic qualities of England going to quash the fire and talent of the West Indies? Maybe dreams do come true! Tony Grieg directed the field with the exuberance of a just-rich Las Vegas millionaire. He was like a showman at the circus. West Indians in the crowd grumbled at their team's struggles. Inter-island rivalries were never far away. A successful West Indies team would keep a lid on the sometimes fragile peace and harmony. A losing West Indies team might just open up a few wounds and island resentments.

In England's second innings, David Steele and Brian Close scored 64 and 46, resisting some seriously quick bowling from Roberts and Holding. Michael Holding was recovering from an illness that stopped him playing in the First Test, so he was feeling his way back to top form and pace. Again, the feeling that England was 'hanging on' prevailed, and that sooner, the West Indies fast bowlers would run amok. There was no respite from this fast bowling attack. Resisting it required extreme skill and bucket loads of concentration, determination and courage. Eventually, through mental fatigue more than anything else, the batsmen would succumb. One player likened it to 'being in the firing line'. David Steele had been bought in to face Lillee and Thomson in the previous summer and had proved to be a revelation. He was a solid professional on the county circuit who was braver than most when the fast stuff was flying around your ears. Batsmen could be classified as falling into two groups when facing fast bowling: those who 'that didn't and kidded everyone they liked it' and those 'that didn't and showed it'. David Steele was neither: he loved and embraced fast bowling. He had found his calling.

Others had seen little to suggest that the uncapped 33-year-old averaging in the low thirties would take to Test cricket with such aplomb. Yet the gloom started to lift as Steele memorably dubbed, "The bank clerk who went to war," – walked out of that unremarkable career with "unfashionable Northamptonshire" and straight into the crosshairs of Lillee and Thomson.

Famously, on debut at Lord's, Steele's grand entrance was not so much gladiatorial as farcical, redolent of another quintessentially English character first seen on the big stage that summer, Basil Fawlty: "I went down a flight of stairs too many and almost ended up out the back of the pavilion. Then when I got out there, Lillee started calling me Groucho." Jeff Thomson expressed his opinion more crudely and brutally, "Who the fuck is this old bloke coming out to bat?"

But Steele was no comedy act. Gritty rather than pretty, he didn't so much strike a blow for ordinariness as for the extraordinary lurking within those considered ordinary, and with each over-my-dead-body block and defiant hook off his helmetless head he slowly turned the tide of the series, perhaps the national mood. "We'd been down. People told me it was Churchillian. I just came and got stuck in and gave them a bit of inspiration and that's why the country got behind me."

Steele's new-found fame came with perks. A Northamptonshire abattoir owner offered to pay him a lamb chop for every run he scored up to 50 in the third Test at Headingley, and a steak for every run after that. Steele made 72 on day one.

"I got a telegram the following morning," says Steele. "'Dear David, I owe you 50 lamb chops and 22 steaks. Take your time in the second innings – I'm running out of lamb." In his second dig, Steele scored 92. "I didn't earn much money that summer, but I was eating lamb chops and steak for two years solid."

Bob Woolmer and Tony Greig added a few late order runs and England were bowled out for 254. Andy Roberts had another 'five for', with 10 in the match. He was on the Honours Board. Michael Holding had taken 2–56 off 27 overs. He had felt his way into the match, allowing Andy Roberts to receive the well-deserved plaudits. The bowling in this match would improve his form and fitness for the mayhem that was to come. The West Indies needed 323 to win in a day's play. They would be facing spinners Derek Underwood and Pat Pocock on a fifth day test pitch, taking some spin, so the task was not going to be easy. England smelt victory. Underwood and Pocock bowled over 50 overs between them taking just 3 wickets, albeit economically. Roy Fredericks scored 138 at a decent strike rate of 55. Fredericks loved pace on the ball and was a fine player of fast bowling. His 169 against Lillee and Thomson the previous year of only 145 balls on the super-fast track at Perth in Western Australia had become a knock of legends.

ESPN described it, "In just 145 balls, he scorched to 169 against an attack that included Dennis Lillee at his most fearsome and Jeff Thomson at his fastest. His hundred came in 71 balls. This was not a one-dayer, but a test match, for God's sake."

Freddo smashed the ball continuously, especially when he batted at the Members' End, where he hit with the strong south-easterly that blew like a mini-cyclone. His slash through backward point travelled with the velocity of a tracer bullet and was nigh on impossible to catch.

There was Lillee hurling down his thunderbolts and Thomson bowling like the wind, and Freddo cutting and pulling like a man possessed. There was many a time when he cut at lifting deliveries, and at the precise instant he struck the ball, both his feet were well clear of the ground.

The Fremantle Doctor added to Australia's woes, for the wind reached 50kph. Add that to the speed of Freddo's ferocious strokes. Surely the good doctor, who with his cooling hand comes to the rescue of the people of Perth every afternoon in summer, could have given Freddo a calming pill to save the poor Aussies from a terrible hiding.

Fredericks had shown superb patience and restraint against two slow bowlers in Underwood and Pocock on a slow English wicket. Useful contributions from Lloyd and Kallicharran saw the West Indies finish on 241–6, just over 80 runs short of victory. England was 4 wickets short of victory. Tony Greig was confident in his post-match interview that England could go on and win the series. Honours were even and the battle moved to Manchester where the West Indies hoped Viv Richards would return. Both the summer weather and test series were warming up. Soon both would reach boiling point. After the game, the West Indies went straight to Northampton and would play a further 3 counties: Yorkshire,

Derbyshire and Leicestershire with only 1 rest day before the third test match on July 8th. Touring in 1976 was intense. At times, it resembled a Tour of Britain coach holiday.

Northamptonshire were one of the weaker county teams and the West Indies batted first scoring 413/3 declared, scoring at nearly 5 an over. Collis King and Larry Gomes enjoyed some gentle batting practise putting on 303 for the third wicket. Gomes was 166 not out with King dismissed for a belligerent 163. Northamptonshire scored 172 in reply with David Steele scoring 1 before being dismissed LBW from a Wayne Daniel thunderbolt. Geoff Cook top scored with 53 and reliable Raphick Jumadeen took 5–47. The West Indies enforced the follow on and dismissed Northamptonshire for an improved 256. This time David Steele top scored with 56 with useful contributions of 44 from both Richard Williams and Pakistani test player Musthaq Mohammed. The West Indies won easily by 10 wickets.

The weather was now warming up. June had seen progressively rising temperatures in a long spell of quite calm and sunny weather dominated by high pressure. The lack of ground moisture resulted in a high proportion of the sun's energy being utilised to heat the air, rather than being used for evaporation. Whilst the month started damp by the second as the Azores high ridged towards up and into the country the south became settled although and as it moved further east a southerly flow moved up right across the UK allowing temperatures to rise towards the mid to upper twenties centigrade. By the end of the first week, the constant sunshine and dry ground temperatures rose into the low thirties in parts of the south east, though the heat was not widespread. The middle of June was mixed with unsettled weather in the north, but the high pressure remained across the south so these parts stayed dry.

It was the last ten days though of June that saw the real heatwave. High pressure developing across south east England allowing a continental flow from Spain and temperatures then exceeded 30C every day until the end of the month. From the 23rd June through the first week of July, there were 15 consecutive days when the temperature exceeded 32C somewhere in the country and five days exceeded 35C. On the 26th June, 35.4C was reached at North Heath (Sussex) and East Dereham (Norfolk), this is the earliest date in the 20th century that 35C was exceeded. The old London Weather Centre in High Holborn, central London, also recorded a rooftop maximum of nearly 35C (34.8C) on the 26th, whilst Southampton's Mayflower Park recorded a maximum of 35.6C on the 28th. Nights were particularly uncomfortable for sleeping, especially in the cities with falling to 20C at times. Brush and heath fires developed too across the south given the very dry conditions. The New Forest was particularly badly affected. Even along the coast there were quite high temperatures reported as coastal breezes were suppressed by stable high pressure inhibiting convection of the hot air inland. Temperatures above 30°C were recorded at numerous coastal locations in the latter part of June.

Chapter 9

The First Gig
Sheffield, July 4th

'I mean, like, rock n' roll was always about spirit and fun' –
Joey Ramone
*'Batsmen who say they like facing fast bowlers are common
liars'* – Justin Langer

The Clash had reformed and been invited to play their first gig
at the Black Swan in Sheffield on July 4th. Gene Vincent was
in the crowd. This was the moment he had been waiting for.
The story of The Clash would begin here. The Clash was
supporting the Pistols. John Lydon had taunted Joe Strummer
for weeks about being on the undercard to anyone who cared
to listen. Word had reached Joe Strummer on the punk network
of Lydon's taunts. The organisers had warned both The Clash
and the Pistols they wouldn't be paid should any trouble occur.
Gene Vincent had been mentoring Mick Jones to stay calm and
concentrate on the music. This was like Genghis Khan
teaching his tribe about the joys of celibacy.

The Pistols and The Clash were on opposite sides of the
Black Swan exchanging stares. For the Pistols, Steve Jones,
Paul Cook and Glen Matlock were calm. John Lydon was the
antagonist, the agent provocateur. The lead singer of any group

was usually a problem. Keith Levene had spoken to John Lydon, but that had been the only verbal contact between the rivals. There was unfinished business from the Patti Smith gig on May 16th. The Clash were showing their nerves.

The relationship between Mick Jones and the other members of The Clash, after the night at Louise's where Mick and Gene Vincent had connected, had been different. Mick Jones went to great lengths to explain that Gene Vincent was mentoring him. They were meeting daily and Mick Jones would pass on the fruits of their discussions, Joe Strummer was a great fan of rock n'roll, rockabilly and Gene Vincent.

The idea of Mick Jones and Gene Vincent tutoring the band was not a problem with the rest of the band. Joe Strummer loved Gene Vincent. The three of them had conversations though Joe couldn't see Gene Vincent. Mick Jones was the man in the middle. The setup was unorthodox, but it worked. One of the many wonderful things about Joe Strummer was his ability to take on the unusual. If it worked... it worked. He didn't have set boundaries. He was a very spiritual person. The gift just came to him in a different way. He was on a higher plane of consciousness. No idea would shock or faze him. If Gene Vincent was helping them, then that was brilliant. Joe didn't need to see him to connect. Gene Vincent had become a member of The Clash. Paul Simonon was cool with the Gene Vincent membership. They'd seen the vision. They knew it wasn't a Gene Vincent impersonator. It was no double or look alike person. They had that moment at Louise's. They knew something special was being played out. Friction in The Clash manifested itself from their ambition, hard work and commitment. Gene Vincent was never a problem.

185

Terry Chimes and Keith Levene were ambivalent. They wanted out. They didn't see their future with The Clash. It was not easy being a member of The Clash. As Strummer said, it was Stalinist in its approach. There were big egos in the band. They worked 12 hour days, 7 days a week. Arguments could be personal and vicious. It wasn't for everyone. Terry Chimes would play on and off for The Clash up until 1983. He also played for Black Sabbath and is now a chiropractor in Essex. Keith Levene had been instrumental in forming The Clash. Levene was responsible for helping to persuade Joe Strummer to leave the 101ers and join The Clash, on that night of destiny in Fulham. However, Keith was more inspired by John Lydon, and joined him when Public Image Ltd was formed. Levene's guitar work was later imitated by others, including the Edge of U2. Levene was one of the first guitarists to use metallic guitars, such as the Travis Bean Wedge and Artist as well as the Veleno, the latter of which was nicknamed the "Leveno" in his honour.

The Clash were raw, and that's putting it kindly. It was inauspicious start, but it was a start that fitted in with punk's DIY ethos. They could only get better. At least, they had the guts to do it. The benchmark had been set. Mark Twain once commented, "The secret to getting ahead is getting started." That was a perfect ethos for The Clash and punk in general.

Paul Simonon was struggling musically and the writing of Mick Jones and Joe Strummer was in its infancy. Keith Levene and Terry Chimes didn't really fit in with the other members of The Clash. What they did have was an amazing work ethic and the manic ambition of Joe Strummer and Mick Jones. Failure was not an option. For them and Paul Simonon, the alternative was the dole queue or worthless, low-paid jobs with an idiot supervisor or manager shouting at you all day. 1976 with 1.5 million on the dole queue felt like that. They would work 7 days a week to avoid the apocalypse for the underclass of 1970s Britain. The next gig was going to be much better. It was a matter of life and death. This was life on the edge.

A reporter in the NME commented on their July 4th gig, "The Clash was just a cacophonous barrage of noise. The bass guitarist had no idea how to play the instrument and even had to get another member of the band to tune it for him. They tried to play early '60s R 'n' B and failed dismally. Dr Feelgood is not one of my favourite bands, but I know they could have wiped the floor with The Clash."

The band's feeling of their first gig, in a later interview, was enlightening as to their rawness and punk DIY ethos.

Joe: 'The line-up for the first gig was Terry Chimes on drums, Paul Simonon, Mick Jones, myself and Keith Levene, so we had a three-guitar set-up at that time'.

Mick: 'I don't think we had been rehearsing that long before the first gig'.

Joe: 'The first gig we ever played was at what we used to call the Mucky Duck (actually called the Black Swan) in Sheffield. We had a song we did called Listen , which had a bassline that went up in a scale and then down a note to start, and Paul was so nervous that he just kept going up the scale, and we all fell over laughing 'cos we didn't know when to come in'.

Paul: 'The day The Clash started really was when we played the Mucky Duck with the Pistols, which was great. It was the first time that I had ever played on stage. The night before it felt frightening, but once we were on the way there then I began larking about. I tied one of Keith's shoes to a piece of string and hung it out of the back of the van and the door had to be open anyway so we could breathe. So there we were sitting with all the amps and luggage with a plimsoll bouncing around behind us and all the cars behind us slowing down to avoid it. But the moment that we walked out on stage, it was like I was in my own living room. I felt really comfortable. Things went wrong during the evening, and Mick had to come over and tune my guitar, but it didn't bother me. I just wanted to jump around, but Mick wanted it to be in tune'.

Another eye-witness reported, "The Clash were billed as "The 101ers" on the posters... and Mick Jones and I were born on the very same day. The only song I remember was Steve Hibbert's *Pressure Drop* which I knew well from my old Trojan collection. There was a lot of shouting and political grand standing."

Mick Jones went on to comment, "We played our first gig at the Black Swan in Sheffield. We went in the back of a removal truck with the gear piled up next to us. We all sat in the back. It had a gate on the back, and it was open like an old army truck, and we put someone's shoes on a string and put them out the back and they bounced along! And the gear was going like this (waves his hand about, laughing). It was quite hairy!"

"It was the back room of a pub. There were fifty people there, a couple of punks. It was interesting, wherever you went you would see a couple of them in the early times. Then you would see them getting more all the time they would tell their friends. It was a big thing."

Gene Vincent had seen their performance alone. Bess and WG were working on a project in London. He was excited to be there, but disappointed with what he heard and seen. He couldn't hide his anger.

Gene Vincent made his way straight to Mick Jones after the gig. Mick Jones could sense Gene Vincent wasn't impressed. They had been talking daily for 2 weeks since that night at Louise's that had changed everything. The outcome of that evening had been momentous.

Mick Jones had got in touch with Bernie Rhodes the following day after that famous night at Louise's. The reforming of The Clash had been straightforward. Bernie Rhodes had been worryingly easy to win over. Everyone had calmed down. Bernie Rhodes had been like a little puppy dog when Mick Jones approached him. Everyone knew they were onto a good thing with The Clash and could see sense. They had all met at Goldhawk Arms in Shepherd's Bush to confirm the reforming of The Clash. The date was 18th June. They drank all night.

"So how do you think it went, Gene?"

"You've a long way to go, Mick. That was raw. In fact, it was crap."

"We've made a start," Mick felt awkward and couldn't think of anything else to add.

Gene went closer to Mick as if to stop people hearing, "I know. But you need some songs. We talked about this. You're a second rate covers band at the moment. Make that third rate."

"We're working on them, Gene. I promise you."

"I know you are, but if you take out the incompetence a wedding band would have more attitude than you."

"That hurts Gene," Mick Jones sounded rather lame and pitiful.

"Well, for fuck sake, get some of that attitude you keep talking about," Gene Vincent was on a roll now. "You live in a shithole with no future so talk about that. And learn how to play your instruments. The Blue Caps and Wild Angels were great musicians."

Gene wasn't finished, "Paul can't even play bass. And your drummer isn't at the party. He looks fucked off with all of you. The drummer is the most important man in the band."

"We'll look for another drummer Gene."

"That'll help, but you need a rock n'roll attitude and you haven't any. Doris Day is more rock n'roll than you."

"Fuck off Gene. We're not that bad."

"For fuck sake, get some attitude. Fucking upset people. Do something. Stop acting like a bunch of pussies."

Mick Jones recoiled from the brutality of Gene Vincent's critique. He couldn't hit him, but Mick's fist was clenched. It just didn't seem right to strike your spirit guide, especially when he's right.

Gene Vincent had given Mick Jones and The Clash the wakeup call they needed. They were posturing as a punk band, but weren't actually one.

Gene Vincent wasn't finished. "You love the idea of punk and being part of something. But you don't know what to do. You're fucking clueless. Where are you going?"

Mick Jones looked chastened, "Help us, Gene. Don't give up on us. We'll get better."

"There's nothing wrong in pissing everyone off. At least, people will write about you and remember you. You can't create too much of a stir."

Joe Strummer and Paul Simonon wanted to know what Gene Vincent had thought of them.

Joe went first, "Did Gene like us, Mick?"

"Not exactly."

"Why?"

"We've no real material. He told us to get writing. Too many covers."

Joe was indignant, "We've written some stuff."

"Have we, Joe? We've got ideas. It just scribbles on bits of paper. Nothing real."

Joe Strummer looked crestfallen. Paul Simonon was angry.

Joe put it together, "Ok. This is day zero again. Gene is right. We write everyday. We'll be poets of the Westway."

Paul Simonon had his say. "Did Gene say anything about how we played? How were we musically?"

Mick Jones shook his head. "We've got to play our instruments right. He said we were shit. The Wild Angels and Blue Caps were much better. And we need a proper drummer."

Far in to the future, Mick Jones would add the following comments to that night in Sheffield and the struggles of their first gig.

"Very often, people got it completely wrong. But in a way, you couldn't get it wrong; it wasn't formed. We were just starting to find out what it could be. You didn't think about it too much really. When you are young you think about it after in the post-match analysis! By the time everyone had sussed it, it was already over."

"We were dressed in black and white. A couple of us had ties on, black and white shirts with suity bits. It was punk style... not good suits, a bit ripped. Kind of tight suits, slightly different. We were dressed fairly straight and well-behaved in a way. There was maybe a rip here and a little splash of colour there. A couple of pin-type things, not safety pins. The look was still formulating."

The same night as The Clash's debut up in Sheffield, the Ramones played the Roundhouse in Camden, and nearby Dingwall's the following night, supporting the Flamin' Groovies. Playing to 2000 people at the Roundhouse was their biggest gig yet, the first time they had played outside small clubs. These were also their first shows in the UK, and proved to be pivotal moments in the early punk scene. The Ramones had the exoticism of coming from the States and New York. They weren't coming at it with a London or English template. There weren't the rivalries that English punks had. They looked and dressed so differently.

They came onto the stage after The Stranglers had played. The Guildford Stranglers were confined to a similar circuit. It was 1975 before they ventured into even the London suburbs. They shortened their name to the less parochial Stranglers and were now, in the summer of 1976, firmly on the punk bandwagon. At this time, they were a little more polished than many of the punk acts.

Their early songs displayed their top drawer punk credentials, radiating an aggressive attitude and some biting lyrics. They had songs such like *Peasant in the Big Shitty*, *I Feel Like a Wog*, *Down in the Sewer*, and *Ugly* They were both ugly and wonderful.

Then The Ramones made their appearance. They looked like four New York hoodlums in torn jeans and biker jackets, sporting Byrds-style mop-tops. They tried to act New York tough, but it was good. They were different and the crowd took to them. They played loud, fast and aggressive with a 'fuck you' attitude. The crowd had come home. They knew straight away The Ramones were special. Within a minute, they were converts. It was like that Patti Smith moment again from 6 weeks earlier. New York punk was winning over London. For many, it was also the start of the revolution. No group liked 'multiple starts' as much as punks. A 'Start' had that magical feeling you couldn't recreate quite as well again. Like that moment of first love, the feeling of pure joy and innocence as if nothing else matters. 'Starts' couldn't be bettered. They were the purest feelings in the world.

One member in the crowd, Alan Butts, commented, "I knew we were at the right event when a hippy turned to me and muttered 'it all sounds the same!'" Well, that was the point, but to quote John Peel on those early tracks, "They're all the same, but they're all different – if you know what I mean."

Rose Williamson called it brilliantly, "The excitement of the audience and of the band themselves was testament to the fact that they weren't only tapping into the anger and discontent, they were turning it into something new. Momentous in its simplicity, political in its refusal of politicisation, their acknowledgement and simultaneous creation of punk was changing music and the way it could be."

NME's review of The Ramones gig named it 'the hottest, sleaziest garage ever'.

T-Rex leader, Marc Bolan, was in attendance at the Roundhouse show and was invited on stage. Gary Webb was there as were Viv Albertine and Chrissie Hynde. The ripples of that evening would last for years.

The Flamin' Groovies/Ramones double bill was successfully reprised at the Roxy Theatre in Los Angeles the following month, fueling the punk scene there as well. The Ramones were becoming ambassadors for global punk. Another performance in Toronto in September energised the Canadian growing punk scene. Punk wasn't just exploding in London and the North West of England.

The Ramones' debut LP was greeted by rock critics with glowing reviews. The Village Voice's Robert Christgau wrote, "I love this record – love it – even though I know these boys flirt with images of brutality. For me, it blows everything else off the radio." In Rolling Stone, Paul Nelson described it as, "Constructed almost entirely of rhythm tracks of an exhilarating intensity rock & roll has not experienced since its earliest days."

At Dingwall's on July 5th, all the faces from the London punk scene were there. The evening ended up in a brawl outside the venue. It's been called 'the battle of Camden 1976'.

The self-styled bard of Camden 'Sir' Johnny Green was there to break up a fight between JJ Burnel of the Stranglers and Paul Simonon of The Clash. He was helped by Gene Vincent. The Clash had come back from Sheffield the previous evening with criticism ringing in their ears. Gene Vincent was there that night to see his fellow countrymen The Ramones perform and look after The Clash. Bess and WG were there also. They were leaving the following day to travel to Manchester for the third test. And, of course, Billy Idol was circulating.

There was something in the air that night. London was steaming hot with temperatures over 90f. Tempers were on short fuse. The Pistols were back from Sheffield and John Lydon was giving his opinion on the Ramones for anyone who cared to listen. The Clash were standing on the bonnet of their car. They had the 101ers' *Keys to Your Heart* to give to The Ramones. Joe Strummer and John Lydon were keeping their distance. They just snarled at each other from 20 yards. Tonight, the true punks were there to pass their opinion. The Ramones didn't know what was about to hit them. Welcome to London!

The Damned and 'Bromley Contingent' were waiting in the heat outside Dingwalls. The future members of the Slits: Ari Up, Palmolive, Tessa Pollit and Suzie Gutsy were sitting on the gates of Camden Lock. Future Slit member, Viv Albertine, was there again. There were too many egos for something not to happen. Camden was combustible at any time. Now it was like a tinder box. Captain Sensible and Rat Scabies were mock fighting and ended up in the Regent's canal. Dave Vanian pulled them out with the help of Chrissie Hynde, Jimmy Pursey and Viv Albertine. Even the waters of the Regent's canal were at record temperatures so Captain and Rat weren't cooled off.

The fuse was lit as The Stranglers left Dingwalls after their performance. JJ Burnel of The Stranglers barged into Paul Simonon of The Clash or something like that. Anyway, a disturbance and melee then ensued close and onto the Regent's Canal. Billy Idol tried to act peacemaker, but was felled. A JJ Burnel punch had been enough for him. Poor Billy Idol was always getting hit by some punk. The Clash were taking on The Stranglers. The Pistols were hitting anyone and purely non-partial as were most of the 'Bromley Contingent'.

Siousxie Sioux was kicking out and ruling the roost. A still damp Captain Sensible hit JJ Burnel. Soon nobody knew who was hitting who. A Wild West saloon had nothing on the 'Battle of Camden'. The tensions had been brewing for a long time.

Bess loved the fight and wanted to join in. She was pure punk at heart. WG was disapproving, then a Moses 'parting of the waves' moment took place next to Camden Lock.

'Sir' Johnny Green arrived with Gene Vincent on his shoulders singing *Be Bop a Lula* cutting through the melee. Ray Davies of the Kinks had got them together. Everyone could see Gene Vincent. The sight was so bizarre and incongruous that everyone stopped fighting, applauded and then broke into the words of *Be Bop a Lula*. 'Sir' Johnny Green took JJ Burnel and Paul Simonon aside to make their peace. Gene Vincent was still on his shoulders. This time he was belting out *Lotta Lovin'*. The punks were singing *Lotta Lovin'* as well. Gene Vincent had all the punks on a string and playing to his tune. Bess and even WG were belting it out. Rock n'roll was back. Gene Vincent smiled in satisfaction. Even Billy Idol smiled holding a sore jaw. His pouting was better than ever. Captain Sensible was hailing the 'new messiah'. Job done.

'Sir' Johnny Green, the self-styled bard of Camden, would go on to be the road manager for The Clash. He loved Gene Vincent and rock n'roll. You could say that he had a very personal experience with the king of rock n'roll. Seemingly, Gene Vincent belting out *Be Bop a Lula* made him visible to all.

The press was speculating that England had weathered the storm and that the West Indies might be tamed. In between the second and thirrd test matches, the West Indies had played 4 counties. The tough schedule had honed their skills and they were ready with Viv Richards back in the team. The wicket at Old Trafford looked strange and would crack likely at some stage. The warm weather had taken a toll on the preparation of the pitch. There was some pace in the wicket as well and some of the West Indies bowlers were licking their lips at the prospect of bowling on it. England needed slow, very slow pitches to prosper and nullify the West Indies pace attack. Their best prospect was to bore the West Indies to defeat. It was the English way.

The West Indies batted first and were soon 26–4. Mike Selvey, on debut, had replaced the injured John Snow and taken 3 of the four batsmen to fall including Viv Richards. Viv Richards was bowled for 4. Mike Selvey must have thought he was in heaven and that test cricket was easy. The ball was swinging in hot, humid conditions and the pitch was offering lateral movement. Hendrick was back in for Chris Old, who had been ineffective and expensive at Lord's, and he took the valuable wicket of Clive Lloyd for 2. One man stood in their way though and that was Gordon Greenidge. He would go onto score a majestic 134 out of a total of 211, one of the highest ever percentages of runs scored by a player in any innings. He had some support from Collis King who scored 32, but precious little else was offered from the other batsmen. Mike Selvey finished with 4–41. Derek Underwood took 3–55 and England cricket was buzzing again. Whisper it quietly, but 'these West Indies might not be all they're cracked up to be'. They were 2 and bit test matches into the series, and if you exclude Viv Richards's 232, they were going toe-to-toe. Tony Greig looked confident as England walked off at the end of the West Indies innings. He was laughing with his team. This was the highlight of the English cricketing summer and the calm before the storm. The missiles were about to be unleased. Tony Grieg wasn't going to be laughing much more. A painful grimace would be more his look.

At the end of day one, England was 37–2. John Edrich and Brian Close had gone cheaply, but England were still in the game, if they could put together one decent partnership. Friday morning was hot and humid again. Clive Lloyd had urged his players for more effort. This was the moment that could decide the series. His players responded brilliantly. England were blown away for a meagre 71. Michael Holding, or 'whispering death' as he was often called, bowled with extreme pace to take 5–17. His pace and bounce was too much for England. Only David Steele with 20 made it into double figures. Andy Roberts took 3 wickets and Wayne Daniels took 2. Tony Greig made 9, the second highest score in the innings. Wayne Daniels had uprooted his off stump much to the delight of the West Indies players. Tony was no longer smiling. The England players looked haunted as if the Grim Reaper had stepped into town to collect their souls. Stunned silence from the English supporters spoke volumes. In that moment, England were finished and 'shot through'. There was no way back. The West Indies had breached the dam. English resistance had been smashed. In a Boxing bout it would have been stopped to cease any further brutality and possible damage. There is a moment in some test series where the pendulum swings in one team's favour and the psychological balance falls one way. The moment had just happened.

The English bowlers were devastated. On Friday morning, they would have been looking forward to a day with their feet up after the exertions of the previous day. Even at

37–2, they would have felt reasonably comfortable. To be back out bowling again before lunch was not on the agenda. This could alter the mood and balance of any team. Bowlers would feel aggrieved at the batters for depriving them of much needed rest. They would also feel that their efforts of the previous day had been wasted. This could niggle at a team psyche and was like waking up on xmas morning to rubbish presents and a day of preparing and cooking for ungrateful relatives. Naturally, the English players appeared somewhat deflated as they took to the field. They needed early wickets to improve the mood.

The West Indies sensed that the series had turned, and now full of confidence, were in for the kill. They put on 116 for the first wicket which adding to England's anger and frustration. Eventually, Roy Fredericks went for 50 hit wicket bowled Hendrick. Fredericks had toppled onto his stumps whilst hooking Hendrick for 6. This situation always felt a little unsatisfactory for the purists. The batsman has clearly been unlucky and the wicket is hardly deserved for the bowler. Ripping the batsman's middle stump out and knocking it back 10 yards would feel much better. At this point, England were just grateful for a wicket, however earnt. Then Viv Richards walked to the crease, strutting to the crease with a mixture of dominance, arrogance and relaxed menace. The bowlers shuddered. This was knockout time. Fortunately, there was still something in the pitch for the bowlers, so Viv was quite restrained. WG had built him up for this moment. His ears were still ringing from WG's criticism at his first innings shot that saw him fall to the bowling of Mike Selvey. WG had pulled himself away from rekindling his love of music to go back to his first love, Cricket. He and Bess were having an away day holiday for spirit guides. WG had given him the bollocking of his life at the hotel in Manchester after the first day. The 'telling off' had gone like this:

"Hello WG. Thanks for coming up to watch."

WG was in no mood for small talk, "What was that shot, Viv?"

"Selvey was pitching up so I thought it was right for the drive. The wicket was doing quite a bit."

"You should have seen off the new ball. The conditions were always going to calm down," WG was preaching like a convert to the Geoff Boycott school of batting.

"If the ball is there I'll drive it," Viv sounded assured and non-repentant. "You've got to score."

"There was time for that later. I liked to whack the ball as well. You're not the only one."

"I live by the sword, WG," Viv was in a bullish mood. He'd never been this forthright with WG before.

"You looked a fool out there. Mike Selvey is just another one of those county trundlers. He'll live off this wicket for the rest of his career. He's crap and you made him look a world beater."

"I can't always score hundreds, WG. Everyone fails at some point."

"I know. But you're giving your wicket away Viv. You're better than being bowled by a Mike Selvey. I know I'm always on your case, but I want you to do well."

"I know you do."

"I've said it before and I know it's boring. Play straight, late, keep the ball on the ground and in the V."

WG left without another word. Viv Richards had been admonished and was left standing there like a naughty schoolboy. Only someone of WG's stature could have got away with it. His captain Clive Lloyd and manager Clyde Walcott had never spoken to him like this before. WG felt a little guilty slating Mike Selvey. He admired the way Mike Sevey had bowled first innings, but he wanted to motivate Viv. He asked the cricketing gods to forgive him.

Gordon Greenidge was in dominant form again. He had endured a horrible winter at the hands of Lillee and Thomson in Australia. They had blitzed him with pace and their aggression. He scored 0, 0, 3, 8 in 4 innings and was dropped twice from the team. Australia had been chastening for him on and off the pitch. Touring Australia in 1975–76, the racist abuse the players received from the crowd was both distressing and formative. "Being bombarded by comments and behaviour… well, I'd encountered some ignorance before, but this was very different, very very different... it degraded me and downgraded me a great deal," said Greenidge.

Gordon Greenidge had a troubled relationship with some of his fellow West Indian players. The reasons were complex. In 1965, when Greenidge was 14, he left Barbados for Reading where differences in culture and climate were exacerbated by racism, making for a miserable time. But he developed as a cricketer, joining Hampshire and going on to form a legendary opening partnership with Barry Richards. Then, in 1973 and after rejecting England, he returned home to play himself into West Indies' test team, and was picked to make his debut at Bangalore a year later with Viv Richards. Pre-match, the chatter concerned how a rain-affected strip might assist the Indian spinners, and then West Indies won by 267 runs with Greenidge scoring 93 and 107. His friend and mentor was the great John Arlott, a cricket commentator and writer unsurpassed. Some players and supporters thought him as more English than West Indian. The West Indies team and many of its players were on a mission on many fronts. There is little doubt that England players were motivated as a team, but seemingly, there were many West Indian players with points to prove and with careers at stake. This just added to the edge they had over England.

Gordon Greenidge was out for 101, his second century of the match. However, the third day belonged to Viv Richards. Eventually, he was dismissed for 135 lbw to Pat Pocock. He had hit eighteen 4s and no 6s. The innings had taken him 261 balls and his strike rate was only 51.72 which was excellent, but not up to his usual high tempo scoring. Restraint and discipline were two new words to his batting vocabulary. WG was euphoric with his protégé's success. At least this time, he had Bess to share his joy.

Derek Underwood and Pat Pocock had bowled 62 overs between them for only 2 wickets. Mike Selvey had taken another 2 wickets, but went for 111 off only 26 overs. England were being flogged and slayed to all corners of Old Trafford and the weather was Caribbean hot to add. England were firing blanks with poppy guns. Soon after, the West Indies declared on 411/5 setting England an improbable 552 to win. Now the guns would be fully loaded with armour piercing bullets. Roberts and Holding were getting ready. 1976 was getting ready to explode fast bowling style. For the next 90 minutes, Michael Holding and Andy Roberts went for England with some of the fastest and most hostile bowling ever witnessed. Brian Close and John Edrich survived to be 21–0 at close of play. No words could do credit to their incredible skill and courage. No words can adequately describe the hostility of the bowling. You have to view the footage to appreciate what those two openers faced. No longer did England fans care about winning. What mattered to them was Edrich and Close surviving in one piece. Health was more important than saving a Test match. The umpire Billy Alley intervened warning Michael Holding and speaking with Clive Lloyd, the captain. At the end of play Edrich was 10 not out with Close undefeated on 1. They were cheered off as heroes. They could each have scored a double hundred against Australia and the reception would have paled into insignificance to the applause the crowd at Old Trafford gave them that night. Predictably the Sunday papers were full of criticism of the fast bowling assault on Close and Edrich. For them it had crossed the line and wasn't 'Cricket'. There was 'outrage' everywhere. England was 'shell-shocked'.

In analysis, it's important to look at several factors. Firstly, the pitch was dangerous, with unpredictable bounce. Secondly, the West Indians had suffered at the hands of Lillee and Thomson the previous winter and were going to dish out that treatment rather than receive it going forward. The Australian tour had left its psychological marks on the West Indies team. They had beaten India with hostile fast bowling back in the Caribbean just before the tour. Now it was England's turn. They would soon get their revenge on Australia in the sweetest of all revenges. But for Packer, it would have come sooner. This was the way they were going to play now. Lastly, every team and especially England, would do the same if they had the same weapons. Englishmen enjoyed dishing out the heat as much as anyone and their fans reveled in it; albeit, the occasions were rare. Something in the game was wrong if England were losing. The West Indies had heard it all before and it didn't and never would 'cut' with them. For West Indies fans, this moment was sweet. The colonial masters were getting battered at their own game.

In the words of Bob Marley, and adjusting those words to Cricket, "Who are you to judge the life I live? I know I'm not perfect – and I don't live to be – but before you start pointing fingers, make sure your hands are clean!"

The words of WG to Viv Richards later that evening were touching and full of emotion. He praised Viv for his innings. "Well done, Viv. That was excellent. You played really well. That innings was as good as any I've ever seen. Better than Trent Bridge," Viv was emotional hearing such words. There were tears of joy in his eyes. WG hugged him.

WG scratched his head, "That Holding bowled quickly. I've never seen anything as fast. How can you play bowling that fast?" He collected himself for a moment. "I knew he was quick but that was something else."

Viv was intrigued, "You never faced anyone that quick?"

WG chuckled, "Spofforth was fast, but nothing like Holding. Let's not forget Andy Roberts. I'm glad I wasn't out there."

WG was enthralled. He had never watched a day's play that had been so exciting. This was his game. He was home. Nothing could beat cricket and he was relieved the game had been in good hands during his absence. Bess had to calm him down.

The days play had left its mark on England. For the next 24 years, England would fail to win a series against the West Indies. They would twice be 'blackwashed' in 1984 and 1986. Every series would see English batsmen facing a battery of great West Indies fast bowlers: Holding, Roberts, Daniels,

Marshall, Garner, Clarke, Croft, Ambrose, Walsh and Bishop. They hunted often in packs of four, sometimes being called 'The four horsemen of the apocalypse'. July 10th 1976 was the day the cricketing world changed. The wickets may have fallen the previous day with England all out for 71, but the impact of that last session on the Saturday would reverberate for years. English test careers would be defined as to how you played the West Indies fast bowlers. Graeme Hick was destroyed by them, but for Graham Gooch, it made him. Graham Gooch batting against the barrage of West Indian fast bowling greats for the next 15 years was as good a cricketing contest as you could ever witness. Graham's 154 undefeated against the West Indies at Headingly in 1991against the great Malcolm Marshall with the support of Curtley Ambrose and Courtney Walsh is the greatest test innings by an Englishman that I've ever witnessed. The West Indies would go on to rule the cricketing world for the next 15 years. England fans would view series with the West Indies from behind the settee, grimacing at the ensuing horror. This was cricket's version of TV's *Casualty*. Poor Andy Lloyd never recovered his cricketing confidence when hit from a skiddy Malcolm Marshall bouncer in 1984. And who can forget Malcom Marshall picking out bits of Mike Gatting's nose from the ball in 1986 after Gatting ducked into a Marshall bouncer? It was Colin Croft who would say 'pace can kill'. Paul Hardcastle wrote a song *19* explaining the horrors of the Vietnam War on young American troops. The song was adapted to England batsmen facing the barrage of West Indian fast bowling greats and was sung by 'The Commentators', narrated by cricket fan Rory Bremner. Great commentators like John Arlott, Brian

Johnson, Richie Benaud and Jim Laker were mimicked affectionately in the song.

On the Monday, England was bowled out for 126 giving the West Indies victory by a mammoth 425 runs. This time Andy Roberts was the destroyer with 6–37. At one stage England was 54–0 with Close and Edrich gritting their teeth and showing old school discipline and resolve. Michael Holding and Wayne Daniels took 2 apiece. Once Close and Edrich were dismissed, England was blown away. They looked timid and frightened. Michael Holding bowled Tony Greig for 3, but this time, the celebrations were muted. The message had already been delivered to Tony Greig. Greig looked haunted as he walked back to the pavilion. The end couldn't come soon enough. For England supporters this was painful and dispiriting. You felt as if all life had been sucked out of the England team. You could see in their eyes that England weren't coming back. They were beaten in mind, body and spirit. The white flag was flying even if you couldn't see it. Pace bowling played with your mind. It could eat away at you. It could destroy you. There's no way you could explain it to people, who had never faced it, and had that terror keeping you awake at night. To be hit in the face with a cricket ball travelling at 90mph could be a life changing experience. Not everyone was as brave and skillful as John Edrich and Brian Close.

After the game, Tony Greig at the press conference gave out the rallying message. You had to admire his acting abilities. He was fooling nobody. The West Indies fans were joyous. The fires of Babylon were burning bright.

Whilst Bess and WG were in Manchester, Gene Vincent continued to talk daily with Mick Jones.

Mick Jones and Joe Strummer were writing furiously. Mick Jones was teaching Paul Simonon the basics of playing bass guitar. They were either in Camden or Shepherd's Bush. Night and day blended into one. You couldn't fault their effort. The 10,000 hour rule to expertise was starting at a fast pace.

Gene Vincent was happy. He was part of a band again. The boys of The Clash were his sons. He could feel Eddie Cochrane looking down at him and approving. That horrible night in Wiltshire 15 years ago, and its memory, was fading.

Chapter 10

Montreal Olympics

"The water is your friend... you don't have to fight with water, just share the same spirit as the water and it will help you move." – Alexander Popov

The opening ceremony of the 1976 Summer Olympic Games was held on Saturday, July 17th 1976 at the Olympic Stadium in Montreal, Quebec in front of an audience of 73,000 in the stadium. An estimated half billion watched on television

The opening ceremony of the 21st Olympic Games in Montreal was marred by the withdrawal of 25 African countries. The reason was New Zealand's sporting links with South Africa.

The International Olympic Committee's refusal to ban New Zealand, whose rugby team was currently touring South Africa, had resulted in the boycott. South Africa had been banned from the Olympics since 1964 for its refusal to condemn apartheid.

A spokesperson for the New Zealand Olympic Committee said the All Blacks tour of South Africa had been arranged by the New Zealand Rugby Union which was an autonomous body and nothing to do with the Olympics.

In a statement issued just hours before the opening ceremony, Kenya's foreign minister James Osogo said, "The government and the people of Kenya hold the view that principles are more precious than medals."

He said the decision by the IOC not to ban New Zealand would give 'comfort and respectability to the South African racist regime and encourage it to continue to defy world opinion'.

The list of those boycotting the Olympics was: Libya, Iraq, Kenya, Zambia, Nigeria, Gambia, Sudan, Ghana, Tanzania, Uganda, Algeria, Ethiopia, Madagascar, Central African Republic, Gabon, Chad, Togo, Niger, Congo, Mauritius, Upper Volta and Malawi.

The first week of the games were dominated by the sports of swimming and gymnastics.

In the pool, two countries dominated the medal table split by gender. In the women's events, the German Democratic Republic took 11 out of a possible 13 gold medals. Kornelia Ender was the star of the team winning 4 gold medals. At the time, swimmers were suspicious of this achievement. The story would end in tragedy for everyone involved. The swimmers would suffer awful future health issues and nobody cared. 14 year olds girls weren't going to be able to resist the pressure of a brutal totalitarian regime hell bent on beating the hated 'west' and 'capitalists' at all cost. Pressure wasn't just exerted on the swimmer, but families and friends. Jobs, flats and money could be taken from your parents. People in the 'west' would have done the same. Denying this is just kidding ourselves. And then there were those swimmers deprived of medals. Swimmers who were clean and had trained morning, day and night were cheated of their fame and a legacy. They had earnt medals with their talent and sweat that were denied to them. It makes you cry for everyone involved, apart from the politicians. To the politicians, they deserve all the shame heaped on them. The Kornelia Enders, Petra Thumers, Ulrike Richters deserve our sympathies. They were innocent and pawns in a political power struggle.

The highlight of the Mens swimming events was the Mens 100 metres backstroke on July 19th. In the past two Olympics, Roland Matthes had won both the 100m/200m backstroke. He had been undefeated for seven years from 1967 to 1974 when American John Naber defeated him. Matthes was called the 'Rolls Royce of swimming'. The 200 metres backstroke in the 1972 Munich Olympics defined his legend status. Matthes qualified fastest from the heats with Americans Mike Stamm and Mitch Ivey either side of him. They tried their best to psyche him out. They talked big before the Final. The US Mens swimming team were strutting around the pool like Donald Trump at a NATO Summit. Matthes took an early lead. At 100 metres there was only one winner. Just before the 150m mark Matthes hesitated, turning mid stroke to his coach in the crowd, and gave her the thumbs up. He had broken his rhythm and lost much time. There was no panic. This was a man amongst inferiors. Matthes went onto win in 2.02.82, equalling his world record and beating the Americans easily. He looked nonchalant, almost disinterested, in the extreme as he waited for the others to finish. There was no wild fist pumping or exaggerated celebration. He looked as if he'd just been for a stroll to collect the morning newspapers, and was about to sit down and listen to his favourite Beatles records. For a 10 year old backstroker from Bexley swimming club this was the coolest sporting triumph he would ever see. Doping then was not a thought.

Matthes's technique was revolutionary and classical. Rumours would persist he was part of the GDR sponsored doping system. He always denied this. Matthes never appeared on the Stasi files. He was inspirational. However he was past his peak at 27 and still recovering from appendicitis.

He was part of what could be called 'the greatest swimming race that never was'. Mark Spitz won 7 gold medals at the 1972 Munich Olympics and deserved all the plaudits coming his way. One of his victories was in the 100 metres butterfly. Matthes was fourth over a second behind. Before the race, there was anticipation of two 'greats' clashing. Spitz admitted that Matthes was the one man he feared, even though Matthes was an occasional butterfly swimmer. The gun went off for the start. Matthes thought it was a false start and stood up. The other swimmers were oblivious. Matthes was still on the blocks with Spitz in the water. He had lost a lot of time. Would he have beaten Spitz? Sadly, we will never know. We had to wait 32 years before another clash of that greatness when Ian Thorpe, Michael Phelps and Pieter Van Den Hoogenband clashed in the Mens 200 metres Freestyle in Athens 2004.

On July 19th, John Naber beat Roland Matthes in a time of 55.49 seconds, a new world record. The crown had passed. Matthes came third in 57.22 seconds.

In the 200 metres backstroke, John Naber won gold again, becoming the first man to break the 2 minute barrier in a time of 1.59.19. Naber was a worthy wearer of the crown.

From a British perspective, David Wilkie was the outstanding performer. His win in the Mens 200 metres

Breaststroke in 2.15.11 was the reward for years of hard work and a supreme talent. He beat his great rival John Hencken in the process. The race execution was perfection. Wilkie stayed on Hencken's shoulder for the first 100, turning in 1.06.48 to Hencken's 1.06.09. Wilkie, with his greater stamina, blew Hencken apart on the third 50. At the 150m, there was only one winner. The margin of victory was 2.15 seconds. Wilkie's gold medal was Britain's first in the pool for 16 years. They would not shake hands on the rostrum. Their rivalry had been bitter and alive since the Munich Olympics 4 years earlier. David Wilkie had the last word with a gold medal around his neck. For many it was worth staying up to 3am to watch talent, class and style.

The U.S. men's swimming team won all but one gold medal. John Naber won four gold medals and a silver medal. In winning the gold medal for the men's 100m freestyle, Jim Montgomery became the first person to break the 50 second mark in the event, taking first place in the final in a time of 49.99. One of Britain's greatest ever female swimmers, Sharron Davies, made her Olympic debut at the tender age of 13.

It was later revealed that after injecting athletes with performance-boosting drugs at the Montreal Olympics, East German officials dumped the leftover serum and syringes in the Saint Lawrence River.

Secret-police documents would later confirm the worst. In defense of Roland Matthes, he was not part of State Plan 14:25, a systematic doping programme. In a 2006 confession, Dr Helge Pfeifer, one of the senior sports scientists who knew about the East German state doping programme, stated that Matthes' coach, "Marlies Grohe-Geissler, was the only GDR coach for whom refusal to comply with the Stasi-run drugs regime did not mean instant dismissal. His success predated 14:25 – nor did Matthes need such 'means of assistance'."

On 18th July 1976, Comăneci made history at the Montreal Olympics. During the team compulsory portion of the competition, she was awarded the first perfect 10 in Olympic gymnastics for her routine on the uneven bars. Comăneci's perfect 10 thus appeared as '1.00', the only means by which the judges could indicate that she had indeed received a 10.

"I felt I had done a good routine," Nadia Comaneci said of the moment she finished on the uneven bars in the team competition, on the second day of the Montreal 1976 Games, "So, I didn't care to watch the scoreboard because I thought I was going to get a 9.9 or something like that, which was good as a start. I was already thinking of the balance beam because once the score comes, the music comes on and then we had to march onto the next apparatus. So I was putting that routine away and not paying attention to the scoreboard, until I heard the noise in the arena." Arguably, the defining moment of the Montreal Olympics had just occurred.

In one of the most celebrated technical lapses in history, the arena's scoreboard struggled to deal with Nadia Comaneci's brilliance. History recalls that OMEGA, the Olympic Games official timekeepers and scorers since 1932, had asked organisers before the 1976 Games whether the scoreboards needed updating to accommodate four digits. They were told it was not necessary.

"I looked around to see what was going on and then I saw the problem or whatever was happening with the scoreboard," Comaneci laughed. "I didn't understand it, but I was like, whatever it is, it's something wrong so I am just going to concentrate on my next event.

"One of my team-mates said, 'I think it is a 10 or there is something wrong with the scoreboard'. I knew at least I was going to get a 9.9 – because a 1.0 was way too low."

A photograph wonderfully captures Comaneci's slightly perplexed, bashful expression as she joins the world in realising, or sort of realising, what she had just done.

"In the back of my mind, I said to myself, 'I guess I did better than I thought'. I underestimated myself. I thought I could get a 9.9 and when it was a 10, I was like, 'Oh that's much better, let's see what I can do on the beam'," commented Comaneci.

"Of course I knew that the 10 was the highest score, but I didn't know first of all that it was the first 10 in Olympic history; no one had told me, even though I wouldn't have listened because I would have gone, 'Okay, let me think about that later'.

During the remainder of the Montreal Games, Comăneci earned six additional tens. She won gold medals for the individual all-around, the balance beam and uneven bars. She also won a bronze for the floor exercise and silver as part of the team all-around. Soviet gymnast Nellie Kim was her main rival during the Montreal Olympics; Kim became the second gymnast to receive a perfect ten for her performance on the vault. Comăneci also took over the spotlight from Olga Korbut, who had been the darling of the 1972 Munich Games.

Nadia Comeci continued, "I would have been happy with 9.95, but now I think about it, it wouldn't have been history."

While Comaneci missed out on the team gold, it was her performances in the individual and all-round disciplines that catapulted the teenager to fame.

"People ask me what the definition of perfection, I said it's none, and there is no definition of perfection. At some particular time when I was 14 years old, I've done something that people didn't expect," Comneci said. "It's a ladder that you climb in life, and I got there first."

The final words confirm Nadia Comneci's greatness. "You have to have a lot of passion for what you do, to be able to work hard and to have a lot of motivation because you're going to go to places that you're never going to believe."

In the second week of the games, athletics became the main focus. Two significant performers hailed from the Caribbean. One was Hasely Crawford of Trinidad and Tobago. The other Alberto Juantorena of Cuba.

Hasely Crawford won the Mens 100 metres in 10.06, just ahead of the great Jamaican Don Quarrie. 1972 Olympic champion Valeriy Borzov was third. The much fancied Americans Harvey Glance and Johnny Jones were fourth and sixth. This was the first time someone from the Caribbean had won the men's 100 metres. In 2000, he was named the Trinidad & Tobago Athlete of the Millennium. On returning home, Hasely Crawford had both a jet and a stadium named after him. During his reign as the 100 metre Olympic champion, he also appeared on postage stamps and was awarded Trinidad and Tobago's highest honour, Trinity Cross, in 1978.

Alberto Juantorena became the only athlete to win both the 400 and 800 m Olympic titles in Montreal. In the 800m Olympic final, he led the field for most of the race, eventually winning in a world record time of 1:43.50. Three days later, he also won the 400 meter final, setting a low-altitude world record at 44.26. Later, he became Minister for Sport of Cuba, and Vice-President, later Senior Vice-President of the Cuban Olympic Committee, after retiring from athletics in 1984.

Alberto Juantorena was nicknamed 'El Caballo' (the horse) and inspired one of the finest commentary cock-ups, from the great David Coleman, that became known as 'Colemanballs'.

David Coleman, as Juantorena ran to greatness could not help himself. 'The big Cuban opened his legs and showed the World his class.'

Headingly test match. July 22–27. The West Indies won the toss and batted. At lunch, they were 147–0. Roy Fredericks and Gordon Greenidge took England's attack apart that morning. They cut, hooked and drove England to pieces. England was hoping to strike back and tie the test series with a victory. Tony Grieg was the ultimate frontman of a band. If he could have sung he would have been superb. He was bravado, swagger and personality with verbal diarrhea. His eyes told a different story. England was going to come out fighting and a comeback was imminent. He was pushing it hard but nobody believed. There was more chance of a 3 foot snow blizzard hitting Britain in July 1976.

Alan Ward and Bob Willis replaced Mike Hendrick and Mike Selvey. John Snow was back for Pat Pocock as Headingly was a wicket that favoured pace over spin. Bob Willis was a tearaway young fast bowler who had taken 6–56 against the West Indies for Warwickshire in the preceding game. He had been on the county scene for 5 years or so, but had never cemented his England test place. He was prone to injuries and losses in form. However, he had pace. The England selectors had seen what Holding and Roberts had done to England at Old Trafford. Alan Ward was one of the fastest bowlers on the county circuit so pace was the antidote to England's woes. Medium pacers with a little bit of 'nip, nibble and wobble' hadn't overly worried the West Indies batsmen so far. No longer was England firing a poppygun, but more of a World War 2 semi-automatic rifle. They were still underpowered compared to Holding and co. Also, the lesson here was skill. Pace was good but you needed skill, control and accuracy. 90mph leg side half volleys would be food and drink to Viv Richards, Greenidge and Fredericks. The extra pace would mean they'd score faster and heavier.

Also, Brian Close, Mike Brearley and John Edrich were dropped. Frank Hayes, Chris Balderstone and Peter Willey were placed in the firing line instead. The English selectors had wielded the knife in a desperate attempt to save the series. You couldn't fault them for effort. So far it had been business as usual. The extra pace was pure pleasure to the West Indies batsmen. They wished that England had fielded this attack from the start of the series. The selectors had played a blinder. Roy Fredericks scored 109 and was the first wicket to fall at 192, bowled Willis. They had been going at more than 5 an over. Fredericks must have thought he was back at super-fast Perth. This was a celebration of batting Caribbean style and now Viv Richards was walking to the crease wetting his lips in anticipation. There was going to be fireworks. He looked like Smokin' Joe Frazier at Madison Square Gardens preparing for the knockout blow. England was already on the floor. Alan Ward, the Derbyshire speedster, looked like a startled rabbit in a headlamp yearning for green top wickets in the shires against county journeymen. He was like a non-swimmer chucked into the English Channel with 2 miles of water below him in a Force 9 gale and 10 foot waves.

Viv Richards was quickly into his flow passing 50 at just under a run a ball. He looked nonchalant as if it was all too easy. Even Derek Underwood was feeling the heat. Richards marched down the wicket regularly hitting him over the top. Underwood looked bewildered. The wheels weren't coming off. They were already off and running at speed downhill towards Leeds city centre. Greenidge was dismissed for 115, his third consecutive hundred. English supporters had given up hope and were now consigning themselves to a West Indian run fest. They had decided to celebrate the world class show that was happening before them, reaching that pivot point all too familiar for English cricket fans. There's little point making yourself miserable. Just thank God you're at the cricket, watching something special, because you're privileged to be there. Celebrate it!

There's that moment when greatness just has to be admired and all nationalistic sentiments ignored. You had that same feeling as a miracle goal from Pele, a Beckenbauer pass, a Nadia Comaneci perfect 10, a Michael Jordan interception and jump into orbit for a basket. They're just worth celebrating. Then it was over. Big bustling Bob Willis induced an edge to Alan Knott. Viv Richards was out for 66. Viv Richards looked shocked with Bob Willis running past him, he of the long curly mane and wild eyed mania, to congratulate Alan Knott. Time stood still. As an English fan you felt a little cheated. You'd set yourself for an afternoon of Richards mayhem and now it was over. There was a feeling of anticlimax rather than euphoria, as if you'd been cheated. Even

WG was speechless. He just accepted that even Viv Richards could fail and that Bob Willis had bowled well. Not that 66 was a failure, but in the circumstances and with the mood of the crowd, it felt like Viv had underperformed. That's the pressure of greatness.

That night WG went up to Viv Richards at the team's hotel in Leeds. "Well played, Viv. You're the man. I wish I could have played like that," Viv looked shocked.

The bollockings were over. WG sensed his job was done. The reactions of the crowd at Headingley had confirmed his arrival. He had got there arguably after his 232 at Trent Bridge, but now, there was something different. Cricket fans now talked of him as if he had an aura of greatness. The word 'promising' had been dropped. The pupil had possibly overtaken the master. WG's creditability with Viv Richards had been his own greatness, and of course that was still there. However, WG conceded that Viv was better. That changed their dynamic.

"Shame I couldn't get a hundred for you, WG," Viv felt he had to apologise. WG's meekness had freaked him out a little. He felt awkward.

"You always say that. Willis bowled well in that afternoon session. Sometimes you nick them," WG was philosophical.

Viv explained, "I'm glad England played faster bowlers."

"I sensed you liked that extra pace on the ball. You just wanted to put Willis in his place. He irritates you a little."

"A little. He has an attitude. I like that as well."

WG's final words to Viv Richards that night were special. "You've responsibility to the game now Viv. Your life is going to be different. Stay humble. Don't bat as if you're bigger than the game."

Lawrence Rowe added a classical 50, but the rest of the West Indies batting offered little. They were all out for 450, albeit off just 88.4 overs. England's bowlers were able to take some cheap wickets to massage some unpleasant bowling figures. Snow took 4–77 and Willis 3–71. Thankfully, Alan Ward took 2 wickets in 2 balls, to finish with 2–105 off 15 overs. He looked shell-shocked, a familiar English look that summer, leaving the field.

Lawrence Rowe had played with classical elegance in his first test appearance of the summer. The Jamaican had scored 214 and 100 not out on debut against New Zealand in 1972. In 1974 he scored 302 against England in Bridgetown, Barbados. Michael Holding described the innings as "I have not seen such perfection since." Lawrence looked as if the mantle of greatness was too much for him. He was the talent that 'got away'. He should have followed the likes of Walcott, Weekes and Worrell as a great of West Indian cricket as he was that good. But it all went wrong. Illness, attitude were some of the reasons. He should have been up there with Viv Richards. He ended up in the 1980s on rebel tours to apartheid South Africa much to the horror of fellow West Indians. It was like watching the prodigal son go bad. He would never be forgiven and ended up emigrating to the USA. An attempt to forgive and honour him by renaming a stand at Sabina Park, Jamaica after him failed after local protests. The sadness of Lawrence Rowe would stand poignantly next to the greatness of Viv Richards. Maybe there is a Lawrence Rowe out there for all the greats of sport we celebrate. He was something special to watch. There is a tear for what might have been, the tragedy of Lawrence Rowe. Please forgive and spare a thought for him if you can.

England started cautiously on a slow pitch. Frank Hayes and David Steele went early. England were 80–4 and struggling and Holding was off injured after only bowling 8 overs. England could breathe a sigh of relief. Chris Balderstone and Peter Willey batted slowly but started the recovery. Both were out in the '30s. Tony Greig was batting well for the first time in the series. He was taking his time. When Alan Knott joined him on 169–5, the pace of the innings picked up. Alan Knott was all unorthodox and improvisation. He'd move about the crease and play eccentric shots, placing the ball in unusual positions. He scored quicker than most English batsmen and he averaged nearly 40 in test cricket. He could have played for England solely as a batsmen. To mark 150 years of the *Cricketers' Almanack*, Wisden named him in an all-time Test World XI. On the occasion of England's 1000th test in August 2018, he was named in the country's greatest test XI by the ECB. He was regarded as one of the best wicketkeepers to have ever played the game. Knott was known for his idiosyncratic behaviour on the field. His trademarks included always keeping his shirt collar turned up to protect him from the sun; his sleeves rolled down to safeguard his elbows when diving; and, after a tip from former Northamptonshire and England wicket-keeper Keith Andrew, warming his hands with hot water before going on the field. He had a handkerchief coming out of his right pocket. Arguably, he was England's only world class player. The partnership of caught Knott bowled Underwood was famous in the game.

Tony Greig and Alan Knott shared a stand of 152. Both scored 116. Greig seemed inspired by Alan Knott. Knott was that type of person and he was punishing Wayne Daniels and

Andy Roberts any time they overpitched or bowled short and wide. He wasn't afraid of pace, and had played Thomson and Lillee as well as any English player. England were bowled out for 387, their best score of the series. The innings had taken over 133 overs and taken a decent amount of time out of the game.

Vanburn Holder was the workhorse for the West Indies. He was solid and reliable. He had played at Worcestershire in English county cricket for years so was well versed in bowling on English pitches. He took 3–73 off 30 overs with his fast medium pace bowling and was a perfect foil for the faster bowlers. The likes of Roberts and Holding owed him, when they took the glory and ovations. Without Vanburn Holder their jobs would have been much harder. He was the typical unsung hero and gave the batsmen nothing. Captains loved to have bowlers like Vanburn Holder in their teams. They bowled reliably and didn't get injured.

In their second innings, and with a lead of 64 close to the end of day 3, the West Indies needed to score quickly. In no time they were 23–2 with both Fredericks and Greendige gone cheaply. Viv Richards was soon in his stride taking early boundaries off Willis and Snow. At the end of Day 3 Viv Richards was unbeaten on 32 with West Indies 56–2. Lawrence Rowe had played carefully for 4 not out. Willis, Ward and Snow had bowled well on a wicket was starting to help the bowlers. On the 4th day, Bob Willis was inspired and ripped through the West Indies taking 5–42. Alan Ward enjoyed himself a little more than the first innings taking 2–25. Viv Richards fell for 38, an addition of just 6 runs. Willis had breached his defence, disturbing his off stump. The crowd was torn between celebrating and lamenting his dismissal.

After Viv Richards' dismissal, only Collis King contributed with a run a ball 58. He was harsh on John Snow, who bowled too short. Collis King was another West Indies batsmen who loved pace on the ball, and was prepared to take the bowlers on. He wasn't there to defend but to play his shots. The West Indies were dismissed for 196, giving England a target of 260 to chase victory and tie the series. There was hope. The West Indies were having none of it. Davis Steele was dismissed for a duck second ball. Hayes went for a duck and Balderstone for 4. Andy Roberts had taken all 3 wickets and England were 23–3 and looking at defeat one again. He had looked a little tired in the first innings, but he was now fired up. Clive Lloyd was asking for a big effort. He wasn't going to let England back in. Michael Holding was bowling within himself, but was still dangerous. He had more than pace to his armory. Bob Woolmer and Peter Willey withstood the storm to give England hope again. 'Mr Reliable' Vanburn Holder trapped Woolmer for 37. Tony Greig came to the wicket again. His first innings century had restored some confidence. He took the attack to the West Indies scoring heavily off Wayne Daniels, who had struggled with his line and length throughout the match. Maybe, Tony Greig could turn from villain to match winner for the day. He had self-confidence and guts. Willey went with the score at 140 after scoring a gutsy 45. He was another 'West Indies' specialist who was only ever picked to play for England when the Four Horsemen of the Apocalypse were threatening to run riot, and everyone else, was too battle fatigued for another effort. He was all bravery and defiance, making the most of his limited ability. Overnight, England was 146–5. West Indies required 5 wickets to win. England needed 114 to win. Tony Greig was England's hope.

Wayne Daniel found his form and ripped out 3 England wickets for an addition of 13 runs. Snow, Underwood and Knott went quashing any hope England had. Knott's wicket was particularly demoralizing. Alan Ward came in and added 46 runs with Tony Grieg taking England to 56 runs away from victory. His contribution was 0 off 29 balls before edging Holding to wicketkeeper Deryck Murray. Tony Grieg was going for broke. Realistically, he had no alternatives. He took the attack to the West Indies fast bowlers, and again, was brutal on Daniels. However, the young Bajan had come to the party that morning. Wayne Daniels would only play 10 test matches in his career. The fast bowling competition for places in the West Indies team was fearsome. Within 2 years Colin Croft and Joel Garner – tall, powerful and ferocious, would be bowling for the West Indies. Malcolm Marshall, arguably the best ever West Indian fast bowler, came onto the scene in 1979. Sylvester Clarke made his test debut in 1978. The list of talented fast bowlers was endless. If Wayne Daniels had been English or from any other nation he might played over 100 test matches. He was a stalwart for Middlesex for over 10 years in English county cricket enjoying much success, County cricket batsmen feared him. He caused many a county batsman to have sleepless nights.

The end was nigh. Bob Willis went first ball to Holding, who would be on a hat-trick for the next test match at the Oval. West Indies had won the match by 55 runs and the series. Their players celebrated joyously. Their supporters were ecstatic. There was no disgrace for England. Superior skill and talent had won the day as it always should in sport. Tony Greg had a very decent match with 116 and 76 not out. He was very generous of the West Indies in the post test match interview. For Clive Lloyd, the result was particularly satisfying.

Clive Lloyd was a captain that had unified a squad of players of different nationalities. Many fans failed to realize that Barbados, Jamaica, Trinidad and the other islands were rivals economically, politically and in major sports to the islands like athletics. Their domestic cricket was an inter-island contest. The West Indies was a union of these nations and inter-island rivalries had raised their ugly head before. Bajans and Jamaicans had been known to protest if a local hero was omitted from the test team for someone else from another island. Any West Indies captain had to be acutely aware of these sensitivities. Winning helped, but there was more to West Indies team dynamics than that. That's why sometimes opposing team captains would hint at these rivalries and the impact on morale to gain a psychological edge. Clive Lloyd had the ability of a diplomat. He had the respect of the team as a batsman, though his series so far, had been average. He had one 50 and a few other starts, but no big score. Clive Lloyd was a fast learner and the wounds of the 5–1 defeat had concentrated his mind on the way the West Indies would play in future. The talent and ability was always there. The islands produced great fast bowlers, dynamic batsmen and wonderful spin bowlers. At the time the spinner Lance Gibbs held the record for the highest number of test wickets. A ruthless professionalism was missing. They didn't have the mental edge of an Australian team. The previous winter in Australia had exposed some weaknesses. Clive Lloyd's mantra was 'never again'. Time would show he was true to his word.

Collis King was a supremely talented cricketer. 41 years on from 1976 Collis King would face the biggest battle of his life.

After his test career Collis played in the northern leagues and county cricket for Glamorgan and Worcestershire. He would spend the summer in the UK and the rest of the year in Barbados. He was still playing for Dunnington at the age of 66. In 2017 he wanted to spend more time in the UK with his wife that he decided to apply for a spousal visa. When that was turned down, his nightmare began. He had to return to Barbados to make the application.

When he flew back to Barbados, his Bajan passport was confiscated by Heathrow staff. It was only returned at the top of the airplane stairs when it touched down in Bridgetown. He was told it could take months for a hearing on the spousal visa, whilst in Barbados and away from his wife who lived in York. Fellow Bajan, Hartley Alleyne, who played county cricket in the 1980s, spent three years waiting for his case to be resolved. Many of the Windrush generation cases have been going on for years.

"It really hit me hard, that experience," King said. "But now it is all a waiting process. I am a fit person and play club cricket when I can. I love cricket and whether playing years professionally or as an amateur, I have always put something back. I coach voluntarily and it is saddening, really."

Collis King continued. "The Windrush generation went to the UK and helped rebuild the country after the war. My situation is not quite the same. I sympathise with the people who have gone over there from all of the Caribbean states, done all that work and then after 50 years realise they have nothing. That is really hard," Collis King went on to add. "I hope the country sticks by those people, they deserve it. It is hard when you live over there for 50 years and then find out you have to go back."

The Clash needed practice. Gene Vincent was in despair after the concert at the Black Duck in Sheffield.

He confided in Billy Idol and WG as they sat in the garden of the George and Dragon in Bromley. The date was July 14th.

"They were hopeless. They couldn't play an instrument, Mick apart, and they had no materials."

"How are you helping them?" asked WG.

"Their drummer wants out. A band is only as good as their drummer."

Billy agreed, "That's true."

"They're writing new material. Lots of it was just scribbled down."

Billy came up with an idea, "We need to get them some low key gigs. Start them up nice and easy."

"The Black Duck was a shithole. Hardly anyone was there." Gene Vincent wasn't convinced.

Billy was philosophical, "I thought after that night at Louise's that everything would be easy. I guess life doesn't work that way."

"You saved The Clash for what?" asked WG. "You need to make it happen Gene. I want you to make it work. As much for you as them."

Gene Vincent explained, "Viv Albertine said they're working 12 hours a day, 7 days a week."

"I hope so," Billy Idol looked worried. "But it needs more than that."

"I'm speaking with Mick Jones every day. The message is getting through the band. Paul and Joe are with me. They're getting better. Trust me."

"It's like you're a member of the Clash, Gene."

"I am Billy. They'll make it. It might be the death of me, but they'll make it. I'm mentor and saviour."

Gene Vincent looked at Billy Idol, "I need you, Billy, to get them some gigs. I can't do it. I can shape them but they need gigs. This is about getting out there and showing the people what they're about.". There's the Goldhawk. I hear they use Loftus Road. We could go there. I don't fancy Camden again."

"That's not easy, Gene. I can't get my own gigs."

Billy Idol was slightly hesitant. "Leave it with me. Siouxsie can help."

Gene was getting agitated. "They need to matter. Playing in front of fifty people in a northern pub isn't going to help. That isn't going to start a revolution. London is where it needs to happen."

"The North is important. It's got to be everywhere Gene. It's just not London exploding but Britain exploding. The North has the Buzzcocks."

"Billy. I love the North. That's where I hooked up with the Beatles. I played all over the North. I know Liverpool, Manchester, Leeds and Newcastle. I've happy memories there. But this is about the Westway. The Westway is leading it. That's the centre of the punk revolution."

WG spoke with purpose, "Speak with Bernie Rhodes or Siouxsie. There's the Goldhawk. I hear they use Loftus Road. We could go there. I don't fancy Camden again."

"That's not easy WG. I can't get my own gigs." Billy looked pained. I'm going to go out on my own. I need my own identity and to make my own name."

"I can understand that, Billy, but you saved your family's name now," WG reached out to him.

"Have I? Your men did something with their lives. I need to do the same. I'm not just a shit that does drugs."

"But you're still with Siouxsie aren't you Billy?"

"Of course I am Gene. We're like brother and sister."

"Then ask her for a favour. That's what family is all about Billy."

"I guess a man who had 4 wives would know about that." WG had the last word.

They sat in silence for over 10 minutes digesting what had been said. The conversation had been as emotional and profound as they had ever experienced together.

Billy explained, "I hear The Clash are playing 'screen on the green' in Islington at the end of August. There's a new club called the Roxy, off Oxford Street, that'll be running a 100 day punk event at the end of the year. It's going to be every night. Every punk band might be there including The Clash. Also, the 100 Club, in Oxford Street, is running a 2 day punk festival in late September."

"Oxford Street is where punk is happening," WG was excited.

"We need those gigs, Billy. They need that edge. That's where you learn your craft. Practising isn't enough. They need to be at their best for the Roxy and Islington."

"I'll try. I'll get Siouxsie to help." 3 days later, a gig was arranged for the Goldhawk on July 18th. A further gig was arranged at Loftus Road for July 25th. This gig would be played before QPR's pre-season friendly against Arsenal. Fate was offering a generous helping hand.

July 18th was seriously warm. The temperature had exceeded over 90f. The evening was still warm and humid. The Goldhawk Arms was full to the rafters.

Over 100 people were packed in. The pub was close to the Shepherd's Bush Empire and Green. Gene Vincent was nervous at coming back to the Green.

"I don't like this place, WG. The Green gives me the creeps. There's something weird going on here."

Bess explained, "It's a plague pit, Gene. Thousands of bodies were buried here. Dig deep enough and you'd find all the bodies. "

"All those germs are still incubating I reckon," WG was having some fun.

Gene Vincent was changing colour, "I'm going to be sick." Gene Vincent was on his knees retching.

"Pull yourself together, man. You're a spirit. You can't be sick," WG wasn't sympathetic.

The Clash were ready. Gene Vincent, Bess, WG and Billy Idol were at the front. Gene Vincent was still feeling a little under the weather.

The Clash played: *Keys To Your Heart, Rock'n'Roll Petrol, Sweet Revenge, Rabies, Police and Thieves, Deny, I Know What to Think of You, How Can I Understand the Flies, Janie Jones, Protex Blue, Mark Me Absent, Deadly Serious, What's My Name, Sitting at My Party* and *48 Hours.*

The line-up was Joe Strummer, Mick Jones, Terry Chimes and Paul Simonon. They were on their home patch. Friends were in the audience. Two weeks earlier, Sheffield had been like alien territory.

Joe Strummer was furious and electric. He was explosive and dynamic. Energy pulsated from The Clash. Mick Jones and Paul Simonon were jumping around constantly. Paul Simonon would lower his guitar and run towards the audience. Terry Chimes was aggression and power. Keith Levene added the style. There was a connection. There was love. The rough edges were still there, but nobody cared. In Sheffield they'd been timid and nervous. Now, they played with a fuck you punk attitude. People were having a magical evening. The heat was unbearable. Beads of sweat were flying around like confetti at a wedding yet nobody cared. A Finnish sauna would have been cooler. The stage was taking a pounding. The walls shook. The lights came on and off. The Goldhawk felt like it could have exploded into outer space. This was a wild orgy of a party in your front living room with your best mates ever. People came onto the stage. It was a free for all in true anarchic punk style. It was truly magnificent. The Clash finished the night with *Be Bop a Lula*. Gene Vincent was up on the stage with The Clash, as was most of West London. He and Joe Strummer were belting out the words together. Joe knew he was there. Gene Vincent had never felt better; he belonged to the Westway. The Beatles and Shea stadium was good, really good. But this felt better. This was for Eddie Cochran. This was raw, exciting and personal. It was a beginning to something special and a start. Nothing felt better than the sweet moment of a beginning. Everyone could sense it and feel it.

They were much, much better than 2 weeks earlier at the Black Swan in Sheffield. Paul Simonon had worked really hard with Mick Jones on bass guitar. They'd practised every day since Sheffield. They had found their mojo.

Afterwards, Mick Jones was talking with WG, Gene Vincent and Bess. Everyone was ecstatic. It was safe to say they'd never experienced an evening like this before. Victorian London music halls had their own unique atmosphere, but this had been something else.

Mick Jones spoke first, "You saw punk tonight. That felt special."

Gene Vincent agreed, "You're right, Mick. That was fucking kickass fucking rock n'roll. It was fucking beautiful. I'm emotional." Gene Vincent had made a great recovery. The plague pit on Shepherd's Bush Green was no longer affecting him. He hugged Mick Jones.

"I was manhandled tonight. I might be a spirit, but I was seriously mistreated. This was the best evening of my life." WG was in shock.

Bess added her opinion, "I've never experienced anything like this before. I would have loved to have performed on a stage like this. That was electric."

Mick Jones laughed, "You're more punk than we are. You're a Victorian Siouxsie Sioux, Bess."

On July 25th QPR were playing Arsenal in a pre-season friendly. The Clash were the half time entertainment. The half time was extended to 30 mins and The Clash were allowed to play a 25 mins set. A crowd of 20000 were at the game. The game was a London derby and expectations were high. QPR had just had their best ever season. The ground was on South Africa Road 400 yards south of the Westway sitting close to the South Africa council estate and the BBC. White City, Shepherd's Bush and Shepherd's Bush market were the nearest tube station. This was classic Clash territory close to various squats that Strummer and Mick Jones had lived in. Half a mile west of the ground was Davis Road where Joe Strummer, in a squat, formed the 101ers.

They played in front of their biggest crowd ever. They wouldn't play to such a large crowd until they toured America in the '80s. The crowd were supportive of a local band, though punk was unknown to many of them. Pink Floyd, Genesis and Disco were more their style. The atmosphere was very different to the Goldhawk. This was more stadium rock, something they detested. The Cash were about connecting with the audience in small intimate venues, as if they were one. The crowd weren't meant to be dots on the horizon, all cold and impersonal. There was a sense of anti-climax after the high of that night at the Goldhawk. The Clash belted out some of the same tracks as they performed at the Goldhawk, albeit their performance was much shorter. They had broken into Loftus Road to practice. They knew the stewards and all the people that worked at the ground. Many had turned a blind eye to them practising at Loftus Road. Again, Gene Vincent was in the crowd. His work with The Clash was pulling him away from WG, Bess and Billy Idol. WG and Bess were in Leeds for the fourth Test. Billy Idol was practising with the Banshees and Siouxsie Sioux. At least they were on their own patch. They could see the Westway. The crowd just needed time.

WG, Gene Vincent, Bess and Billy Idol were meeting once a week now at the George and Dragon in Bromley. They had gone their separate ways out of necessity. Gene Vincent was rock n'roll. WG was cricket. Inevitably, they would spend

233

more time on their interests. Gene Vincent and Linda had become friends. However, she had her entourage of lesbians to look after. Malcolm McLaren had them booked for 'screen on the green' in Islington for the end of August.

Chapter 11

The Oval, 5th test match
August 1976

*"When you play test cricket, you don't give the Englishmen
an inch. Play it tough, all the way. Grind them into the dust."*
– Donald Bradman

After winning the test series at Headingley on July 27th, the
West Indies were back on the road the next day, playing Essex
at Chelmsford. The West Indies batted first and were dismissed
for 190. Possibly they were feeling the effects of the previous
day's celebrations from winning the test series. It's not
unknown for cricketers to celebrate these events for days.
They wouldn't have been the first and warm days fielding and
bowling certainly build up a thirst. They were coming to the
right place to continue their celebrations. Essex played hard
but knew how to enjoy themselves. They had a team of
characters. They were a team in transition from fun loving
underachievers to serial winners. Thankfully, in their glory
years to come, they still kept the fun side. The likes of Ray
East, Graham Gooch, JK Lever, Brian Hardie, Stuart Turner
and the 'gnome' Keith Fletcher were heroes of the county
cricket circuit on and off the pitch.

The West Indies batted first with Gordon Greenidge scoring 71 and Lawrence Rowe contributing 47. Very little came from the other batsmen as they were dismissed for 190. Part time bowler and future England cricketing legend Graham Gooch turned his arm over and took 5–40. Gooch could often swing the ball and there was also some assistance in the Chelmsford pitch this morning. In the Essex innings the South African Kenny McEwan scored a sumptuous 76. Graham Gooch contributed a decent 43. The Essex tail wagged and Ray East scored 49 undefeated with 31 not out from JK Lever. Essex declared at 294/8 with a lead of 104. In the West Indies second innings Gomes scored 74 with useful contributions from Findlay and Fredericks to reach 306. Essex had to score 203 to win the game. Essex had one of their all too familiar collapses and were dismissed for 97 giving the West Indies victory by 106 runs. Wayne Daniels destroyed the top order. Clive Lloyd with his part time medium pacers and off spinner Albert Padmore finished the job. Only Captain Keith Fletcher and all-rounder Stuart Turner offered any resistance. For Essex it was another one of those matches where almost certain success is then snatched away at the last moment. There was such love and pain supporting Essex.

Bajan Keith Boyce was not playing for Essex in this match. Keith Boyce played 21 times for the West Indies, touring England in 1973 and 1975, taking 19 wickets at an average of 15 in the three Tests of 1973. In the Prudential World Cup Final of 1975 Boyce's versatility gave the West Indies the decisive edge over Australia. He played for Essex from 1966 to 1977. Arguably he was one of county cricket's finest overseas players. Boyce scored almost 9,000 runs and took 852 wickets at an average of 25. He was made for one day cricket with his athleticism, fast bowling and powerful hitting. Add his one-day career and his 215 first-class catches, his loss to Essex and cricket, after 12 summers in England, through injury at the age of 34, was enormous. He had given his fellow Essex cricketers a front row view of what they could be and what was needed to succeed. His zest for life also suited Essex and their approach to cricket.

Once told to block out for a draw, Boyce responded by hitting an enormous six before being stumped yards out. His response to his captain's rollicking was: "I thought it would waste more time if I kept hitting it over the pavilion."

When all did go right for Boyce it was the opposition who suffered. He once went in to bat at 12.30 and scored a century (125) before lunch at 1.30. He was the first to 1,000 runs and 100 wickets in the Sunday League.

Sadly, his return to Barbados was far from happy. Domestic difficulties including the loss of his house in a storm and the break-up of his marriage broke his spirit. He lost his life at the all too young age of 53 and was buried in an unmarked grave. He will be remembered with pride and affection in Essex, for he was one of the names who helped move that county from the backyard to the front room of county cricket. Some years later, a few Essex cricket members on holiday in Barbados found his unmarked grave and paid for a headstone.

After the Essex game, the West Indies went to Lords for the third time this summer to play Middlesex. WG was there and watched the entire game. Viv Richards was playing. After each day's play, they would meet up for a chat. There was more than cricket to talk about now. The pressures of test cricket were forgotten for awhile.

Viv was keen to catch up with news on Gene Vincent, "What's Gene been up to?"

"He's been very quiet. He's mentoring Mick Jones at the moment. The Clash are playing a serious gig in Islington at the end of August with the Pistols and the Buzzcocks."

"How did their first night at Sheffield go in early July? I forgot to ask you at Headingley."

WG looked reflective, "It was awful. But they made amends the other night at the Goldhawk. They did a small performance on their home patch and they rocked. They fucking rocked."

"They were that good?"

"They were 100% rock n'roll. They were 200% punk."

"That's good. I'm pleased for Gene and The Clash boys."

"I thought the Goldhawk was going to catch fire. They were fucking hot. The crowd were mental. I've never seen anything like it before. The place was shaking. Nobody will ever forget that night. It was the most exciting night of my life."

"Crikey, I wish I was there."

"At least they've made a start and it can only get better. Mick and Joe Strummer are writing some new material."

"What are they writing about?" Viv was intrigued at to what punk meant.

"London, I think. And how crap things are. They've a lot of anger to channel."

"Are things that bad here?"

"I guess they are. There's a lot of suppressed anger on the streets. London feels it's about to explode with all this heat as well," WG spoke like a social commentator and expert on these matters.

"How do you know?" Viv's tone was more inquiring than critical.

"Gene Vincent and I have spent most of the summer walking the streets of London looking for The Clash. We've felt it growing."

"Do you think it's going to explode soon?" Viv was concerned.

"Definitely, Viv."

"What can be done?"

"It requires a voice for those who are angry. That's what The Clash are trying to do with all the other punks."

"Do you think it's down to colour and race?" inquired Viv.

"In different ways, it is. White youth are using punk rock to rage against no hope and despair. The black community has had enough of being treated like scum and criminals. Black people need a voice."

"People don't respect us."

"Exactly. They need people like you Viv. Success changes people's perceptions. It shouldn't have to but it does." WG thought some more and added, "You're someone now who people admire. They'll listen to you now. That's just the way it is."

WG's last comment gave Viv Richards much to think about.

On July 31st, the West Indies batted first and were dismissed for only 222 in less than 50 overs. Gordon Greenidge brutalised the Middlesex attack for 123 with his customary powerful square cuts and savage drives. They played like millionaires, but on this day, the roulette table wasn't turning in their favour, Greenidge apart. Mike Selvey dismissed Viv Richards for 4 in identical fashion to his first innings dismissal at Old Trafford. With Gordon Greenidge scoring over 50% of the team's runs it was almost a carbon copy of that first day at Old Trafford. The batsmen seemed disengaged and frivolous. Clive Lloyd was furious. Wily England veteran spinner Fred Titmus, aged 43, took 5–41 and ran through the West Indies batting. Mike Selvey took 4–58, getting a decent amount of swing.

The fact that Fred Titmus could bowl was a miracle. He suffered a horrific boating accident in the Caribbean in 1967–68, when he caught his foot in the propeller and lost four toes. He was back in action for Middlesex by May 1968 and finished the season with 111 wickets, and also topped his county's batting averages. The man was tough, loyal and durable. The label 'county stalwart' fitted him perfectly.

Fred Titmus played in 53 Tests between 1955 and 1975, claiming 153 wickets at 32.22, including a best of 7 for 79 against Australia at Sydney in 1962–63. Fred was a decent bat also and had a highest test score of 84 not out. In his first class career he took a staggering 2,830 wickets. His legend wouldn't end there. Fred was the basis for what has been described as "The funniest song ever written about an England and Middlesex cricketer." The band was Half man Half biscuit who wrote some of their greatest songs a decade after 1976. The song, *Fucking 'ell, It's Fred Titmus!* was memorable.

Half Man Half biscuit also made reference to Vanburn Holder in one of their songs with the line "Where Vanburn Holder joins a local grindcore outfit." To my knowledge, they've made no other references to cricket. Another sporting iconic song from Half Man Half Biscuit must be mentioned; 'All I want for Christmas is a Dukla-Prague away kit' was pure punk. Music broadcaster Andy Kershaw described Half Man Half Biscuit as 'England's greatest folk band' and 'the most authentic British folk band since The Clash'. Folk and British punk were comfortable bedfellows.

When Middlesex batted, MJ Smith scored 95, Mike Brearley 39 and young off spinner Phil Edmonds smashed a belligerent 53. Middlesex were all out for 257, a lead of 35. The West Indies had bowled their spinners Padmore and Jumadeen for most of the Middlesex innings. Padmore took 6–69, but Jumadeen went wicketless. Andy Roberts bowled a gentle 13 overs after his efforts at Headingley. For him, it was no more than a warm down 'net'. The West Indies had scaled down their gears of intensity

The West Indies gave a more determined showing in the second innings. Greenidge scored well again with 67. Viv Richards came to the crease and struck a measured 53 before he was bowled again. This time, the bowler was Fred Titmus. He looked as nonchalant as a man can possibly look. Viv Richards could have been driving an open top Ferrari on the French Riviera in an Armani suit with Miss World next to him. The whole team looked as if they were in first gear and tired. The tour had been tough with very few days off. Three months of coach journeys and hotels were beginning to take their toll. With one test match at the Oval to go and three one dayers the team needed to recharge. The itinerary would be unheard of in today's game. The West Indies got to 308 thanks to some late hitting from Andy Roberts who reached a rare 50. Middlesex needed 274 for victory. An opening partnership between Mike Brearley and MJ Smith set them up well. MJ Smith scored 108.

Mike Brearley contributed a patient 62. Roland Butcher came in first wicket down and scored 45. A cousin of Basil, a famous West Indian test batsman, Roland Butcher had come to the United Kingdom at the age of thirteen from his native Barbados. He was an aggressive middle-order batsman, who represented Middlesex between 1974 and 1990. His intuitive batting style was more West Indian than English. He became the first black player to represent England, making his Test debut at Bridgetown in 1980–81.

The spinners Jumadeen and Padmore were bowling the bulk of the overs again. Again, Andy Roberts was contributing gently with some very unlike 'Andy Roberts' bowling with the aim of just ticking over. The juices weren't flowing. They weren't machines. The aim was to peak for the Oval and the fifth test match. The team needed a dip first.

Middlesex won by 4 wickets. Padmore took 4–78 for 10 in the match. Jumadeen went wicketless again. He had been bowling at the wrong end! The game was over and the West Indies were on the coach heading to the Devon Riviera to play the Minor Counties. Nowadays, touring teams would never play such a game. The gulf in talent and class was too much. The trip was a holiday with some very gentle cricket in-between. If the Middlesex game had been gentle, this would be taking gentleness to a new level. This was carnival cricket on the beautiful Devon Riviera. Mind, body and spirit were rejuvenated in the bracing sea air. The Minor Counties scored 123 and 329. In the second innings, once again, the spinners Jumadeen and Padmore bowled most of the overs. The ever reliable workhorse Vanburn Holder took 7 wickets in the match. The man was as reliable as a Volkswagen beetle. The West Indies scored 354 and 100/3 winning by 7 wickets. Viv

Richards scored 98 in the first innings whilst Clive Lloyd got himself into some form with an undefeated 145. The Minor Counties had put up a very decent performance. Their bowlers would be able to tell their children and grandchildren that they had bowled at Viv Richards. This was like George Best playing non-league football.

The match against Glamorgan was the last game before the fifth test at the Oval. Clive Lloyd had words with the team before the game. His message was clear. The team had won the test series but they wanted a 3–0 series victory with a resounding win at the Oval. The Oval would have more West Indian supporters than any other test ground. It was important to win in front of so many West Indians. They had a responsibility. It was time to refocus after some relaxed performances since Headingly. Brixton was next door to the Oval and they would make it feel like a home Test match. It was time to 'switch back on'.

Sadly, for Glamorgan, the West Indies were refocused. Poor Glamorgan were 'brutalised'. There is no other word for it. The West Indies started off slowly with Glamorgan batting first. Michael Holding was loose and expensive. Albert Padmore was putting in another decent performance and holding up an end. With Andy Roberts and Vanburn Holder rested, all looked relatively calm. A number of scores in the 20s and 30s plus a dashing 64 from Malcolm Nash saw them score 266. This was a small revenge for Malcolm Nash. Swansea was the same ground where 8 years earlier the great West Indian Sir Garfield Sobers had hit Malcolm Nash for six 6s in an over. Then the West Indies batted. Roy Fredericks, playing for his home county went for 2. Maybe he felt sorry for his Glamorgan. The rest of the innings was painful for

Glamorgan Viv Richards and Gordon Greendidge put on 224 for the second wicket at 5 an over. Gordon Greenidge went for 130 and Viv Richards soon after for 121. This was simply the starters for the main course and a sumptuous banquet of batting. In walked Clive Lloyd who'd had a quiet summer up to this point. In the next 2 hours he scored 201 not out, the fastest ever double century. Lawrence Rowe scored just 88 in this time. They put on 287 for the fourth wicket. Barry Lloyd went for 162 off 23 overs. Allin went for 128 off 19.3 overs. Malcolm Nash bowled just 12 overs but went for 77. He must have hated bowling at West Indians in Swansea. Bajan Tony Cordle was the 'pick' of the bowlers going taking 1–83 off 16 overs. Over twenty 6's were hit in the innings. West Indies declared on 554/4 off just 83 overs. In Glamorgan's second innings, Michael Holding and Bernard Julien did the damage. They reached 73–1, but once they lost their captain Alan Jones, all the fight went out of them. Pakastani test batsmen Majid Khan played some delightful hook shots off Wayne Daniels and he looked in good touch, oozing time and style. Sadly, for the crowd, he was bowled middle stump by a Michael Holding thunderbolt for an all too short 21. Six dismissals in the innings were clean bowled. They had bowled fast, skillfully and straight. The Oval was coming.

The Oval looked like a beach. The summer was officially in drought.

Dennis Howells, Minister for Sport and a Birmingham Labour MP, was appointed Minister for Drought. There was widespread water rationing and public standpipes in some affected areas. Reservoirs were at an extremely low level, as were some rivers. The cricket was about to get even hotter.

WG had met up with Viv Richards the night before the 5th Test at the team hotel. They were refocusing back on cricket after their wider chats at Lords during the Middlesex game.

"You've got to control your emotions tomorrow, Viv. The Oval will be like a home test match."

"I know. I know. Trust me."

"If you go out there and play like a headless chicken, I'll be waiting for you. This is your chance to cap a great summer. Don't fuck it up," WG was back to his best. The Master pupil dynamic that had been disturbed at Headingley was back to normal. WG never swore unless it was talking about a Clash gig.

Viv was taken aback, "I'll play sensibly."

WG was on a mission, "The wicket is gorgeous for batting. I had a good look at it today. I overhead the Groundsman say it was 500+run wicket. The outfield is like lightning."

"I'll make it look like an 800+ wicket when I get going."

"You need to calm down. It's my fault as I'm putting too much pressure on you," WG realized he was cranking up the expectation levels on Viv.

"I know you want me to do well. Both of us need to calm down. You're more into this than me."

WG was contrite, "I apologise. Just keep it in on the ground. The Oval is a big ground so don't try hit sixes. I don't want you trying to hit the gasometer. I know a man who lives next door.

Viv looked at WG strangely, "Okay. I guess you do."

"Try and avoid the catshit. Ian Dury lives there."

"Have you lost it WG?"

"Ian Dury! You stopped him beating up his mate back in June on the Kilburn high road. They were musicians. Ian lives in a squat called Catshit Mansions next to the gasometer."

"Strange name for a home. Yes, of course. I do remember."

"That helped Gene find his confidence when he found Ian Dury."

"I'm responsible then? I didn't know he lived here." Viv was laughing.

"I think you are Viv. Gene would never have gone on to find the Clash but for that day over there with Ian Dury. 1976 has been your year Viv."

"Its not over yet WG. I'll salute Ian Dury tomorrow when I score a hundred."

Viv Richards had higher concerns though. He was making himself a legend and a hero to his people.

Both felt there was something special in the air. The Oval had been where WG had first seen Viv play and the place was special for that reason for both of them. The Oval would be where the West Indies would have the crowd on their side. The other test match in London at Lord's had a very unique, slightly class conscious, cosmopolitan feel. Lord's was special with its MCC members, Long Room and dress code. The Oval was special as well but for different reasons. In amongst the council flats of South London and with the unique catshit mansions squat next door it was never going to be Lord's. There was a slight earthiness to the Oval. The Oval to Lord's was like comparing light and shade. He'd always have a special connection to the Oval. WG loved both grounds though he didn't have any gates named after him here. However, there was a plaque to commemorate his 152 against Australia in 1880. This was the first ever test century scored by an Englishman against Australia. WG had two of his brothers playing in that Oval test of 1880. Sadly, FR Grace lost his life two weeks later from pneumonia. In 1878 WG Grace had a serious latercation with some Australian players outside the gates at the Oval. He had 'history' with the Oval.

Ian Dury was sitting in his squat writing new material. WG had tried to persuade him to come to the cricket the previous day but he wasn't interested. He had recovered from the Kilburn's last gig nearly two months ago at Walthamstow after spending time with friends in Brighton. Gene Vincent was his inspiration now. Who said "never meet your heroes?"

The Oval test started on August 12th. The West Indies batted first, and very soon, Greenidge was LBW for 0 to Bob Willis. Viv Richards strode to the wicket. He was motivated, but his emotions were under control. The West Indians in the crowd cheered him to the wicket. He could see several Antiguan flags. This and the passionate West Indian support made him feel 10 feet tall. The England bowlers were going to suffer. And suffer they did. Roy Fredericks and Viv Richards put on 154 for the second wicket. The off spinner Geoff Miller, making his debut, snared Fredericks for 71.

Viv Richards was playing sensibly, but still scoring at a decent strike rate. His batting was world class, keeping the ball on the ground, but driving anything overpitched and pulling short deliveries. His defence was compact and correct. He was getting to the pitch of the ball and hitting straight. There was no silly playing across the line. WG approved as he watched on from the Pavilion. He hadn't seen Viv play better.

The West Indian supporters were joyous. Every boundary was celebrated as if the Notting Hill Carnival had started early. England's bowlers were resigning themselves to another day of slaughter under the sun. Tony Grieg look harassed. The West Indians were shouting 'who's groveling now Tony Greg'. He was getting both barrels. Lawrence Rowe was playing sublimely. He caressed the ball as if he was having a 'net'. The sound of the ball on their bats was different. With Viv Richards it was like a pistol shot when he pulled a short ball to the boundary. A gentle whisper was the sound of a Lawrence Rowe drive to the fence. Both were a joy to behold but in different ways. Something special was happening that you didn't want to end. This was like Headingley all over again, but just a little calmer and more sublime. It was as if Pele and Di Stefano were playing in the same team. This was the sport of the Gods and an afternoon to remember forever. WG thought he had died and gone to heaven. Then with half an hour to go, and almost perfect dismissal occurred. If Lawrence Rowe had to be dismissed then this was as close to perfection. He was stumped Alan Knott bowled Underwood. The dismissal was made in Kent. Underwood had flighted a ball outside off and Lawrence Rowe had gone down the wicket only to be beaten in the flight and by some decent spin. Alan Knott had completed the dismissal with the quickness and efficiency of an eagle going in for their prey. A stumping was rare in test cricket, but was worth waiting for. Also, Alan Knott had beaten Godfrey Evan's test record of dismissals for a wicketkeeper with this classical stumping. He now had 220 dismissals. Alan Knott is the best wicketkeeper I've ever seen. He's England best test cricketer in my view of the last 50 years. Kent churned out 'wickies' out on a production line with

Alan Knott following Godfrey Evans and Les Ames as England greats. A stumping was something special for a wicketkeeper, and to break a world record, in such a way, bought smiles to every Englishman on a day where they had been made to suffer. I salute you Alan Knott. Every England player applauded and congratulated him warmly. He truly deserved those accolades. At close of play the West Indies were 373–3. Viv Richards was 200 not out having completed his double century in the last over of the day. People were already talking of him beating Sir Garfield's record test score of 365 the following day. His reception as he left the field of play was one of pure delight. Every West Indian now felt 10 feet tall. They could look anyone in the eye and say 'Am I not your equal? Look who we are'. It had been a very special day.

Something significant had happened with an hour to go on the first day. Tony Greig looked at the West Indian crowd, who were still baying him, and got down on his knees. "We're groveling now," was his call. The West Indians roared in delight. Then some clapped. Tony Greg's comments may have been forgiven by some if not forgotten. A 'sort of peace' and apology had been made. Tony Greg was not everyone's 'cup of tea', but he was no racist. The West Indies fans left the Oval that night in a state of delirium. They wanted to bottle that moment and feeling forever.

Viv sat in the changing rooms at the Oval and took in the day. West Indians were desperate to talk with him and his supporters waited outside the pavilion for a glimpse. When he did appear the reception was spine tingling. WG was overcome with emotion as he waited with the West Indies fans. He wasn't going to get a chance to speak with him tonight. Viv made his way out of the Oval just before 8pm.

Viv thought of Sobers' test record that night but not for too long. He managed to get out seeing some distant family members in Brixton. They had a party and Viv didn't make it back until 1am. Everybody wanted part of Viv Richards.

The next morning, Viv was set to start again as if he was on 0. That's what the experts told you to do. England had set defensive fields so the scoring rate slowed a little. They were in damage limitation mode. Clive Lloyd had got himself back into form with his double hundred at Swansea. He was happy to play a supporting role. Again, the atmosphere seemed quite calm and predictable. A wicket would be a shock. Then just after lunch Viv Richards was out, bowled by Tony Greig. There was this overwhelming feeling of anti-climax, disappointment and disbelief. The crowd went quiet for 10 seconds digesting the impossible. Even England fans couldn't celebrate and felt a weird sadness. Then the applause kicked in for a batsman with 291 against his name with a style and panache unmatched. Everyone at the Oval had witnessed something very special. The crowd's feelings were all over the place. He was just 74 runs away from Sober's record and 9 away from a triple century. The feeling of deflation was tangible. However, the emotions of the crowd were tinged with excitement over witnessing something that would be talked about for the next 100 years. But it was still much worse than the end of the best Christmas ever. Even Greig celebrated his wicket quietly. The villain of the series seemed on a strange valium induced auto pilot. The showman had come back down to earth. Tony Greig struck again to dismiss Clive Lloyd for 84. Collis King scored 63 but the scoring rate was quite sedate. England were bowling to no slips. They were beaten. The white flag was flying. Michael Holding came in to increase the scoring rate and scored 32 off 15 balls. The West Indies declared on 687/8 so to have nearly an hour bowling at England before close of play. England reached 34–0 when the Umpires called time. In the West Indies innings, Willis and Selvey had only bowled 15 overs apiece. Underwood bowled over 60 overs. Tony Greig returned 2–96 off 34 overs. Even Chris Balderstone, a part time county trundler at best, bowled more than Willis and Selvey. Greig's reputation as an aggressive, attacking and dynamic high risk captain was damaged. They might as well have played with only 2 main line bowlers.

Later that evening, Viv Richards explained to WG, "I should have got Gary's record but the England's bowlers were too slow and they put 6 guys on the boundary. Grieg didn't bowl Selvey or Willis."

WG gave his summary, "The pitch looked slow as well. It looked dead. "

"It was tougher than it looked out there. They've taken any pace out of the pitch to stop Mikey Holding and Andy Roberts."

WG was philosophical, "You'd probably do the same if you were English. You've battered them. They're all shell shocked."

"That's cricket. If you can't take the heat then get out of the kitchen. I want to squeeze every bit of cricketing life out of them." Viv Richards looked steely eyed. He was like 'Spartacus' talking about a victim at the Coliseum in ancient Rome. No quarter was given.

WG changed tract to a slightly softer tone, "I thought Greig and his captaincy has been struggling so far. The 'Grovel' comment has got to him."

"Do you think so?"

"He saw you and Lawrence Rowe scoring easily. He just cracked. Its been a long summer for him."

"Tony Greig has only got himself to blame. He made his bed. Look who is groveling now." Viv Richards fixed WG with a glare that made him nervous, "No mercy."

The next day, Dennis Amiss, playing his first match of the series, held England together with a score of 203. It was his second double century against the West Indies. In the 1973–74 series, he scored 262 not out in Kingston, Jamaica to save a test match. He had adopted a very front on style covering his off stump to combat the pace of Holding and Roberts. Nobody else could cope with the pace of Michael Holding other than Alan Knott and David Steele who scored 50 and 44 respectively. Michael Holding took 8–92 with arguably the fastest and finest fast bowling ever seen. Six of his dismissals were bowled. The other two were LBW. There was no pace in the wickets so edges weren't carrying to the slips and wicketkeeper. English batsmen didn't hook so Michael Holding bowled fast, straight and full of length. His pace through the air was too much though England did score 435. Andy Roberts took 0–102 and Holder 1–75. Wayne Daniels bowled just 10 overs for no reward. Roberts, Holder and Daniels looked tired and ineffective on a slow pitch which underlines just how brilliant a performance was Holding's 8–92. Later on the Jamaican DJ, I-Roy, would make a record called 'a tribute to Michael Holding' that referenced his 8–92 performance at the Oval. This was special. This was sporting 'magnificence'.

WG thought it was the best fast bowling performance he'd ever seen. The West Indian fans were just as ecstatic with

Holding's performance as with the batting of Viv Richards. When Holding bowled Tony Greig for 12 on Saturday night the crowd exploded. The noise around South London seemed to shake every nearby building. People outside the ground stood still as if a maelstrom of redemption was whipping through the streets of Kennington. Every West Indian in London seemed to let out a cry of celebration and liberation. The atmosphere was spine tingling. The sights of Greig's stumps flying towards the wicketkeeper Deryck Murray was one of the photos of the series. Michael Holding was classical and smooth in his run up and delivery stride. He could have been very possibly an International class 400m runner. He'd made his debut in Australia the previous winter with little success. However the pace and potential was there and he was recorded as bowling faster than Thomson, Lillee and Roberts. He struggled with inexperience. At one stage he had broken down with the stress of competing against battle hardened Australians like Ian Chappell, when an umpiring decision went against him. Now all the moving parts were coming together. His nickname would be 'whispering death' as umpires could not hear his approach to the stumps, and the end result was usually batsman annihilation.

The West Indies decided not to enforce the follow on as they'd been out in the field for 130 overs and their bowlers needed a rest. England's spirit in the field had deserted them completely. In 32 overs the West Indies scored 182 without loss and then declared. Fredericks was undefeated on 86 and Greenidge was not out 85. England bowled from the start with men on the boundary and the bowlers looked uninspired. England and Tony Greig were on their knees. Defeat and the end couldn't come soon enough. You wanted England to be put out of their misery. This was painful to watch.

England required 435 runs for victory and they weren't too many people putting money on an England victory. The openers Amiss and Woolmer looked determined. They got to 49 before Holding dismissed Amiss. David Steele showed his usual customary grit and fight making 42 in over 3 hours. Sadly, this would be his last test innings. He wasn't selected for the winter tour to India where spin was on the agenda, and pace bowling was an alien concept. In his 8 test match career he faced Thomson, Lillee, Holding, Roberts and Daniels. He had faced constant 'chin music' and now he was discarded and sent back to county cricket. The daily treadmill of motorway journeys, cheap hotels and cricket tea and lunches awaited him in all its glory. His moment in the limelight was over. At least, he had enough lamb chops and steaks to keep him going for a few years. The rest of the innings was predictable. The pace, accuracy and skill of Michael Holding wore England down again. He took 6–57 for 14–149 in the match. Three of his victims were bowled. Alan Knott defied Holding for awhile with a patient 57. Chris Balderstone, in his second test match, bagged a pair. Holding had bowled him both times. He never played another test match. The West Indies had won by 231 runs and their fans ran onto the pitch to celebrate. The Oval belonged to them.

In the end, superior skill, talent and ability had won through.

West Indian intellectual, CLR James said decades earlier. "Here, on the cricket field if nowhere else, all men in the island are equal, and we are the best men in the island." He must have foreseen the Oval in August 1976.

One more quote from CLR James would further summarise what had happened. "It seemed like a classic ploy by the conquerors: games, particularly so restrained and ritualistic a game as cricket, could be imposed upon the colonies to tame them, to herd them into the psychic boundaries where they would learn the values and ethics of the colonist. But once given the opportunity to play the master's game, to excel at it, the colonials gained a self-esteem that would eventually free them."

The Antiguan singer, 'King Short Shirt' wrote a song *Vivian Richards* to celebrate Viv Richard's great series of 1976. In the song, he heralds Viv Richards. In his words, "The cricketer's attributes are the stuff of ecstasy, with breathtaking late cuts, plundering drives, a classical and noble defence, and cunning manipulation of opposing fieldsmen drawing, in evocative phrase, 'people applauding for runs like bread'."

King Short Shirt explains that, "Richards is terrified by no bowler." He mentions Thomson, Lillee, Bedi and Chandrasekhar.

The West Indies had no rest and the next day were playing Worcestershire. They had 3 one day internationals to prepare for. A tour of England in the 1970s meant a tour of all the counties and the test matches. Truly it was a tour of England. The wear and tear on all the players, especially the fast bowlers, was a danger. In many of the later tour games against the counties, Clive Lloyd would bowl the spinners and bowl the faster bowlers very lightly so they would be at their best for the test matches. This match was no different. Worcestershire rattled up 358/8 declared with Phil Neale scoring 143. Holding bowled just 5 overs taking 2–16. Padmore bowled 36 overs for 2–121. Roy Fredericks took 3 wickets! In reply the West Indies scored 408 with Collis King scoring 109. In Worcestershire second innings they collapsed to 86 all out with Roy Fredericks taking 3–10 and Larry Gomes 2–5. The West Indies won easily by 8 wickets. You felt the West Indies couldn't lose. Worcestershire with its beautiful ground next to Worcester Cathedral was very different to the Oval and a pleasant contrast. The match was a much needed comedown from the intensity and emotions of the Oval in front of their own fans. Middle England rolled to its own genteel vibe. Vanburn Holder was able to hook up with his county teammates. Worcester had been a delight.

The day after Worcester, the West Indies were playing Gloucestershire in Bristol. The home team had their overseas stars in the team in sharp contrast to present day touring matches. Sadiq Mohammed and Zaheer Abbas were established Pakistan test players. Mike Proctor was a South African test player, who for the evils of apartheid, would have become a great of the game. The West Indies batted first scoring 349/8 declared with Collis King scoring 108. All-rounder Bernard Julien helped himself to 89. Gloucestershire replied with 265. England rugby international Alistair Hignell scored 119 with Padmore and Jumadeen doing the bulk of the bowling again. Outside of the test matches both of them had bowled a healthy number of overs. The tourists went for quick runs in the second innings with Gomes leading the way scoring 111. The home team were set 327 to win the game. In the end, it was a very exciting chase with Gloucestershire finishing on 282/9 and the match drawn. Mike Proctor scored 97 and until he was out a home victory was very possible. Again, Jumadeen and Padmore were the unsung heroes of the West Indies team, sharing 7 wickets.

The one day internationals were due to start, a format new to WG. The international one day game was just over 5 years old, but the 1st World cup had been held the previous year, with the West Indies the worthy holders. If ever there was a team born to play the fast pace, fast scoring, dynamic game of one day cricket it was the West Indies team of 1976. The forthcoming contest against England would be like pitting a Ferrari against a Ford Fiesta in a race for speed. It almost felt unfair. A team with the mind-sets of bank clerks against a team overloaded with Caribbean flair and exuberance just wasn't cricket!

Chapter 12

<u>Anger rising</u>

"What history had I inherited that left me an alien in my place of birth?" – Reni Eddo-Lodge

The background to the Notting Hill riots of 1976 was complex and multi-dimensional. A significant event occurred nearly 6 years earlier on 31st October 1970. A demonstration had taken place in Notting Hill organised by the Black Defence Committee.

Matters came to a head when Frank Crichlow and seven others, including the late writer and broadcaster Darcus Howe, were arrested and charged with a variety of offences including affray while protesting against police harassment. The trial exposed racism in the Metropolitan police 30 years before the Macpherson inquiry. All nine were acquitted of the key charges against them.

Darcus Howe, who was working at the Mangrove, urged Critchlow to look to the community for support. Together, Howe, Critchlow and the local Panthers organised a March. On 9 August 1970, 150 protesters took the streets, flanked by more than 700 police. Police intervention resulted in violence and Critchlow, Howe and seven others were charged with inciting riot.

The march sent shockwaves through the British polity. Special Branch was called in, and files at the National Archives show that the Home Office considered trying to deport Critchlow. Meanwhile, the Mangrove Nine made legal history in demanding an all-black jury, taking control of the case and emphasising the political nature of police harassment. Police witnesses described Critchlow's restaurant in lurid terms, as a hive of "criminals, ponces and prostitutes," Critchlow fought back with numerous character witnesses who defended his reputation as a respected community leader.

After 55 days at the Old Bailey, Critchlow and his fellow defendants were acquitted. What is more, 28 years before the Macpherson Report, the judge publicly acknowledged that there was 'evidence of racial hatred' within the Met. Horrified, the Assistant Commissioner wrote to the Director of Public Prosecutions seeking a retraction of the judge's statement. The Home Secretary, Reginald Maudling, arranged a meeting between the judge and senior civil servants, but the statement was never withdrawn.

The case did not end institutional racism, but as Critchlow put it, "It was a turning point for black people. It put on trial the attitudes of the police, the Home Office, of everyone towards the black community. We took a stand and I am proud of what we achieved – we forced them to sit down and rethink harassment. It was decided there must be more law centres and more places to help people with their problems."

Notting Hill and Brixton were the two main areas where Windrush migrants settled. The majority who arrived in

Notting Hill came from Trinidad, and at the very heart of this community was the Mangrove restaurant, at 8 All Saints Road.

The Mangrove restaurant was established in 1968 by the same Frank Crichlow who hailed from Trinidad. Crichlow set up the Mangrove Community Association to provide practical help for the community, from accommodation for older people to support for women coming out of prison.

The Mangrove, which served the cuisine Critchlow had learned from his mother, soon became the beating heart of Notting Hill's West Indian community. The restaurant was a meeting place for black radicals who wanted to discuss the revolution in the Caribbean, or the fortunes of the American Black Power movement, as well as bohemian 'whitebeats' looking for an alternative to square English culture. The community aspect of the Mangrove was evident in the pages of The Hustler, a small community newspaper edited by Courtney Tulloch which was produced on the premises

But the thriving restaurant soon came under attack. 'The heavy mob', a group of officers who, according to The Hustler, policed Notting Hill like a colonial army and raided the Mangrove 12 times between January 1969 and July 1970. They claimed that the Mangrove was a drugs den, in spite of the fact that their repeated raids never yielded a shred of evidence. The police pursued Critchlow on a host of petty licensing charges, including permitting dancing and allowing his friends to eat sweetcorn and drink tea after 11pm. Critchlow stood resolutely against this persecution. "Unless you're an Uncle Tom," he protested in an interview with The Guardian in 1970. "You've got no chance."

Police harassment of Crichlow continued, however. In 1979, he was charged with drugs offences but was again cleared. In 1988, Mangrove was raided again by police and Crichlow's bail conditions prevented him from going near the restaurant for a year.

Police persecution of the Mangrove never wholly ceased. In 1989, Critchlow was in court once again, this time accused of drug-dealing, and again, church leaders, magistrates, community leaders, black and white, all spoke out in his defence. Again, he was acquitted of all charges.

The final victory was Critchlow's; in 1992, he sued the Met for false imprisonment, battery and malicious prosecution. The police refused to admit fabricating evidence but paid him a record £50,000.

Speaking at the time, he said that the money would help, 'in a small way, but it is no compensation for what they did'. "Everybody knows that I do not have anything to do with drugs. I don't even smoke cigarettes. I cannot explain the disgust, the ugliness, not just for me but for all my family that this whole incident has caused."

Looking back, Lord Gifford commented, "Frank was determined to build a business in and for the North Kensington Community. He persevered in the face of adversity and harassment. His restaurant was a place where all people of good will were welcome. He was a hard-working pioneer who was not recognised as he should have been." For his friend Darcus Howe, Frank Critchlow was simply, "A Caribbean man who did ordinary things in extraordinary ways."

Frank Crichlow died in 2010, aged 78, but his legacy endured. In 2018 community activists, generations of Windrush residents, lawyers and musicians gathered to mark the 50th anniversary of the restaurant's opening.

As well as providing an opportunity for celebration, the anniversary resurfaced some darker memories. Clive Mashup Phillip, was a regular at Mangrove in its heyday and endured many struggles with the police himself. "When I came to this country from Trinidad in 1961 I knew nothing about racism and I didn't expect to find this kind of situation."

Phillip went on to add, "Back home, we showed people so much respect, especially white people. We came here to the mother country and found ourselves not wanted, abused and laughed at."

Phillip said that until 20 years ago he was regularly harassed by police, "We stood up and fought racism as a group. I felt safe being around Mangrove, it was like family. I was often charged with obstructing police officers. When I saw someone being abused by police in the street I would help to defend him and they did the same for me when I was in that situation."

Phillip said he met many celebrities at Mangrove, including Bob Marley and Marvin Gaye. "I used to talk a lot with Marvin Gaye," he said.

Jeb Johnson, who describes himself as a Windrush baby, remembers Marley frequenting the restaurant. "He was a vegetarian and he used to eat rice with butter."

Johnson said a community hub like Mangrove was needed more than ever today. "We need something like this for our young people to give them an alternative to the life some of them have at present."

The community activist Lee Jasper, another Mangrove veteran, said: "The history of Mangrove embodied the spirit of British black civil rights resistance against racism and injustice. Our 50th anniversary reunion on All Saints Road is a celebration of one of Britain's foremost radical black political organisations. One day we will buy the entire street and turn All Saints Road into a world heritage site celebrating its unique black British history."

Crichlow previously ran the Rio Cafe in nearby Westbourne Park Road, a venue frequented by John Profumo and Christine Keeler. His new venture attracted artists, musicians and activists from around the world. Bob Marley, Marvin Gaye, Jimi Hendrix, Nina Simone, Diana Ross and the Supremes, and Vanessa Redgrave all flocked to the Mangrove to enjoy traditional Caribbean food, share ideas and discuss politics.

The growing racial tensions on the streets of London were not helped by the growth of the far right. John Tyndall became the National Front's chairman in 1972. Under Tyndall's leadership, it capitalised on growing concern about South Asian migration to Britain, rapidly increasing its membership and vote share in urban areas of East London and Northern England. Its public profile was raised through street marches and rallies, which often resulted in clashes with anti-fascist protesters, most notably the 1974 Red Lion Square disorders and the 1977 Battle of Lewisham

WG was a little uncertain as to how one day cricket would work. However, he was prepared to give the new format a chance. In truth, the last few weeks had been a little tame after the excitement of the fifth test match at the Oval. Gene Vincent was still mentoring Mick Jones every day. They met up once a week so as to keep in touch, but it wasn't the same. He didn't think he'd ever say it, but he was missing the excitement of trying to find the saviour of rock n'roll. He looked back with a certain amount of nostalgia at the days in

May, June and July of walking along the Regent's canal, the Westway, Camden and the Thames trying to find Joe Strummer and The Clash. Then there had been the conversations with Viv Richards and watching the test matches. The gigs they had seen… Bob Marley, Ian Dury, Patti Smith, the Pistols. Now, everything seemed sorted. There was a slight feeling of anti-climax. Though, a trip to Scarborough with Bess, seemed ideal. The sea air, the crashing waves and the excitement of the seaside was enticing. WG had never seen a one day, limited overs match so was full of anticipation for this new form of the game. Bess had done a long stint at Louise's so needed a break. The girl she was mentoring from Bromley called Kate was away with her family. Also, Viv Richards was missing WG and wanted to catch up. The Scarborough trip would be short as Bess and WG wanted to be back in London for the second one day international at Lord's, 'Screen on the Green' and the Notting Hill Carnival.

The first one day international took place at Scarborough on August 26th. England gave one day debuts to 5 players. Two of those players would go on to become greats of English cricket, namely Ian Botham and Graham Gooch. They helped transform England cricket from its grey, timid conservatism into something more dynamic, entertaining and vibrant. Graham Gooch had made his test debut a year earlier, being manhandled by Lillee and Thomson, and then sent back to county cricket. He hadn't been the first. Now this was his comeback into international cricket if not the test team. Ian Botham was making his international debut, the start of a great career that made him arguably the most entertaining and best all-rounder in the world of his generation. Botham and Gooch were coming together with the start of Punk. Hope was everywhere, if not always visible. This was Phoenix from the Ashes for music and cricket. The one day team was similar to the test team for the West Indies.

England were still licking their wounds after the heavy defeat in the test series. England batted first and score 202/8 of their 55 overs. Graham Barlow, on debut, made 60 not out. Graham Gooch scored 32 and Dennis Amiss 34. Holding and Roberts did the damage with 6 wickets between them. It was business as usual. As if to re-iterate the BAU concept, Viv Richards scored 119 not out of 133 deliveries. He was in the form of his life and treated his friend Ian Botham with complete disdain as the West Indies cantered to victory by 6 wickets with 14 overs to spare. This was men against boys stuff. You had the feeling the West Indies were toying with England and could move through the gears at will. There was nothing England could do. The West Indies were more skillful, more talented. In football terms they looked like a first division team playing a team 3 divisions below them. The West Indies were world champions at this format. The one day game was made for their collection of inspired, dynamic and attacking flair players. England's chief weapon of boring a team to defeat was even less effective in this format. The only upside for England was that the game only lasted a day. The pain was brief.

Viv Richards had met up with WG and Bess after the game. They were overlooking the sea.

"Did you enjoy your first one day game, WG? It's the game of the future. We're the world champions, winning at Lord's last summer."

"So I hear Viv. You played well again. I guess you take a few more risks in this form of the game. Your head was all over the pace today and you played across the line. It's not really proper cricket."

Bess gave her views, "Sorry, Viv, WG is a boring old fart. I really liked it today. The game wasn't so slow as normal. There was plenty of excitement. It was like cricket on speed."

Viv laughed at Bess's comment, "I'm glad you liked it Bess. This is the new game. I wanted to go out there today and give it a blast. I was playing some crazy shots out there."

"I suppose I can't argue too much with someone who has just scored a run a ball century." WG went over to WG and patted him on the back, "Don't think I'm going to ask you to go easy on England. You murder them. I thought it was good to see them blood a few youngsters."

"My best mate, Ian Botham, was making his debut today."

"You didn't go easy on him did you? Young Botham felt the heat of your blade."

"No chance. I wanted to hit him all over the place." Viv gave WG the 'look' again. For a moment, the Scarborough seaside became Ancient Rome and the Coliseum.

Bess got up to leave. "I'll see you at Lord's Viv. WG and I are going to enjoy the sea air for a while."

The second international was at Lord's 2 days later. WG and Bess were there in attendance. The West Indies bowled first and scored only 221 and were 7 overs short of using their allotted 55 overs. But for Viv Richard's 97 they would have been in serious trouble. England was hopeful of a rare victory. Tony Greig had dismissed Viv Richards and Derek Underwood had found some turn on a very dry Lord's pitch. Within an hour England were 62–6. Andy Roberts took the first four wickets and snuffed out any England hope. He was back to his best after a quiet Oval test match. Derek Randall, on debut, scored 88 with his quirks and strange mannerisms to take England fairly close. England were bowled out for 185 handing the West Indies victory by 36 runs. Derek Randall had given England a lift with his innings. He looked relatively comfortable against the pace of Holding and Roberts. Also, his magnificent fielding added much to England's athleticism in the field.

Bess loved the cosmopolitan atmosphere of Lord' There was the cachet of being with someone who had his name all over the place. The place had a unique atmosphere. Viv Richards met then in the Long Room after the day's play. There had been a rain delay and the game would go into a second day.

"Are you having a good time, Bess?" Viv was drinking in the atmosphere of cricket's most famous room. So were WG and Bess.

"Crikey, Viv, it ain't half posh for a girl from Hoxton. Luckily, WG was quite well connected in his day so I've been to Lord's before. I've never been to the Long Room though. They don't like ladies here."

WG explained, "She knew a few MCC chaps in her day as well."

"Don't tell him all my secrets, WG."

Viv laughed, "I don't know if the Long Room has heard too many conversations like this before."

"I could tell you a few stories Viv about cricketers in my day. They were an unruly lot. Especially this one," Bess looked towards WG.

"We knew how to have a good time. Why not? Cricket is tough. You're out in the field all day in the scorching sun. You need something to pick you up.

"How many times have I heard you say that WG?" Viv and Bess asked the question together."

Then a strange apparition appeared. Billy came into the Long Room at Lord's in full punk regalia.

WG nearly collapsed, "What are you doing, Billy? You can't come into the Long Room dressed like that. The stewards will kill you. The members will do you worse."

To the Lord's members, it looked as if Billy Idol and Viv Richards were in deep conversation. They couldn't see Bess or WG. They were starting to get uneasy... seriously so. Some were outraged. Even Viv Richards wouldn't be able to control the fury of the Lord's members. They were coming over.

"I had to avoid some strange looking blokes. I like those yellow and red ties they're wearing."

WG smiled, "Egg and bacon, Billy."

"Where? I'm starving."

WG started to laugh, "No, Billy. That's the colour of the ties. They're like eggs and bacon."

"And you think us punks dress weirdly?"

Three Lord's members came over to Billy Idol.

"Get out of here you delinquent. You're one of those awful punks. This isn't your place."

Billy Idol stood his ground, "I'm cricket royalty, mate. The man who built this place killed one of my ancestors... my great-great-grandfather or something. 1787 was the year. Thomas Lord killed William Broad on this very turf. I'm William Broad."

The look on the Lord's members was priceless. They had never bargained for this response. They were struggling. He had bowled them middle stump with a fizzing googly that Shane Warne would have been proud of. Eventually, one of them spoke.

"Do you know this man, Mr Richards?"

"He's cool guys. I do know him and the story is true. He had two great-grandfathers a million times removed that captained Kent. Both died playing this great game. He's more connection to Lord's than any of us."

The Lord's members looked as if they were about to collapse. More came over.

"Go on, Billy, you tell them," WG was proud.

Billy Idol explained the events of 1739 and 1787.

"He was hanged at Tyburn in 1740 for cricket. He had a good eye and sharp reflexes. Kent won fair and square. The match took place on Bromley Common."

The Lord's members were now asking questions, Billy Idol had them eating out of his hand. The sight was as surreal as anyone could imagine.

"The argument was about gin. Kent won by 20 runs. Every generation of the Broads know the details."

"Billy's family are cricket through and through. This is his home," Viv had his say again.

"William Lord bought Lord's and the first game for the MCC was against Kent. We won by 2 runs. William Broad top scored with 84. He bowled Thomas Lord to win the game. Later, in a duel, Thomas Lord shot him." You could hear a pin drop when Billy stopped talking. Lord's members looked at each other.

"We've pictures of Thomas Lord everywhere. We need a picture of William Broad here. Both of them. They're the history of our game," the Chairman of the MCC had just spoken.

Billy Idol punched the air. A tear could be seen running down his cheek if you looked close enough.

WG hugged him. He didn't know what to say. The moment was too profound.

The Chairman of the MCC spoke, "I think the ghost of WG Grace would approve." The Chairman deliberated for a moment and then continued. "You're forgiven Billy. The Broads are innocent. Your cricket's first family."

An hour later WG, Bess and Billy Idol were walking around the outfield at Lord's. Billy was still euphoric. WG was content but reflective. Billy picked up on his mood.

"Are you okay WG?"

"I'm good Billy." WG wasn't convincing anyone.

"You'd like to play still? Watching is all right, but it not the same is it?"

"That's true Billy."

"Come on WG. Let's take you home." Bess held his hand and took him away.

Yet through all the grief of losing his daughter and son, Grace continued to play cricket, playing at club level in south-east London. His last season was in 1914 when he captained Eltham CC's second XI. He was as enthusiastic for the game as when he had made his debut 50 years earlier. WG just wanted a game of cricket. He embodied why sport matters as offering comfort and hope for the sorrows and disappointments of life. Some people scoff at sport as meaningless and the preserve of the sweaty and unwashed.

They see it with their pseudo intellectual snobbery as the pursuit of the inferior, as if the participants lack any meaning to their existence. Let the story of WG Grace persuade them otherwise.

"It will be a jolly match, do try and come," WG explained to a friend in 1914 as he tried to arrange a side for a game in Woolwich. He was 65. At the end of his life, WG loved cricket so much that he wanted to play for ever. The cricket field was one place he felt comfortable, safe and confident. The music halls were where he could forget his worries. These places were his sanctuary. Many in sport have felt the same. Ask Paul Gascoigne and many others. Cricket has been called the suicide sport, as brilliantly portrayed by David Frith. The game was so all consuming, that retirement for many cricketers left too big a void in their life.

29th August 1976 was the day punk in the UK exploded again. Punk explosions had been the feature of the summer. The Screen on the Green was McLaren's big play – his first opportunity to show that three bands was indeed a movement. The three key bands played together on the same stage for the first time. The event was the Buzzcocks first foray to London. Also, it was The Clash's third public gig billed as The Clash, after the Goldhawk and Loftus Road. The Sex Pistol headlined with a storming set to underline their dominance. And the punk crowd came out to play in all their finery, putting on their best bin bags, safety pins and strutting their stuff. The Clash and Pistols were getting on reasonably well. The fight after The Ramones gig on July 5th during the summer heatwave had eased much of the tensions between some of the punk players. Joe Strummer was still uber competitive but was channelling his incredible energy and aggression more positively. Keith Levene's relationship with John Lydon had helped smooth the waters. John Lydon and Joe Strummer still eyed each other suspiciously.

Chrissie Hynde and The Slits were there as were the Damned. The Bromley contingent had a full turnout. The Stranglers turned up late and Poly Styrene was entertaining everyone with her unique charms. She emanated punk attitude from every part of her body. Paul Weller of The Jam and Shane MacGowan were also there. The night at Beckenham Cemetery in early May was just over 3 months ago, but so much had happened in the punk world since then. The summer had lasted an eternity and it had been hot and dry. The Pistols were touring regularly. The Damned were just a few weeks away from releasing *New Rose*, their iconic first single. Ian Dury had recovered from the famous Wathamstow gig in July and was forming a new band called the Blockheads. He and Gene Vincent were back as a team. After Walthamstow, Ian Dury had gone to Brighton to get his head together. He walked along the seafront taking in Brighton's unique atmosphere and felt himself getting calmer and physically stronger. He was able to take in the experience with Gene Vincent and make more sense of it now. He was back at catshit mansions with Gene Vincent a regular visitor.

The Buzzcocks performed brilliantly having gone on first. The Damned had performed an impromptu and unofficial warm up for them. This was very punk. The Buzzzcockswere tight musically with their own material. They were special, very special. The Clash followed. They were in the groove. The set was exactly the same as they played at the Goldhawk. The venue was more personal than Loftus Road, but not as intimate as the Goldhawk. The Clash did not disappoint. They'd come a long way in 2 months from their chastening debut in Sheffield. Gene Vincent had performed miracles with them. WG and Bess were rocking along in the front row with Billy Idol. Siouxsie Sioux and Gene Vincent were with them. The crowd were engaged. They were feeling it. Some came onto the stage. The anarchy level was 8 out of 10. At the Goldhawk, it had been 10, but it had been enough. It was punk. A young writer called Peter Ackroyd fainted at the anarchy of it all. Twelve-year-old Kathy Burke helped him to his feet. Earlier Kathy had met her saviour in Poly Styrene. Peter required 3 stiff gins to come fully around in the Old Queen's Head.

After The Clash had played, the Pistols came on. Mick Jones was talking with Gene Vincent. Siouxsie Sioux came up to Gene Vincent. They hadn't spoken since she had appeared as Mother Thames at Vauxhall Bridge after they had met Ian Dury for the first time in early June. Siouxsie had mostly been aloof and remote. She seemed all powerful, but always in the background, "Thank you, Gene." The Guardians of London came over to Gene Vincent. They were on Islington Green.

Ray Davies spoke first. "Hi Gene. It's a long time no see mate."

"You've been everywhere this summer Ray. But you disappear as soon as I see you."

"I've been watching you though. Welcome to London Gene. You're one of us now."

"But you're still living. I'm dead Ray."

"I know you've saved rock n'roll and the Clash Gene, but do you want to stay on and help us further, albeit in spirit?"

"Why not? I died when I was 36 and Eddie died at 21. We're both owed a few years."

Ray Davies looked happy. "That's settled then Gene."

Gene Vincent turned to David Bowie. "It's Davy Jones isn't it? Or are you still Ziggy Stardust as well or with the Riot Squad? Maybe the Faces?"

"I'm not Ziggy anymore Gene. I'm David Bowie now."

"I like the name. I knew you'd do well. You look like you're one of the Bromley contingent Davy."

"I'm not one of the 'contingent' though I'm from Bromley, Gene. I went to school there."

"You lived there didn't you?

David Bowie laughed. "Plaistow Grove was the place. And I went to school there as I said."

"Do you know the George and Dragon and Sainsbury's in the high street?"

"Of course I do Gene. I'm the 'Bromley boy' and Marc here is the 'twentieth century boy'. Sorry for the awful joke."

David Bowie went on. "I preferred drinking in the three tuns though and it was more of a music pub."

"I don't know it Davy. Sainsbury's is where I first met Billy Idol."

"So I hear Gene. I could think of no finer place."

"Bromley has a certain magic. It's where Billy's ancestors played cricket," explained Gene.

"That's true Gene. It's a place of mystery. Do you know Marc? Siouxsie and he are big mates."

Gene Vincent looked at Marc in admiration. "I heard a lot about you in the late 60's. You were a poet as well. Didn't you start the glam rock craze? "

"Maybe. I think David here deserves most of the credit for that. He's the master and I'm the apprentice. I really liked your music Gene."

"What was your favourite track Marc?"

"Bluejean bop."

"Thanks. They've been playing your tracks at Louise's Marc."

"I know. I was there that night you met Mick Jones."

"I can't remember seeing you there Marc."

"I was sitting with Captain Sensible, Rat Scabies and Dave Vanian. The Captain is so noisy nobody ever notices the people around him."

David Bowie laughed, adding "The Captain is a very naughty boy. Rat and Dave aren't much better."

Ray Davies scratched his head. "We're all going to have a difficult job controlling the Damned."

WG, Bess and Billy Idol came over.

Billy spoke first. "Bess. WG. I want you to meet my heroes."

"It's Bessie Bellwood isn't it? You're a legend." David Bowie was a fan.

"How do you know me David?"

"You're a star Bessie. You were the face of London nearly a century ago. You are part of all this punk thing as well. You work at Louise's."

"I do work at Louise's. That's so nice of you David. You're such a gentleman."

"Your story was an inspiration to me as well." Ray Davies was another admirer of Bessie Bellwood.

"Crikey! I didn't realise I had such a fan club here."

Marc Bolan was, finally, able to get a word in. "Bess. You look like Siousxsie. Are you related?"

"I'm her great great grandmother."

"Fuck me." The rest of them spoke in unison.

A young Kate Bush came up to Bessie from nowhere. "I think it's time for our singing lesson Bessie."

"I guess you're sticking around then Bessie?" asked David Bowie.

"I might as well. Also, I've got to look after this old man as well as Bromley Kate. He's desperate to catch up on some cricket. The Aussies are coming next year for the Ashes."

"You're a famous cricketer aren't you? Are you more famous than Fred Titmus? I'm a Middlesex fan, albeit from a distance." Ray Davies was interested.

"I hope so. No disrespect to Fred Titmus of course." WG looked slightly peeved.

David Bowie spoke to WG. "I'm more of a Alan Knott fan myself, though I don't know too much about the game. I like Derek Underwood and Kent as well."

Billy Idol stuck his chest out and pronounced. "I'm more cricket than all of you. I'm even more cricket than WG."

Marc Bolan, David Bowie and Ray Davies looked at Billy with amusement.

"My ancestors were hung at Tyburn and shot on Hampstead Heath for the game."

"It's redemption Billy." David Bowie was sympathetic. Everyone fell silent, out of respect, looking around awkwardly.

Bowie spoke again. "We need to get back to Chelsea."

"To the King's Road?" asked Billy Idol.

David Bowie moved closer to Billy Idol. "No. We're going somewhere much better than the King's Road, Billy. Siouxsie and Dave Vanian have prepared a tea party for us back at Chelsea Physic Garden. Dave is dressed like Bela Lugosi."

Chapter 13

Notting Hill Carnival
August 30th 1976

'Why are all the angels white? Why ain't there no black angels?' – Muhammad Ali

London seems to invent fire and destruction – Peter Ackroyd

The atmosphere was deteriorating as the police looked to arrest petty criminals on the Portobello Road. Don Letts was circulating around Westbourne Park Road. One witness, Raymond Hunter, who lived in Westbourne Park Road said he saw a police van set alight.

Gangs of white youths were involved in the violence. The far right was creating trouble knowing they'd be innocent in the eyes of most people and the Press. The Westway was witness to the violence.

Joe Strummer, Mick Jones and Paul Simonon were on Portobello Road. West London was combusting with anger. Simmering resentment had finally turned into a fireball of fury. The West Indian community had had enough.

The police presence was intimidating and oppressive, striking an Orwellian vibe.

"I predict a riot. This is crazy." Joe Strummer was unimpressed. "This is a carnival. It's meant to be a happy day. The police are ruining it."

"This is England. Fucking England," Mick Jones was not impressed.

The background to these feeling can be summed up by paraphrasing Don Letts.

"In the mid-70s, as a young man, I would frequently be trailed through the streets by police. I would stop my car, jump up on the roof and stand, arms outstretched, Jesus-like. 'I'd go, 'Why are you guys crucifying me?' And I'd start taking my clothes off. I did that to get people to start looking. The minute you've got an audience, the cops don't know what to do. The 'sus law' – police powers to stop and search anyone considered to be suspicious (i.e. young black men) – was in full effect and this was the most extreme tactics. Most of the time, I would just leave the house half an hour early because I'd probably get stopped on the way. You know what's really sad about it? You expected it – it was normal. The riots at the Notting Hill carnival in 1976 were triggered by these sort of experiences. Everyone thinks it was a race riot, but it wasn't a black-and-white thing, it was a right-and-wrong thing. The previous year, the trust between the black community and the police had broken down, primarily because of the sus law. We were pissed off and frustrated. Until that point, you just thought it was part of the deal; it was the way things were."

"I can feel this is going to explode," Joe Strummer was certain. His eyes were everywhere. "I can smell burning. London's burning."

"It's everywhere. Definitely. That's cars burning. Fucking hell," Mick Jones agreed.

The situation had worsened for them. Suddenly, the riot was personal.

People were starting to run towards them. The police were running after the fleeing mob. The truncheons were out and innocent people were getting smashed out of the way. Women and children were affected. Blood was being spilt. Residents ran into their houses. Portobello Road was a no-go area.

Paul Simonon wasn't impressed, "Let's get out of here. I don't fancy this." All three of them started to run north towards the Westway, shouting to each other at the same time. A car in front of them was set alight.

Joe Strummer summarized, "The Far Right are stirring this up. They know the black community will get the blame. It's a win-win for them. The police are just going to hit out. They can't control it."

Mick Jones summarised, "This is young coppers hitting out at everyone. They don't know how to handle this. This needs wise old heads and there aren't any. The old bastards are stirring them up instead."

Paul Simonon agreed, "It's young kids who are frightened. They're just lashing out. No judgement. They'll get the shit kicked out of them for this."

Carnival floats had been abandoned. Sound systems, guitars, musical instruments were just lying there. No Jamaican sounds were to be heard. The music of happiness had been replaced with screams and mothers howling for the safety of their children. Young men were fighting back against the police. Twenty years of oppression was coming out in people's reactions. Cable Street 1936 was now Notting Hill 1976. An English civil war was being played out. People were crying for

England. The home of cricket, civility, supposed decency and manners had become a lie.

The three members of The Clash were nearly under the Westway now. A fence stopped them going any further. They were standing on a float that had been belting out reggae tunes 10 minutes earlier, before escape and self-preservation took over.

Joe Strummer was alive and snarling, "This is it boys. We're going to have to fight our way out of this. It's a fucking massacre."

"I'm ready if some young copper wants it. Fucking Nazi wankers," Mick Jones was all defiance.

Paul Simonon was more measured, "We need to be smarter than just fighting. There's got to be a better way."

Nearby, a crowd of about 300 carnival goers were going to be trapped under the Westway with an advancing police force hell bent on destruction. They would be mincemeat.

"We've got to do something, Joe," Mick Jones was panicking.

"You're right. This is going to be total annihilation."

Paul saved the day as divine inspiration took over, "Let's start a song. It might stop them. There are instruments and a mic over there." Both Joe and Mick looked at Paul, "He's right." There was no time to discuss. Instinct and survival was now running the show.

They jumped back onto the float. Joe took the mic that was still live. Mick and Paul picked up guitars. Fate had played its hand. The Clash were meant to be. It was like magic. This would be their true beginning and mean something. A band born out of a riot would be their moniker. The Rolling Stones had never been here. Where was prog rock now? Prog rock was disappearing up its own irrelevant, self-satisfied, smug arse. Punk rock had truly been born now.

Mick called out to Paul, "Get on the drums, Paul. Just make a noise."

Joe looked at Paul and Mick, "I've got a song. I'm going to change the words and meaning a little. London Burning. A drug song. You know it."

"Well, fucking sing it then, Joe," Mick was excited and scared. "Fuck me! This is what The Clash is all about," the mob was getting ever closer. Adrenalin was the rocket fuel for The Clash.

"Ok. The chord of A. You've got it, Mick. You know it," Joe Strummer was leading.

Bernie Rhodes wanted anarchy, riots and catastrophe. He was getting both barrels of it now. The Clash had played at Music on the Green in Islington the previous day. They'd been practising daily. With Gene Vincent as their mentor, they'd come a long way since July 4th in Sheffield. They were 'tight'. The Clash was going to mean something. That night in the Goldhawk in July had defined what The Clash was about but this was another level. This moment would really define them. Were they coming to the party or not? They were playing for more than their lives. The music had to mean something. At this moment, The Clash were truly the only band that mattered.

London's burnin'! London's burnin'!

The police were 100 yards away. The running mob was just yards ahead of them. This was going to be a stampede. A running mob was going to flatten The Clash and all the others stuck under the Westway.

London's burnin'! London's burnin'!

A burnt out police van was no more than 50 yards away. Smoke was drifting over the Westway causing the traffic to slow down. At least 20 police vans were on fire. Several shops on Portobello Road were in flames. Lootings and fighting was everywhere.

The first lines of 'London Burning' had been loud and aggressive. The sound could be heard across the shouts and screams. The music was making a difference. Even the traffic of the Westway could not compete.

"Fuck it, Joe, they're not stopping. We're going to get mashed," Mick Jones was worried.

The police and mob were getting closer. Mick Jones called out, "Sing louder, Joe."

"I can't sing any louder. Oh fuck it!"

Paul Simonon was drumming for his life.

Viv Richards had just arrived in Notting Hill from the third ODI in Birmingham that had been delayed because of rain. He'd been dismissed for a duck earlier. He couldn't believe what he was seeing. He was with Lawrence Rowe and Wayne Daniels. They were coming out of Ladbroke Grove tube station, soon to be closed, into a war zone. They had feeling there was some trouble, but didn't expect missiles, stones being launched as they stepped out underneath the Westway.

London's burnin'! London's burnin'!

Lawrence Rowe spoke first, "What's that sound? This doesn't have a Jamaican beat to it!"

"I've never heard anything like this before," Wayne Daniels looked confused.

London's burnin'! London's burnin'!

Then magic happened. The mob came to an abrupt stop to watch The Clash. Their passion and energy had won the day. The rushing police hadn't seen The Clash who had been hidden by the mob. The Police stumbled over the mob. They went down like dominoes. The Police and mob were scratching around on the ground. The aggressors had been floored.

The scene was pure slapstick comedy. The mob just lay on the ground whilst the police got to their feet with a loss of pride all over their faces. The Clash played on.

London's burnin'! London's burnin'!

The police didn't know what to do with this passive form of rebellion. There were no upright bodies to strike. The police stood there impotently. They were out of their comfort zone. The solution required intelligence and thought. Naked aggression and brutality hadn't worked.

Joe Strummer then tried to address the police and mob. By this time Viv Richards, Wayne Daniels and Lawrence Rowe were walking towards The Clash.

"Policeman, we don't want no trouble. Go home to your families. Enjoy life," The words weren't from Joe Strummer, Mick Jones or Paul Simonon. They came from Viv Richards, Wayne Daniels and Lawrence Rowe.

A few policemen made an attempt to get to The Clash. However, a responsible police officer called Dave Roberts held them back. A cricket fan had seen just his hero. He had been at The Oval to see Viv Richards' 291. He had seen that best day's cricket and greatest innings in his life. A truce had happened.

"That's Viv Richards. Lawrence Rowe and Wayne Daniels are with him. Stay back fellows. Let's go home!" Dave Roberts was shouting the order with passion. His epiphany had happened. The police turned around back down the Portobello Road with their truncheons down. Dave Roberts shook his head in shame. His hero Viv Richards had looked at him eye to eye. There had been pity in Viv's eyes. Dave Roberts would never forget that look. The look had been a hammer blow to his soul. The conquerors had truly been conquered.

"I bow to you fellows," Joe Strummer was struggling for words.

Joe Strummer, Paul Simonon and Mick Jones looked in awe. They didn't recognize the cricketers.

Viv Richards went up to Joe Strummer, "Are you The Clash?"

Don Letts was still around Westbourne Park Road. Shops were on fire with police vans overturned and burnt out. The Police were operating more in smaller snatch groups than on Portobello Road. He was working on his own filming the riot. Therefore, he was a marked man, for more than the colour of his skin. Don Letts was jumping in and out of gardens and shops to avoid capture. He was the lone ranger, cool and detached, but a leader at the same time. People could see what he was doing. He was inspiring people around him. He wasn't going to take this abuse. There was going to be evidence of this massacre, not just hearsay, and what they read in the right wing press. There was another solution other than fighting, though Don appreciated more than anyone, why people would want to vent their anger and frustration this way.

Don turned into Basing Street. The police were concentrated mainly on Portobello Road, Ladbroke Grove and Westbourne Park Road now. More cars were being overturned and burnt. He was unconsciously moving towards the Westway and the sounds of The Clash. His intention was to get over to Ladbroke Grove via the underpass of the Westway. Rumours were spreading there was a serious disturbance happening there. The filming opportunities would be really good.

London's burnin'! London's burnin'!

Don Letts stopped to listen to the music. The sounds were coming slightly to the left somewhere over on Portobello Road close to the Westway. 20 police officers were coming towards him. The crowd behind him were ready for a war and Don Letts was caught up in it. He had to get onto Lancaster Road and slip the police net that was closing in. Lancaster Road was 20 yards away. Momentarily, Don slipped back into the crowd and retraced his steps. The police were coming from behind in a classic pincer movement. Now, he had to get through the terraced houses and onto Portobello Road through someone's back garden. He started to panic as terraced houses didn't afford that opportunity. There had to be some break or alleyway. Don was still backtracking when he saw an alleyway that would bypass the houses. There was a view to Portobello Road but it required jumping a couple of fences. The police from Westbourne Pak Road were closing in. Don Letts sneaked into the alleyway. However, a couple of police officers had spotted him and gave chase. Don Letts was running for his life. Two police officers, out of sight from the public, weren't going to spare him. He had to get onto Portobello Road, and the chances were that the situation there would be just as bad. The music was drawing him in. His natural curiosity meant he had to get to the source of this sound. It was just so unique to his ears. He started humming the words, "London's burnin'! London's burnin'!"

The chasing police officers were so close to Don Letts that they were almost wearing his trousers. The fence was 6 feet high. This was time for a fosbury flop. Don jumped for his life. Pure fright and adrenalin gave him superman strength and he managed to grapple his way over the fence with seconds to spare. He could hear the curses of the police officers behind him. This gave him breathing space as the police officers following took their time to climb the fence. Pure instinct had taken over. The second fence was easy now. Don Letts found himself on the Portobello Road and soon lost himself in the crowd. He was in a new war now. 'Out of the frying pan into the fire' would best summarise the situation. The mob was being pursued by the police. Don Letts was running for his life again. They were now running towards the Westway. The concrete monolith was in sight. Somehow, it seemed that the Westway was offering safety and peace.

Then the mob stopped. Don Letts went flying over the people in front of him. He was on the floor. So was everyone else. People started to get up.

London's burnin'! London's burnin'!

Don Letts then took control. He was shouting as loud as possible, "Stay down brothers. Stay down sisters. If we lay down, they can't touch us." The message soon got over to everyone. Then the police were on top of them. Don Letts had enough about him to look where the music was coming from. A police officer on top of him wasn't going to stop him.

Eventually, the police stood up. The mob was still laying flat. The police looked bemused. They didn't know what to do. The mob soon realized.

Don Letts was still leading, "We've won, brothers, sisters. They don't know what to do. Stay down and listen to the music. Look to the sky and the stars. That's where we're going."

The police started to retreat. Don Letts stood up and went towards The Clash. He stood in front of Viv Richards, Wayne Daniels and Lawrence Rowe. "Thanks brothers." They nodded to him.

Viv Richards went up to Joe Strummer. "Are you The Clash?"